D.E. STEVENSON

ANNA AND HER DAUGHTERS

DEAN STREET PRESS

A Furrowed Middlebrow Book
FM81

Published by Dean Street Press 2022

Copyright © 1958 D.E. Stevenson

All Rights Reserved

The right of D.E. Stevenson to be identified as the Author of the Work has been asserted by her estate in accordance with the Copyright, Designs and Patents Act 1988.

First published in 1958 by Collins

Cover by DSP

ISBN 978 1 915014 48 1

www.deanstreetpress.co.uk

D.E. STEVENSON
ANNA AND HER DAUGHTERS

Born in Edinburgh in 1892, Dorothy Emily Stevenson came from a distinguished Scottish family, her father being David Alan Stevenson, the lighthouse engineer, first cousin to Robert Louis Stevenson.

In 1916 she married Major James Reid Peploe (nephew to the artist Samuel Peploe). After the First World War they lived near Glasgow and brought up two sons and a daughter. Dorothy wrote her first novel in the 1920's, and by the 1930's was a prolific bestseller, ultimately selling more than seven million books in her career. Among her many bestselling novels was the series featuring the popular "Mrs. Tim", the wife of a British Army officer. The author often returned to Scotland and Scottish themes in her romantic, witty and well-observed novels.

During the Second World War Dorothy Stevenson moved with her husband to Moffat in Scotland. It was here that most of her subsequent works were written. D.E. Stevenson died in Moffat in 1973.

NOVELS BY D.E. STEVENSON
Available from Dean Street Press

Mrs. Tim Carries On (1941)
Mrs. Tim Gets a Job (1947)
Mrs. Tim Flies Home (1952)

Smouldering Fire (1935)
Spring Magic (1942)

Vittoria Cottage (1949)
Music in the Hills (1950)
Winter and Rough Weather (1951)

The Fair Miss Fortune (written c. 1938, first published 2011)
Green Money (1939, aka *The Green Money*)
The English Air (1940)
Kate Hardy (1947)
Young Mrs. Savage (1948)
Five Windows (1953)
Charlotte Fairlie (1954, aka *The Enchanted Isle*, aka *Blow the Wind Southerly*)
The Tall Stranger (1957)
Anna and Her Daughters (1958)
The Musgraves (1960)
The Blue Sapphire (1963)

(A complete D.E. Stevenson bibliography is included at the end of this book.)

Chapter One

1

"Are you asleep, Jane?"

It was Helen. She hesitated in the doorway for a moment and then came over and stood beside my bed. There was no need to answer the question for she could see I was not asleep; the lamp on the table beside me was still lighted and I was sitting up writing my diary. I had just written:

> Uncle Leonard came to dinner. We had clear soup and chicken and peas and a cheese savoury. Mother knows that Uncle Leonard likes savouries better than puddings so she had it specially for him. Afterwards we sat in the drawing-room and it was so warm that we opened all the windows. I sat on the window-seat and looked out on to the square. There was not a breath of wind to move the leaves of the trees in the gardens. Every now and then people passed beneath the window and I could hear the click of their heels on the pavement and their voices talking as they went along. (Sometimes you hear funny scraps of conversation and you can make up stories about it, but there was nothing very interesting to-night.) Wintringham Square is a quiet place but you can always hear the hum of London in the distance and to-night it seemed louder than usual. I felt restless and uneasy. Perhaps there was thunder about, or perhaps the queer feeling was inside the room and not thunder at all. From where I was sitting the lighted room looked like a stage . . .

"You still write your diary!" exclaimed Helen. "What on earth do you find to write about?"

She held out her hand for the book but I did not give it to her. There was nothing very secret about it but it was my own private thing—and Helen would laugh. Now that I could see Helen properly in the light of the lamp I realised that it had not been thunder—something had happened. Her face was as white as a sheet.

"What is it?" I asked. "What did Uncle Leonard come for?"

"How do you know he came for anything special?"

I did not reply. Helen had come in on her way to bed to tell me all about it—so of course she would—but Helen liked to keep you guessing; she liked the feeling of power. I knew her too well to try to hurry her.

"How did you know?" she repeated.

"I didn't. It just felt—thundery. That's all."

"Thundery!" she said scornfully. "What a child you are! Nobody would think you were seventeen."

The gibe did not worry me as it would have worried Rosalie. Helen could always get a rise out of Rosalie whenever she liked.

"I suppose Rosalie is asleep," I said.

"Why should you think so?"

"Because you would have gone in and told her—whatever it is."

"It's not thunder. It's an earthquake," declared Helen. She sat down on the end of my bed and added, "Uncle Leonard came to tell Mother that we're penniless."

"Penniless!"

She nodded. "He waited until you and Rosalie had gone to bed and then he said, 'Anna, I've got something very unpleasant to tell you. I scarcely know how to begin.' He began in such a roundabout way that I didn't know what he was driving at. Mother said, 'You mean we shall have to economise? Perhaps we had better sell this house. It costs a lot to run it properly,' and he said crossly, 'Of course the house must be sold. You'll have to move into a small flat'."

"A small flat! But that would be horrible!"

"Horrible," agreed Helen. "Mother thought so too. Mother said, 'But I don't understand! Where has the money gone? I thought we had plenty of money.'"

Helen stopped and for a few moments there was silence.

"Go on," I said. "Can't you remember—"

"Of course I remember! How could I possibly forget? Uncle Leonard was annoyed with Mother. He said rather crossly that the money hadn't 'gone' anywhere. There was none to go. He explained that all Father's money came from directors' fees. Father was a director of several important companies in the City."

"We all know that."

"Yes, we all knew that," said Helen bitterly. "If we hadn't been idiots I suppose we might have known that when Father died there would be nothing for us to live on. Uncle Leonard said, 'He ought to have insured. You should have made him do that,' and Mother never answered. She had never thought of it, of course. She had just gone on spending money like water."

There was nothing I could say.

"Why don't you speak?" cried Helen angrily. "I've told you we're ruined and you just sit there staring like an idiot! Don't you understand what it means? You can't go to Oxford, for one thing, and of course Rosalie can't go to Paris. That's bad enough but it's far worse for me. It's absolutely devastating for me."

"It's worst of all for Mother."

"Worst for Mother! Oh no, it isn't. She's old; she's had her fun."

"She isn't really old."

"Well, anyhow, she's had a jolly good innings," declared Helen bitterly. "Lots of clothes and parties and as much money as she could spend! That's been Mother's life—and now, just when I'm looking forward to coming out and being presented and having a good time, we're ruined! It isn't fair!"

"Couldn't you still—"

"No, of course not. Oh Jane, you are a donkey! It costs money to be a 'deb'. You've got to have masses of clothes; you've got to give parties—and you simply must have a proper background. This house would have been just right—but who's going to bother about a girl living in a cheap flat? A horrid cheap flat in a horrid cheap district!" cried Helen wildly. "A dirty little hole—dark and dingy and smelling of cats! That's the sort of place it will be . . . with a brick wall for a view."

"Is it all settled?"

"Of course it isn't settled. You can't settle things all in a moment—besides Mother said she didn't like flats."

"But I thought you said—"

"I told you what Uncle Leonard said," interrupted Helen. "He said we must find a flat. Mother said she didn't like flats. They're arguing about it now."

2

When Helen had gone I took up my diary and read what I had written only about half an hour ago. It seemed like years and I felt like a different person. You can become a great deal older in half an hour: 'Clear soup and chicken and peas and a cheese savoury!' As if it mattered what we had had to eat!

I had written, 'the lighted room looked like a stage . . .' That was not quite so silly for it had looked just like a stage. I could see it now in my imagination. Uncle Leonard had been sitting in Father's chair and I had thought at the time he was very like Father—but of course he was younger. He was sitting there turning over the leaves of *Punch* but obviously finding nothing to laugh at. Mother had opened the piano and was playing very softly. She often played like that—as if she were talking to herself. Helen was sitting beneath the standard lamp, sewing something frilly; Rosalie was sprawled upon the sofa reading a book.

Helen was 'the pretty one' of the family. Indeed she was more than pretty, she was beautiful and elegant and graceful. Her hair was golden and naturally curly; her skin was white and clear and her eyes were blue. Rosalie was very like Helen but somehow she was just a pretty girl. She did not glow and sparkle, her eyes were paler. They took their good looks from Mother—everyone said so. I was different; thin and awkward with straight dark hair—not pretty at all.

I put out the light and tried to sleep but there was too much on my mind. One day we had been well-off and secure; the old grey London house had been 'home' and we imagined that our lives (which had been running along on smooth lines ever since I could remember) would continue to run smoothly for ever. The next day it was all gone. Helen had said it was an earthquake, and so it was. The ground which had seemed so solid was shaking.

Presently I got up and knelt at the window and looked out. The night was still and sultry with thunder growling in the distance like an angry lion. The sky was covered with a blanket of cloud so it was dark except for the pools of light beneath the lamp-posts. There was not a creature to be seen—except a stray cat which ran across the road, and paused, and then leapt over the railing and disappeared into the gardens.

We had always been fond of the gardens. They were unusually pleasant gardens for a London square. We had played in them when we were children so we knew every corner, every tree, practically every stone. There were all sorts of memories connected with the gardens; they were mostly happy, but not all. There was the day when Helen had fallen off the swing and dislocated her arm; it had hung down at her side in a strange helpless way. Rosalie had burst into tears and sobbed uncontrollably, as she always did at the slightest provocation, but Helen merely set her lips and walked back to the house.

There were other days, summer days, when we had taken our tea and had it in the shade of a chestnut-tree; days when we had played tip-and-run with the other children who lived in Wintringham Square. There was the day Father and Mother had been to a Garden Party at Buckingham Palace and had come out into the gardens on their return; Father looking tall and solemn in his tail coat and grey top hat; Mother gay and pretty in a pink lace frock and a hat trimmed with roses. Perhaps I remembered that day especially because it was the first time I had ever looked at Mother properly and seen her as other people saw her. I had heard two people talking; one of them had said, "Mrs. Harcourt is a pretty creature, isn't she?" and the other had replied, "Yes, and she's nice as well. There aren't any airs and graces about her, she's the same to everyone."

I could have gone on for hours thinking about all the different events that had taken place.

The gardens were part of our childhood, part of our lives. Now we were going away and they would not belong to us any more. We would have no right to walk in the gardens, we would not have a key to the gate.

It was foolish to think of a little thing like that in the middle of an earthquake, but somehow it seemed—sad.

Chapter Two

1

Next morning Uncle Leonard came again and there was a family conclave. We all sat round the dining-room table and Uncle Leonard explained exactly what had happened. It was not difficult to understand. The plain fact was we had been 'living up to our income'. There were no debts but nothing had been saved. Mother had very little money of her own and when everything was arranged and the house had been sold we should have about five hundred pounds a year.

"But that's quite a lot!" cried Mother in surprise. "I thought you said we'd have nothing!"

"My dear Anna," said Uncle Leonard. "You've been spending more on clothes."

"Have I?" said Mother vacantly. "Clothes cost a lot—so perhaps I may have spent all that—but it was necessary, you see. Gerald liked me to be well-turned-out; he said it was good for business. We went to parties and we entertained, so of course I had to have pretty frocks. If I had gone about looking different from other women Gerald wouldn't have liked it."

"I know," admitted Uncle Leonard. "I'm not blaming you for that. You were very 'good for business'. Gerald would never have done so well if it hadn't been for you."

"Thank you, Leonard," said Mother with a little tremor in her voice.

There was silence for a few moments; then Helen said,

"But Uncle Leonard, we can't possibly live on five hundred a year! It's fantastic!"

"You will have to get a job," he told her. "As a matter of fact your Aunt Thelma and I have been talking it over and she thinks you could get a job as mannequin at one of the big fashionable dressmakers'. She knows a lot more than I do about these things and she says it wouldn't be difficult, with your looks and general appearance. Rosalie had better take a course of secretarial training."

"I'll be a mannequin too!" cried Rosalie.

"My dear girl we must be realistic," said Uncle Leonard. "You're very pretty—nobody could deny it—but you haven't got quite the—the—um—er—elegance—"

"I'm like Helen! Everyone says so!"

"Oh well, we must see what we can do," said Uncle Leonard uncomfortably. "It's very upsetting. Very wretched indeed." He hesitated and then added, "I'm afraid Jane will have to give up all idea of going to Oxford."

"Oh no, not that!" cried Mother. "Couldn't we possibly—"

"I don't see how—"

I did not see how, either. I had realised last night that all our plans must be changed. It would be silly to pretend I was not disappointed—of course I was disappointed—but it was really my own fault. If I had worked harder I might have got a scholarship. Miss Clarke had wanted me to, but it had seemed unnecessary (I was keen on games and you can't do both unless you are brilliant). I saw now that I should have taken her advice—but it was too late.

"It's all right," I said. "I can get a job."

"Hair-dressing," suggested Rosalie. "I mean Jane is frightfully good at hair. She always sets our hair for parties—and does it as well as any proper hair-dresser."

"Oh no!" cried Mother. "No, that wouldn't do at all!"

I said nothing. It was true that I was 'good at hair' and liked working with it, but my idea had been to take a course of training and get a job as secretary.

"What an ass you are, Rosalie," said Helen. "Jane has got brains—of a sort. She could get a post as assistant in a library."

"That sounds more like the thing," agreed Uncle Leonard.

I thought so too. In fact the idea of working amongst books was rather pleasant.

Uncle Leonard sighed. He said, "I know it sounds grim but lots of girls have to work for their livings, and you've got us behind you. Thelma and I will do all we can to help you—I needn't tell you that. The first thing to do is to sell this house and find a suitable flat."

"I don't like flats," said Mother.

"Well then, a small house," said Uncle Leonard.

"No," said Mother. "There's no need. We aren't going to live in London."

"You aren't going to live in London!"

Mother shook her head. "I've listened to all you said—and it sounds too frightful. I couldn't bear it. We're going back to Scotland."

There was a moment's horrified silence.

"You don't mean it!" cried Helen.

"Of course I mean it," declared Mother. "I didn't say anything about it before because you said we were penniless, but with five hundred a year we could manage—"

"You couldn't," said Uncle Leonard. "You don't know anything about money. You haven't thought it out."

"Scotland," said Mother firmly.

"Listen, Anna," said Uncle Leonard. "All this has been a blow to you and knocked you off your balance—that's quite understandable of course—but we've got to think of the best thing to do. It's no good rushing off to the ends of the earth without proper thought."

"I was born and brought up in Scotland."

"Yes, I know, but—"

"It's my home, Leonard."

"It hasn't been your home for twenty years."

"It has always meant home to me."

"My dear Anna, do please be sensible. Take my advice and make the best of it. I know it will be difficult at first but we'll find a nice little flat and the girls will get jobs and you'll all settle down—"

"No, Leonard," said Mother softly.

"You've got friends here," he continued. "Your friends won't desert you."

"Not at first, perhaps, but if you can't afford to entertain you soon fade out." She smiled and added, "I'd rather go out with a bang."

"You've got friends here," repeated Uncle Leonard.

"I've got friends in Ryddelton."

"People you haven't seen for twenty years!"

"But they're real friends."

Uncle Leonard was beginning to lose his temper. "I don't understand you, Anna. Surely you'd never think of going to Ryddelton! If you *must* go to Scotland it had better be Edinburgh."

"Too expensive," said Mother softly.

"Ryddelton is a deadly little town," declared Uncle Leonard. "What would you do with yourself in a place like that? Good heavens, you'd be bored stiff in a couple of months! You've lived in London ever since you were married and—"

"I'm not really a London sort of person."

He looked at her—from the top of her beautifully waved hair to her sheer nylon stockings and her high-heeled shoes.

"Oh, I may look it," said Mother with a little smile. "But I'm not really."

"If we've got to find jobs—" began Helen.

"You won't have to. We shall manage quite nicely."

"On five hundred a year!" exclaimed Uncle Leonard. "It would be hopeless. You couldn't afford a maid."

"I can cook," said Mother.

To my knowledge Mother had never cooked so much as an egg. Even during the war we had had a staff composed of a few elderly servants who kept things going fairly comfortably. Mother was the sort of person who could always get people to work for her.

"It's not fair!" cried Helen with blazing eyes. "It's all very well for you to talk of 'going back to Scotland' but it isn't 'going back' for us. It's going away from London—leaving all our friends—burying ourselves in a miserable little country-town!"

"You aren't thinking—of us—at all," added Rosalie with a little sob in her breath.

"Poor lambs!" said Mother gently. "I know it's hard, but it won't be as bad as you think. It won't be nearly as bad as staying in London; living in a poky little flat with no money for nice clothes and entertainments; seeing your friends drifting away and forgetting all about you—"

"They wouldn't!" cried Helen.

Mother was silent.

"They wouldn't," repeated Helen. "And anyhow I'd rather be in London. Uncle Leonard says I can get a job—and he's right. I'm sure Madame Peridot would have me as one of her mannequins; she always says my figure is perfect."

"She says that to all her customers," murmured Rosalie.

"She means it when she says it to me," retorted Helen.

"I shall get a job too," declared Rosalie. "If I can't be a mannequin I can get some other kind of work. Anything would be better than leaving London."

Mother sighed. "Oh well, you can try it," she said sadly. "I'm afraid you'll be very unhappy but I won't stand in your way."

"Oh Mother—darling!" cried Helen in delight. "I'm so glad you've changed your mind! I'm sure it's the best thing!"

"Very sensible," said Uncle Leonard nodding. "Very sensible indeed. It would have been the height of folly to take the girls to Ryddelton." He collected his papers hastily and rose.

"I'll take Jane, of course," said Mother.

Uncle Leonard hesitated and gazed at her in astonishment. "Anna! What on earth do you mean?" he exclaimed. "You don't mean you'll go away and leave Helen and Rosalie alone in London!"

"If that's what they want," nodded Mother.

It was not what they wanted. They wanted us all to remain in London. Helen saw herself as one of Madame Peridot's assistants, wearing beautiful clothes and showing them off to Madame's 'clients'. It was not an unpleasant picture (she had begun to think it might be quite tolerable) but she certainly did not want to be left alone in London. Rosalie's visions of the future were not so clear; she did not know what she wanted.

When they realised the fact that Mother intended to go to Ryddelton with or without her daughters the argument started all over again and everyone repeated what he or she had said before: Mother with unvarying sweetness and good temper; Uncle Leonard more and more crossly. At last he went away, pausing at the door to say that Aunt Thelma would come along at tea-time.

The way he said it sounded like a threat—or at least it sounded like that to me—for Aunt Thelma is a large woman with a knobbly forehead. She wears her hat on the back of her head and talks in a loud voice. Aunt Thelma likes people to do exactly as she tells them and usually they do.

"Thelma will come along at tea-time," repeated Uncle Leonard.

"That will be lovely," said Mother cordially. "I'm always delighted to see Thelma. Give her my love and tell her I shall expect her at half-past four."

2

I went into the hall with Uncle Leonard to see him off.

"What a woman!" he was muttering. "Soft as silk and hard as granite—that's your mother, Jane. How do you like the idea of going to Scotland?"

I hesitated and then I said, "I think Mother is right. It would be awfully difficult to economise here, where everyone knows us, and the girls wouldn't like going to parties without new frocks."

"Wouldn't they?" asked Leonard, standing in the hall and looking at me with an odd sort of expression. "The girls wouldn't like it—eh? What about you?"

"I don't mind so much about clothes. It would be much harder for them."

"I see," he said. "But what about Oxford?"

"Oh well, of course I'm disappointed, but it can't be helped."

"What can't be cured must be endured—eh?"

"Yes."

"I wonder if we could manage—" he began doubtfully.

"No," I said. "It's frightfully kind of you to think of it but Oxford is off."

As a matter of fact it was easier to make up my mind like that than go on wondering and hoping and having the matter discussed—and I knew Aunt Thelma would never let him pay for me to go to Oxford without a lot of unpleasantness. Last but not least if Mother was going to Scotland she would need me to go with her.

"You've made up your mind definitely?" asked Uncle Leonard.

"It wouldn't be fair," I explained. "If the girls have got to give up things . . ." There was a lump in my throat so I could not complete the sentence.

Uncle Leonard nodded. "Perhaps you're right—and perhaps it doesn't matter very much. You can learn a lot of important things without going to Oxford. Don't forget that, Jane."

He gave me a little hug and went away. I think he was relieved that I had said 'no' so firmly.

Chapter Three

1

When Uncle Leonard had gone I looked for Mother and found her sitting at her desk writing a letter.

"I'm writing to my cousin," she explained. "He lives in Edinburgh. He's a Writer to the Signet."

"What does that mean?"

Mother did not seem to hear my question. "Don't go away," she murmured. "I want you to run along to the post. I'm writing to ask him to find us a little house at Ryddelton."

I stood and waited. I wondered what Writer to the Signet meant—it sounded strangely old-fashioned. Perhaps it had something to do with swans (I had been reading about the swans on the banks of the Thames and about the men called swan-uppers who look after them and mark them to show that they belong to the Crown. A cygnet is a young swan of course).

Then I began to wonder about this mysterious cousin, whom I had never heard of before. I wondered if he would be able to read the letter, for Mother's writing was difficult to decipher at the best of times and her pen was dashing over the paper at such a terrific speed that it would be even more difficult than usual . . . and I wondered what he would think when he received a letter out of the blue asking him to find us a house at Ryddelton.

Mother was always ready to do things for other people so she took it for granted that other people would do things for her.

"You haven't seen him for years, have you?" I said.

"No, not for years."

"He never came here, did he?"

"No," said Mother. "As a matter of fact your father never liked Andrew. They have nothing in common. They spoke a different language. Your father was a business man and—"

"Does he speak Gaelic?" I asked.

Mother looked up in amazement. "Gaelic!" she exclaimed. "Do you mean Andrew? What on earth put such an extraordinary idea into your head?"

"You said they spoke a different language."

"I only meant they didn't understand each other," said Mother with a sigh of impatience. She added, "Do be quiet, Janie dear, I'm trying to write this letter."

I waited until she had finished and then ran to the pillar box at the corner—the postman was clearing it so I was just in time—and as I handed him the letter I could not help noticing that it was addressed to Andrew Firth Esq., W.S.

Various thoughts passed through my mind as I walked back to the house. Firth had been Mother's name before she married, so he was that kind of cousin . . . and of course the W.S. after his name meant Writer to the Signet. I realised that he could have nothing whatever to do with swans—it had been a silly idea anyhow—because a young swan, or cygnet, is spelt with a C. I wished I were not so ignorant about The World. You can learn a great deal at school but not things like that. You have to live in The World to learn about it . . . perhaps that was what Uncle Leonard had meant!

It struck me that I knew surprisingly little about Mother's relations. I knew that her father and mother were dead and her only brother had been killed in the First World War. His picture stood on the chimney-piece in her bedroom. It was the picture of a boy in uniform, and there was a strange look of tragedy in his eyes. Somehow you knew at once, without being told, that he had been killed. Unlike Mother he had dark hair and hazel eyes. His face was too thin and bony to be good-looking but there was something very attractive about him and I was always pleased when Mother said I was 'like Robert'. Mother had no sisters and, this being so, I had imagined she had no relations. I had never thought of cousins. I wondered what 'Andrew Firth Esq., W.S.' was like and why he and Father had not got on well together.

By this time I saw clearly that nothing would prevent Mother from going to Ryddelton—neither Aunt Thelma nor anyone else—it might be right or it might be wrong, but at any rate it was settled.

2

It would have been interesting to know whether Helen ever thought of Basil Romford but she never mentioned him and Rosalie and I did not dare to ask. We had known Basil since we were children; he lived in Wintringham Square with his mother and we often met him in the gardens exercising his dog. At first he had not taken much notice of us for he was much older than we were but when he had come back from the war, badly wounded and lame, it had been different. He often spoke to us—and we were full of hero-worship. Then he began to come to the house (Mother knew Mrs. Romford) and when Helen was nineteen he fell in love with her. We all thought Helen would marry him and we were all pleased . . . and then Helen changed her mind. She told Basil that she wanted a Season in London, perfectly free, and if he still wanted to marry her next year he could ask her again. Perhaps she did not put it quite so crudely but that was what she meant.

Basil tried to persuade her to marry him at once—or at least to be properly engaged—but Helen thought he was selfish and told him so. Helen said she wanted a good time before she settled down. There was a great deal of discussion and eventually they quarrelled and Basil went away. Rosalie and I thought Helen was sorry when he had gone but she was too proud to say so and in any case she was looking forward to her Season as a 'deb'.

"Perhaps he'll come back," said Rosalie when we talked it over together. "Perhaps she'll write to him and tell him what's happened."

I did not think so. I thought Helen would be too proud to write.

"Why do you want to stay in London?" I asked.

"Oh, I don't know," she replied doubtfully. "Helen wants me to stay."

Helen and Rosalie could not make up their minds what to do; they talked and argued interminably. One moment they thought they would both get jobs and take a little flat together and the next moment they decided not to. Helen went the length of asking Madame Peridot about a job as mannequin and Madame agreed to take her, but when the salary was discussed, and the hours of work, Helen was somewhat damped.

"There's plenty of time," she declared. "We needn't rush into anything. It will take ages to sell this house and Mother isn't likely to find a house at Ryddelton."

Rosalie could have got a post as receptionist to a doctor, who was a friend of Uncle Leonard's, but she hesitated and he took someone else.

Then suddenly everything happened at once. The house was sold for a very good price and Cousin Andrew Firth wrote and said he had found a house at Ryddelton—a house called Timble Cottage about half a mile out of the town. He added that it was not too bad and in reasonable condition, with a pleasant little garden and an extensive view. Most important of all it was cheap.

"That's splendid, isn't it?" said Mother happily, and she wired to say she would buy it.

"Without seeing it!" cried Helen when she heard the news. "Without having it surveyed! Aren't we going to have it papered and painted?"

"Andrew has seen it," Mother pointed out. "Andrew says it will suit us. We can't afford to have it redecorated. Andrew says there are two public rooms and three bedrooms. One of the bedrooms is quite big so Helen and Rosalie can share it if they decide to come."

"I'd rather have a room of my own," objected Rosalie.

"We can't help it," Mother replied.

It was unreasonable of them to expect Mother to buy a larger house when they could not make up their minds whether or not they were coming.

"If I can't have a room of my own I'd rather share with Jane," said Rosalie crossly.

"That would be much better," agreed Helen. "I'm the eldest," she added.

"Then you've decided to come?" asked Mother.

"What else can we do?" said Helen ungraciously. "You've sold this house over our heads; we haven't had time to look about and find suitable jobs in London."

Mother said nothing—she was very patient with them—but I was angry.

"You could both have had jobs if you wanted them," I said. "The fact is you don't know what you want"—and I walked out of the room before they could answer.

3

"Why do you let them be rude to you?" I asked Mother. We were in the linen-room together, packing the big hampers which we were taking with us to Ryddelton.

"Oh Jane, because I feel guilty! Not guilty about going to Ryddelton—I *know* that's the right thing to do—but because I should have known about our affairs." She was standing still, staring and twisting her hands. "I never bothered," she said vaguely. "Gerald never discussed money with me. I had no idea how much we had. There was always plenty of money. If I wanted money for anything special I just asked him and he gave it to me at once—quite often he gave me more than I needed. It seems extraordinary that I could have been so stupid."

"You didn't know—"

"But I ought to have known. I ought to have asked. Leonard says I should have known what our income was 'and regulated the expenditure accordingly.'"

"He said you were 'good for business.'"

"It was nice of him wasn't it?" she said with a fleeting smile. "But the point is I could have been 'good for business' without spending quite so much. I could have saved if I had known there was any need. I should have thought of the future—but I never did."

"Father should have thought of the future."

"Don't say that!" she cried. "That's what Leonard says, and I don't *like* it! Leonard says he ought to have insured his life. Why should he? How did he know he was going to die—like that—all in a moment?"

It was no good discussing the matter. I just said, "Well, I don't think you should let them be rude. Honestly, Mother, you should speak to them seriously."

"Perhaps I should—but I'm sorry for them," she declared. I thought she meant she was sorry because they had had to give up so much, but she meant more than that.

"Yes, of course it's hard on them," she said. "But that's only temporary. I'm sorry for them because they're the sort of people they are. Helen has always had exactly what she wanted too easily and she thinks she can go on having exactly what she wants. Perhaps she will, too. And poor Rosalie doesn't know what she wants which is almost worse. You and Helen have played 'Pull devil, pull baker,' with Rosalie for years."

"Mother!"

"Oh, perhaps not consciously—but it comes to the same thing. She's had no chance to develop her own personality. I often wonder what sort of lives they will have," Mother continued. "Life is so dangerous. You make your bed when you're very young and you've got to lie on it whether it's comfortable or not. Helen and Rosalie are very different but in one thing they're alike: they don't understand."

"They don't understand what?" I asked in bewilderment.

"They don't understand anything," declared Mother smiling at me rather sadly. "They don't even know that there's anything to understand. They're like horses with blinkers—they just see what's in front of their noses and nothing more. I'm always terribly sorry for horses with blinkers," added Mother with a sigh.

She had never spoken to me like that before—as if I were really and truly grown-up—and I realised that she wouldn't have spoken like that now if she hadn't been upset.

By this time the hampers were nearly packed. Mother was putting all the best linen into the sale and taking the plain cotton sheets and pillow-cases with us.

Horses with blinkers! The more I thought about it the better I understood. In fact it seemed to me that you could divide all the people you knew into two categories: those with blinkers and those without. It had nothing to do with being clever—or not clever—it had nothing to do with what you learnt at school. For instance Miss Clarke, who had taken honours at Cambridge, wore blinkers, whereas Betty Hammond, my special friend (who was quite stupid at lessons) did not.

"Jane! You've put those sheets on the wrong pile! What *are* you thinking about!" exclaimed Mother.

"People with blinkers," I said.

4

Helen and Rosalie ceased to discuss the move to Ryddelton when Mother was present—perhaps she had spoken to them seriously—but they talked about it endlessly to each other and to me. There was a great deal to do and I was busy helping Mother with all the various arrangements, but they did nothing—neither to help nor to hinder.

The night before we were leaving they both washed their hair and as usual I set it for them. They both had beautiful hair, golden and silky. Helen's was naturally curly but Rosalie was obliged to have an occasional perm. I liked doing their hair and as I pressed the waves into shape with my fingers and curled up the ends it occurred to me that there might be worse jobs than this. Perhaps in a small place like Ryddelton I might set up as a hair-dresser and make a little money to help with the housekeeping expenses. In spite of Mother's optimism I realised it would be a tight squeeze to live on five hundred pounds a year.

"You're very good at hair," said Rosalie, taking up the mirror and turning her head to look at her curls. "Helen said I was silly, but I wasn't silly at all. Why don't we all stay in London and get jobs? If we had all three decided to stay in London Mother would never have thought of going to Ryddelton."

"She would have gone herself," I replied (but I said it without conviction, for I was not sure). "And at any rate," I added,

"I don't think I want to go on living in London. I'd rather go to Ryddelton with Mother."

"You're mad," declared Helen. "The cottage will be ghastly."

"Why should it be ghastly?" I asked.

"It's too cheap to be anything else," said Helen promptly.

"And it's got such a silly name," added Rosalie.

"I don't see that the name matters," I said. "We could change the name if we wanted."

"That's not the point," objected Helen. "The point is that a cottage with a name like that is bound to be ghastly."

"I asked Mother about it," said Rosalie. "I asked her why it had such an extraordinary name and she said it was built by an old sea-captain with one leg called Timble."

"What was the other leg called?" asked Helen with bitter satire.

"You know what I mean," said Rosalie crossly.

"Cousin Andrew has seen it," I reminded them. "He said it had a pleasant little garden and an extensive view."

"Yes," agreed Helen. "And he said it was 'not too bad and in reasonable condition'. Sounds marvellous, doesn't it?"

Put like that it sounded anything but marvellous, and I felt a little chill of foreboding. But it was too late for chills of foreboding; we were leaving the very next day.

Chapter Four

1

I WAKENED slowly, coming up from the depths of sleep, and it seemed that my room was full of birds. They were little birds (cheeky robins and finches and tits) swinging upon branches, peeping between leaves—and twittering gaily. I rubbed my eyes and the illusion vanished. The birds were not real, they were wallpaper birds, the twittering came from the open window. This was my first awakening in Timble Cottage and it was delightful.

A few moments passed and then I remembered where I was and all that had happened; the journey was over, we had moved from the big grey house in the London square to the cottage on the hill.

What a journey it had been! How tired we were when we arrived at Ryddelton Station! What a queer little place it seemed!

There was an ancient taxi in the station-yard and in this dilapidated vehicle we had completed the journey, chugging along slowly through the town and even more slowly up the winding road to Timble Cottage.

"It will be empty of course," said Mother as we approached. "The van may not have arrived—or anything—but we'll just have to make the best of it."

Mother had been making the best of it all day.

"Here's Timble Cottage," said the taxi-driver cheerfully. "And you'll not want for company. There's plenty of folks aboot the place."

We had expected to arrive at a solitary cottage, deserted and silent, but Timble Cottage was neither. It was a hive of activity. Certainly there were 'plenty of folks' about the place. The van had arrived and the men were carrying in the furniture; three other men were entangled in telephone wires and an aged individual with a grizzled beard was busily engaged in clipping the hedge.

"Goodness!" exclaimed Mother in amazement.

One of the telephone men approached as we got out of the taxi. "We've nearly done," he said. "We'll be back in the morning to finish."

"But I don't think I want a telephone. I can't afford—" began Mother.

"It's a special order from Edinburgh," said the man in surprise. "It's usually weeks before we get round to a job like this—but it's a special order—from Edinburgh. It's a rush job. The place is kind of isolated and it's not very suitable for leddies living alone."

"Andrew!" said Mother under her breath.

"The leddies will be yourselves, no doubt," added the telephone-man, looking at us with interest.

"Yes," said Mother. "And of course it is—rather—isolated."

"It's nice, though," said the man.

It was nice. The little house was solid and square with a snugly-fitting slate roof and, except that the garden was rather overgrown, it looked in excellent repair. It certainly was by no means the ruin which Cousin Andrew's lukewarm recommendation had led us to expect.

Rosalie exclaimed, "It's a dear little house!"

"Yes, of course," agreed Mother. "Of course it's a dear little house. Andrew would never have recommended it so highly if it hadn't been nice."

There were other evidences of Cousin Andrew's forethought: a young man putting new cords in the window of the sitting-room and an elderly woman in the kitchen scrubbing the floor.

The woman was plump and cosy with a round face and pink cheeks. "I'm Mrs. Gow," she said in answer to Mother's question. "Yon's my man, cutting the hedge. You'll be wanting tea—and I'll need to make tea for the men. Mebbe there's cups in one of yon packing-cases . . ."

"What about milk—" began Mother.

"I got milk fro' the fairm—an' eggs forbye—an' a few wee odds and ends fro' the grocer's. I thocht you'd be wantin' them. Mr. Firdi said I was tae order what I thocht."

"Yes, of course," said Mother. "It's—awfully—kind." Her voice was shaky and she was not far from tears.

There was much to be done in the way of unpacking (and arranging where the men were to put the furniture) but I found time to go upstairs and have a look at the bedrooms. There was a large room and two small rooms—which looked out on to the front garden—and there was a funny old-fashioned little bathroom. There was also a steep wooden stair. I ran up the stair and found the attic.

When I saw the attic I could hardly believe my eyes; it was almost too good to be true! This should be my room—my very own. The girls could have the two front rooms, and Mother the biggest one which looked on to the hill at the back.

The attic occupied half the house, so the floor-space was considerable. The roof was low and in places it sloped to within a few feet of the floor; there were two small windows which faced south and west with breath-taking views of hills and trees and meadows.

I was so enchanted with my find that I rushed downstairs to tell Mother about it.

"An attic!" said Mother vaguely. "Andrew didn't say anything about an attic. He said there were three bedrooms—"

"Come and see!" I cried. "It's a marvellous attic—and I want it for my very own room."

They came upstairs—all three of them—and looked round.

"Oh Jane, you couldn't sleep here—" began Mother.

"I could! I like it!"

"But it wouldn't be comfortable."

"I think you're mad," declared Helen; she had a habit of telling people that she thought they were mad.

"I'm not mad," I said. "I could make it quite comfortable—and it would be my very own."

"Comfortable!" cried Helen. "Look at that horrible sloping roof! Look at the wall-paper! Who on earth could have chosen such ghastly wall-paper, all covered with birds! I never saw anything so hideous in all my life. They would give me the jim-jams."

"I think the room is attractive," said Rosalie. "We could make it nice for Jane—and the birds are rather sweet."

"You *would* think so!" said Helen laughing. "Of course you think it would be 'nice for Jane'. If Jane sleeps here you can have a room to yourself!"

"It isn't that at all!" cried Rosalie indignantly.

"I suppose you realise that there's no electric light," added Helen. "Jane will creep to bed with a candle."

In my excitement I had not noticed this, but I did not care. "I shall have a lamp," I told them. "I've always wanted a room with an oil-lamp. It will be fun. Mother, please—please say I can have this room!"

"Oh well—" said Mother doubtfully. "If you really want it—and if the men can get the bed up the stairs—"

By superhuman efforts the men had got the bed up the stairs and here I was, lying in it!

2

My watch had stopped—I had forgotten to wind it—so I had no idea of the time, but the sun was shining brilliantly and I felt rested and refreshed. I got up and went downstairs and found Mother in the kitchen. She was wearing a large blue overall which for some reason made her look younger, and her hair, which was usually in neat little curls, was a trifle untidy.

"Porridge!" cried Mother gaily, waving a large wooden spoon. "Real porridge, made with salt! Wait till you taste it, Jane! You can lay the table and find a tray for Helen; she was tired last night and she wants her breakfast in bed."

Never before had I laid a table and prepared a tray so it was a new experience and rather a curious one . . . but I would soon get used to it of course. We should all have to help with household duties and I hoped Mother would see that it was fairly arranged. It annoyed me that Helen was having breakfast in bed. We had all been tired last night, Mother had been absolutely exhausted, but Helen was to have breakfast in bed.

Helen was supposed to be the delicate one of the family. Perhaps it was natural that Mother should worry about her for she was the only one who had ever been seriously ill. Long ago, when we were children, we had all had whooping-cough and in Helen's case it had affected her lung. She had been sent to Switzerland for the winter to escape the fogs and had returned home plump and rosy (and prettier than ever). There had never been any recurrence of her illness but it had frightened Mother considerably. Helen made good use of this and sometimes if there happened to be anything disagreeable to do she would complain of a little pain in her side. "Oh it's nothing much," she would say, smiling like an early Christian Martyr. "Of course I can go to the library and change your book. I thought of having a little rest this afternoon but it doesn't matter a bit." Then Mother would make her rest and someone else would change the book—or whatever it happened to be.

Perhaps I was unfair to Helen—perhaps she really did get tired and have a little pain—but no doctor had been able to find the cause and it certainly never prevented her from going to a party.

It struck me, as I carried the tray upstairs, that we had heard nothing about the little pain for months but perhaps now at Timble Cottage we might be hearing about the little pain quite often.

Our first few days at Timble Cottage were full of surprises and not the least of these surprises was Mother. With her foot upon her native heath she suddenly became years younger: there was a sparkle in her eyes which we had never seen before and even her voice seemed different. I saw what she had meant when she said she was 'not really a London sort of person.' Instead of her smart coats and silk frocks, nylon stockings and high-heeled shoes, Mother appeared in tweeds and brogues—and looked right in these garments. She had said she could cook, and her cooking was more than adequate. There were no fal-lalls about our food, for we had to economise, but Mother's soup was fit for a royal table and plain dishes like stews were served in thick brown gravy with a savoury tang. She had said she had friends—and she had. The portly butcher greeted her like a long lost cousin, the baker's wife remembered her as a child.

"Well, Miss Anna!" exclaimed the baker's wife. "Fancy you coming back to Ryddelton after all these years! You could have knocked me doon with a feather when I heard you'd bought Timble Cottage. It's a funny wee place compared to Mount Charles, but it'll be easily run—and that's the main thing nowadays. And is this your daughter? She's not like you, Miss Anna, but she's got a look of Master Robert. Do you not think so, yourself?" Then, leaning her ample bosom upon the counter, Mrs. Fletcher proceeded to discuss her own family and to give Mother a detailed account of what they were doing and whom they had married and how many children they had, while Mother listened entranced and the shop filled up with impatiently waiting customers.

Mother had other friends as well and although she had not seen them for years they had not forgotten her. We had not been in Timble Cottage two days when Mrs. Hunter called. She was a tall slender woman in lovat tweed with eyes to match. I had answered the door and we were still in such a muddle that I was doubtful about letting her in—the sitting-room was cluttered with crates, half unpacked, and the dining-room was worse—but Mother heard us talking and emerged from the kitchen in her overall, crying, "Elspeth, my lamb, how marvellous!" and Mrs. Hunter's greeting was no less enthusiastic.

"The kitchen is the *only* place," declared Mother and they retired to the kitchen arm-in-arm.

It was nearly half-past four and soon we were all called to come and be introduced to Mrs. Hunter and have tea. She had brought a large cherry-cake with her and explained that it was a 'moving-in present.' It was home-made and absolutely delicious and I wondered if she had made it herself. She did not look like a woman who could turn out delicious cakes but only a week ago I should have said that Mother was incapable of cooking an appetising meal and I should have been wrong.

Mother and Mrs. Hunter were too busy talking to pay much attention to us, and quite soon Helen and Rosalie mumbled excuses and drifted away, but I stayed and listened for it was obvious that they did not care whether anyone listened or not. Of course I did not know any of the people they were talking about, but I realised that I soon would know them, and if you are going to live in a place the sooner you learn all about it the better.

"What's happened to the Clutterbucks?" asked Mother.

"The two old Clutterbucks are dead, but Erica is still at Tocher House. She runs the place as a hotel."

"A hotel! Erica!"

"I know," agreed Mrs. Hunter smiling. "But it's a very comfortable hotel and always full. She has a good staff and an assistant to help her to keep things running smoothly. It isn't a job I should like. She's still as rude as ever."

"Rude—but—interesting," said Mother thoughtfully.

"Exactly. Erica is definitely a *person*."

"Is Celia still at Dunnian?"

"Oh yes, it's Celia's house of course. She married an American—a distant cousin called Courtney Dale. He took the name of Dunne so that there would still be Dunnes at Dunnian."

"It was in old Miss Dunne's will," nodded Mother. She added, "I saw the notice about Admiral Dunne's death in *The Times*."

They talked about Admiral Dunne for a few minutes and then Mrs. Hunter said, "You know Tonia, don't you?"

"I don't think so."

"She must have come to Ryddelton after you left. Tonia Melville. She married Bay Coates and they live in that attractive little house in the High Street, next door to the old Smilies. They're dears—both of them—and they've got two amusing children—very naughty but most diverting. Bay lost a leg in the war, he was Bomber pilot, so he isn't able to do very much. All the same he's a useful man in the town—Boy Scouts and Town Council and all that sort of thing. We're lucky to have him."

"What about the Raeworths?" asked Mother.

Presently Mrs. Hunter rose and said she must fly or her husband would get no supper. "You're lucky to have daughters," she declared as she said good-bye. "Daughters can cook and help in the house; sons go away and build bridges in Africa or somewhere—at least mine do. No, Anna, I really must go, but I'll see you again. You must all come over to lunch."

Cousin Andrew was our next visitor and I was very interested to see him. He was tall and rather thin with bright brown eyes which twinkled when they saw something that amused him. His hair was dark with a sprinkle of grey above the ears.

"Well Anna, so you've come back!" he exclaimed. "People always come back to Ryddelton sooner or later."

"Oh Andrew, how good you've been!" said Mother, taking his hand.

He brushed her thanks aside and said it was nothing. "You look a bit older," he added, "but you've not really changed. You're still the same Anna."

I thought Mother might be a little damped by his frankness (in London her friends often exclaimed, "My dear, you never look a day older! How do you *do* it?") but Mother was undisturbed. She laughed quite happily and said, "We're both getting on. I was forty last birthday—and you're forty-three. It seems odd, doesn't it?"

"Very odd indeed."

"Why on earth aren't you married?"

"Couldn't get anybody to have me," declared Cousin Andrew with a twinkle in his eyes.

"Away!" cried Mother. "A fine upstanding man like yourself!"

All this was so unlike Mother—or at least it was so unlike the Mother I had known for seventeen years—that I was quite dumbfounded. I had seen her play hostess—polite and gracious. I had watched her talking to people and wondered how she always managed to say the right thing. She was usually the centre of a little group. People gathered round her to be amused and were not disappointed. Mother had seemed quite happy in London—but here she was gay.

The first time Cousin Andrew came to Timble Cottage he was alone but he came again quite soon and brought Cousin Margaret; she was his sister and they lived together in a comfortable house in Murrayfield Gardens. It was from Cousin Margaret that I learned what Writer to the Signet meant. She explained that Writers to the Signet were lawyers—or solicitors—with special duties and privileges. Long ago they had received this peculiar title because they prepared warrants and charters to be signed with the King's Seal.

Cousin Margaret laughed when I told her about the cygnets, but she laughed in a nice way and said, "Well, how could you know? You can't know things unless you ask—and as a matter of fact there are quite a lot of people in Edinburgh who have heard about Writers to the Signet all their lives and only have a hazy idea as to what it means."

It was during that visit that we arranged for me to go up to Edinburgh for the day and have lunch with Cousin Margaret at her club.

3

Timble Cottage was perched on the side of a hill at the end of a steep and stony road so it was surprising that we had a stream of visitors. Some of them came in cars but most of them walked and brought their dogs. You could see them approaching from a long way off if you happened to be looking out of the window and as there was no other house on the road you knew they were coming to call.

Mother would exclaim, "Jane, put on the kettle. Here's somebody!" and she would seize the field-glasses and clamp them to her eyes. "It's Elspeth!" she would cry. "No, it isn't! Who is it? Could it be Sheila Raeworth? Jane, take the glasses and see who it is." But of course it was no use for me to take the glasses; even if I could see the approaching visitor clearly I could not tell Mother which of her friends was coming up the hill.

Most of Mother's friends were her own age, or older, but some of them had daughters or sons who appeared occasionally for week-ends and could be seen in church or at the tennis club. Rosalie and I joined the tennis club but Helen did not care for games.

I had expected life to be dull at Ryddelton but there always seemed to be something going on; there was the Flower Show and Country Dancing and a big Sale of Work in the Town Hall to raise money for the Old Folks' Treat. Helen turned up her nose at such small-town entertainments but Rosalie and I found them extremely amusing. There was a gaiety about them, everybody seemed cheerful. People went to the entertainments expecting to enjoy them, and this created the right atmosphere for enjoyment. At first it puzzled me a good deal and then I found the answer to the problem: in London, if you wanted a little spree, you went to the theatre—or perhaps to a movie—and sat in a seat to be entertained, but the inhabitants of Ryddelton were obliged to provide their own entertainments, and everybody helped to make them successful.

It was not all fun and games for we had to economise severely and none of us had been used to economise so we did not know how to do it properly. Mother worried a lot about whether we should be able to make ends meet; she kept accounts of all that was spent and pored over them in the evenings.

"I can't remember," she would say. "Rosalie, you were with me. How much did I pay for those apples? Mrs. McBain was telling me about Jean's baby and I forgot to write it down."

Sometimes her difficulties were much more serious and one evening she was almost in tears. "Look, Jane," she said.' "I simply can't make this out. I paid Tom Gow ten shillings for trimming the hedge—but I seem to have paid him twice. I can't have, of course, because he wouldn't have taken it. And I've got one pound four and sixpence too much in my purse."

"It doesn't matter if you've got too much," said Helen smiling scornfully. She thought Mother's accounts were nonsense (her idea was that, if you had spent the money, no amount of adding it up would bring it back); but Mother struggled on, putting down every penny. If she had been too careless about money in London she had now gone to the other extreme and worried far too much.

"Yes, it *does* matter," declared Mother. "I *must* get my accounts right. I know I'm stupid at accounts but I suppose I shall learn in time."

I leant over her shoulder. It was the first time I had seen the account book and it was not as confused as I had expected.

"Tom—10/-," said Mother, pointing out the entry. "That was on Wednesday, and I remember it distinctly. But on Thursday I've written 'Tom—£1. 6. 0', and I've got no recollection of it at all."

It certainly was a poser, and for a few minutes it beat me completely, and then I noticed that the second 'Tom' came amongst a list of 'Pots' and 'Cabs' and 'Bans'. "It couldn't be tomatoes, could it?" I suggested—and then I added hastily "No, of course it couldn't be."

"Tomatoes!" cried Mother, joyfully. "That's exactly what it is!"

"It couldn't be," I repeated. "You wouldn't pay one pound six for tomatoes—"

"One and six," said Mother. "I remember now. I've written down the figures in the wrong columns, that's all. Add it up, Jane, and count the money carefully. Perhaps it will come right."

"Yes, darling, it will."

"But you haven't added it up—and counted the money," objected Mother.

It seemed strange that Mother, who was so clear-headed about other things, should be so muddle-headed about accounts.

Chapter Five

1

The day came for my visit to Edinburgh and although it was not to be all joy—I was going to the dentist—I had been looking forward to it a lot. I had decided to go by bus, for I was anxious to see something of the country. Old Tom Gow was going too; he had some ploy in Edinburgh.

If I had known before that he was going I would have gone by train, for Tom was not my idea of an escort, but it was not until I was sitting in the bus that he climbed in and sat down beside me.

"I'll see after Miss Jane," he said to Mother, who was looking unnecessarily anxious.

Old Tom, in his best clothes, was extremely neat and tidy. He was scarcely recognisable as the curiously-attired individual who had dug the vegetable plot and trimmed the hedge, but all the same I would rather have avoided him—which just shows how foolish I was.

We set off at a good pace through the town and up the hill and for a time he remained silent. Then he said, "Are ye interested in hist'ry, Miss Jane?"

I replied that I was—and at once his brown eyes brightened and he began to tell me about the various places we passed. Sometimes it was difficult to understand what he said, for when he was excited he relapsed into his own broad Doric, and then he would pull himself up and repeat his remarks in language comprehensible to my ignorance.

There were wide moors and rolling hills covered with purple heather—for by this time it was early September and the heather was at its best—and although the road was lonely and wound its way hither and thither Mr. Gow found plenty of history to relate. He pointed out a cart-track and asked if I could see the Roman soldiers with their helmets glittering in the sun. Then, seeing my astonishment, he chuckled and added,

"Aye, that's a Roman Road, Miss Jane. If ye was tae dig doon a couple o' feet ye'd find the stanes, a pavement o' stanes for the sodjers tae walk on. It's interesting, ye ken."

"Yon's Tweed," he said, pointing to a little stream which prattled over grey pebbles beside the road. "There's a wheen o' hist'ry in yon wee river."

Presently we passed a notice at the side of the road which read, "Site of Linkum Doddie."

"Tell me about that," I said.

"Noo ye're askin'," declared Mr. Gow. "I'll no can tell ye the true tale o' Linkum Doddie, but I ha'e my ain explanation. It was a wee village, or so folks say, but I've been on the brae masel' and sairched till ma eyes were sair an' there's no a stick nor stane tae be seen. It's my belief that the De'il ran away wi' it in the nicht," added Mr. Gow solemnly.

I glanced at him in surprise and discovered that his eyes were twinkling.

After a while my companion yawned and said he would take a wee snooze and in a moment he was asleep, sitting bolt upright in his seat, swaying from side to side but never losing his equilibrium. We swept on past fields with sheep and cows grazing in them, past woods and little farms, up hill and down dale. We passed through a little town with quaint old-fashioned buildings which lay in the shelter of a range of rolling hills.

"It's a good thing I woke up," said Mr. Gow suddenly. "Yon's the Pentlands, Miss Jane. You'll have haird o' the Pentland Hills? And there's Swanston where wee Louis Stevenson played when he was a laddie. Mebbe you'll have read *Kidnapped*? It's a grand story."

We talked about *Kidnapped* for several minutes and then we topped a rise.

"Edinburgh!" I exclaimed rapturously.

"Aye, yon's Edinburgh."

"It's beautiful!"

"It's no bad," agreed Mr. Gow. "I've a sort o' liking for the place. I was born there, ye ken."

The city lay before our eyes spread out like a map with its steeples and towers rising above the clustered buildings. There was a faint haze over it—a sunlit haze—and the castle on its rock seemed to be floating in air. Beyond the town there was a stretch of blue water and, beyond the water, green hills.

"Auld Reekie," said Mr. Gow. "There's few days that ye see it clear—and it's no sae pretty wanting it's mist in my opeenion."

"It's lovely!" I cried.

"Aye, it's no bad," he agreed proudly . . . and already I had lived in Ryddelton long enough to know that this was the height of praise.

We parted at the bus stop and Mr. Gow impressed upon me that I must meet him there at ten-to-three—and not a moment later. "You'll not get lost, Miss Jane," he said anxiously. "I telt your mither I'd see after ye. If ye get lost ye'll ask a bobby. See and not get run over," he added. "The traffic's fair awful."

I assured him that I would not get lost, nor run over. "I'm used to London traffic," I said.

That comforted him a little, but when I turned to look back he was gazing after me down the street.

2

Cousin Margaret's club was situated in a wide square with gardens in the middle—it was not unlike Wintringham Square but the buildings here were larger and more dignified. Unfortunately the square was used as a car-park which in my opinion (as Mr. Gow would have said) detracted from its appearance. Cousin Margaret had not arrived so I was shown into the lounge to wait for her.

It was interesting to look round and watch the people; they seemed quite different from the people who frequented Mother's club in London. Their faces were different and so were their clothes. These people were perfectly natural and were not afraid to look like themselves. There were exceptions of course but most of them wore their own faces and the clothes which they found comfortable. (In London it was necessary to be fashionable whether the current fashion suited you or not. The current fashion was practically a uniform.)

I looked round the room at the expressions on the people's faces. Some were relaxed and contented, reading the papers until they were summoned to lunch, others obviously were waiting for friends and looked round every time the door opened. There was one woman who interested me particularly; she was sitting next to me, so near that I could have touched her if I had put out my hand. She was middle-aged and untidy and much too fat, but she was so eagerly expectant that she sat on the edge of the chair with her eyes on the door. Whom was she expecting, I wondered: a husband? A friend? A daughter?

Suddenly the door opened and a young man appeared. He was unusually tall and broad-shouldered; he looked very strong. His hair was thick and brown, his mouth large and generous. He was not really handsome for his features were too decisive but there was a glow about him which caught the eye.

It was the glow of perfect health and abounding vitality.

The young man's gaze swept the room and fastened upon the fat woman. He made a gesture of recognition and threaded his way towards her between the chairs. She had seen him and rose as he approached but they did not greet each other except with their eyes.

"Well?" she asked in a low voice. "Did you have the interview?"

"Yes," he replied. "Yes, and it's all right. I've got the post."

"Definitely?"

"Quite definitely."

"My dear, I'm so glad."

"It's what I wanted—more than anything," he said eagerly. "It's a wonderful opportunity to work with a man like that. I'm to go next year sometime. He's to let me know when he's ready."

"Of course I knew you'd get it."

"How could you? There were half a dozen—"

"But none with your qualifications and enthusiasm. He'd have been a fool to take anybody else."

The young man laughed. "I'm keen, anyway," he admitted. "Keen as mustard. I only hope I can fill the bill."

"Have you phoned Ken?"

He nodded. "First thing I did. Dear old Ken!"

"What did he say?"

"Much the same as you. Oh look, Aunt Edith, we're being signalled!" he added.

They were 'being signalled' to go in to lunch. Hastily 'Aunt Edith' rose and in so doing she dropped her hand-bag upside down upon the floor; keys and letters, a powder compact, a notecase and a purse—and all the other odds and ends which middle-aged ladies are wont to carry about with them in hand-bags—were scattered far and wide.

"Oh goodness!" exclaimed 'Aunt Edith' in dismay.

"It's all right, I'll do it," said the young man quickly and with that he went down on his knees and began to gather up the débris. Some of the things had rolled under my chair so I rose and pushed it back and helped him. The incident had created quite a stir in the room; everybody was looking at us, several other people had moved their chairs and were groping for bits and pieces.

"Thanks awfully," murmured the young man. "Don't worry—I can do it all right—hold on a moment—there's something under the table."

He crawled under the table and retrieved the object. "Good lord, it's a trouser-button!" he exclaimed—and his voice sounded so surprised that I could not help giggling.

I had collected a nail-file, a bottle of smelling-salts, two large safety-pins and a small brass knob. The young man held the bag open and I dropped them in. By this time he, also, had begun to giggle. His face was red with the effort to control himself and his shoulders were shaking. Looking down at him, as he knelt at my feet, I could see how thick his hair was—thick and brown and springy. There was a suggestion of a wave in his hair: it only needed to be damped and pinched to wave beautifully . . . but of course he was not the sort of young man to encourage a wave in his hair!

"Have you got everything?" asked 'Aunt Edith' anxiously. "Oh dear, I'm so sorry! I've given everybody so much trouble—so terribly sorry—"

The next moment it was all over. The young man had risen and restored the bag to its owner and they had gone. The room settled down and everything was exactly as it had been before.

Soon after that Cousin Margaret arrived and as she came towards me several people greeted her in a friendly manner. It was obvious that she knew most of the people in the room and was a popular member of the club. Perhaps she knew THEM and could tell me who they were!

"Oh Jane!" exclaimed Cousin Margaret. "Have you been waiting ages? I meant to be early—"

"It doesn't matter a bit," I told her.

"You weren't bored?"

"No," I said. "No, I wasn't bored."

3

The dining-room was large; it was a long room with windows at each end but in spite of its size it was crowded with people and at first I could not see the young man with the brown hair . . . and then I saw him right at the other end of the room sitting at a table with his aunt. He was talking eagerly and she was listening enthralled. I had intended to ask Cousin Margaret who they were—but I couldn't. He was the only young man in the room. How could I ask who he was?

"Are you hungry, Jane?" asked my hostess. "There's haggis and lamb cutlets and steak and kidney pie. I shall have steak and kidney pie. What about you?"

"Yes, please," I said vaguely.

"You're gazing round as if you had never seen a mob of women before," declared Cousin Margaret. "What do you think of them, Jane? Andrew says they're 'a monstrous regiment of club-women'."

"John Knox said that, didn't he?"

"Nearly," she agreed smiling. "He probably would have said it if I had brought him here to lunch . . . but you haven't told me what you think of us."

"I think you're comfortable," I said.

"Comfortable?" she said thoughtfully. "Yes, I see what you mean. We wear what we like—and people can take us or leave us. As a matter of fact I hate to be all dressed up even for a wedding. I feel all wrong. I'm more myself in tweeds."

"What about the evening?"

"Oh, that's different! I like dressing up in the evening, but even then I like my own special sort of dress. Nothing new or frilly or startling—black velvet and diamonds."

"You would look like a duchess!" I exclaimed.

It was perfectly true; Cousin Margaret had exactly the looks to carry off black velvet and diamonds, her features were finely chiselled and she had wavy grey hair and a complexion that a Society Beauty might have envied.

"A duchess!" she exclaimed. "Oh Jane, you flatterer!" and she blushed like a girl. "We don't go out much in the evening," she added. "Just now and then Andrew and I dress up and go to a ball. Perhaps you would like to come with us. Are you fond of dancing?"

"I'm not very good at dancing—it isn't my line—but Helen loves dancing. I'm sure she would love to go to a ball."

Cousin Margaret nodded. "We'll arrange it," she declared. "Helen must come and stay with us and go to a ball."

We went on talking. She was easy to talk to for she was completely natural and sincere and she spoke to me as if I were her own age. I found myself telling her all sorts of things—things that I had never intended to tell anyone. I told her about Oxford, and how disappointed I had been when I found it was impossible for me to read History and Literature as I had intended, and she asked if I were still keen to go to Oxford.

"No, not now," I said . . . and then I hesitated for I had surprised myself.

"You've changed your mind?"

"Yes, but I didn't know I had changed my mind until you asked me. That's funny, isn't it?"

"Not really," said Cousin Margaret thoughtfully. "Perhaps you've found something else—something that suits you better. Have you any idea what you want to do?"

It was difficult to answer that. I said vaguely, "I think I want to learn more about the world."

When I had said it I thought it sounded priggish and I wished the words unsaid.

"Oh, so do I!" cried Cousin Margaret. "I used to think that when Andrew got married I would go round the world and see all the places I've read about: Greece! New Zealand—the hot springs of Rotorua! Colorado! The South Sea Islands!"

"What a wonderful idea!" I said, looking at her in surprise. It seemed incredible that this middle-aged lady should have dreams of travel. She looked so comfortable and contented and set in her ways.

"I think I would go alone," she continued thoughtfully. "In some ways it would be nice to have a companion, but it would have to be somebody who liked the same things—somebody young and adventurous. I mean I should hate to rush round on a prearranged route like a tourist. I should want to wander about from place to place with lots of time to take things in." She laughed and added, "But what's the use of thinking about it!"

"You mean you won't be able to go?"

"It's only a dream. I could never leave Andrew unless he got married—and he's not likely to get married now. He's forty-three, and I'm fifty," added Cousin Margaret.

"You don't seem as old as that," I said quickly.

"I'm glad," she said, smiling. "Fifty sounds stodgy. It sounds like an overcooked rice-pudding, don't you think so, Jane?"

I knew what she meant, but there was nothing stodgy about Cousin Margaret, whatever her age; indeed I found her so interesting to talk to that I almost forgot the young man with the brown hair... almost but not quite. Every now and then my eyes strayed to the other end of the room and I saw he was still there. We had finished lunch, and were about to rise when I noticed that he and his aunt were on their way to the door.

It was now or never! In another moment they would have vanished and I would never know their names! I had to ask.

"Oh, it's Edith Mackintosh!" exclaimed Cousin Margaret. "I want to speak to her about the bazaar. What a good thing you saw her! Do you think you could run after her and tell her?"

The mission was not as easy as it sounded for by this time several other people had finished their meal and were rising from their tables and blocking the way. I made what haste I could but when I had squeezed past two fat ladies and emerged into the hall Miss Mackintosh and her nephew had passed through the revolving door and were disappearing down the steps. I pursued them and managed to catch them in the road.

"Miss Mackintosh!" I exclaimed breathlessly.

She looked at me in surprise.

"My cousin is there," I said. "My cousin, Miss Firth. She wants to talk to you about a bazaar. She sent me to tell you—"

"Oh yes," said Miss Mackintosh. "Margaret and I are sharing a stall. I must talk to her about it." She added, "You don't mind waiting, do you Ronnie?" and without more ado she turned and went back into the dub.

It seemed natural for me to follow her and I was half-way up the steps when I found the young man at my elbow.

"Couldn't you wait a minute?" he suggested.

"Wait a minute?" I repeated in surprise.

"Yes. You've got to wait for your cousin and I've got to wait for my aunt, so we might as well wait together—if you see what I mean."

Put like that it seemed the sensible thing to do.

"We could go in and sit down, couldn't we?" he added.

I hesitated and glanced at my watch. It was twenty minutes past two so I had half an hour before meeting Mr. Gow at the bus. There was no need to hurry.

By this time we were in the hall and the young man had opened the door of the lounge and was waiting for me to go in.

"Over there near the window," he said. "It's a good place. We can keep an eye on the steps in case our relations forget about us and go off together."

"Forget about us!" I echoed.

"I don't know about yours but mine is a bit vague."

"Cousin Margaret might forget the time," I admitted.

We sat down together on the window-seat.

"That's what I meant," agreed my companion. "If they start talking about a bazaar . . ."

"Yes," I said doubtfully. "But I can't wait very long."

"Please wait," he said. "We could talk about shoes or ships or sealing-wax. It would pass the time."

I did not want to talk about shoes or ships or sealing-wax. I wanted to ask him what his name was (his aunt had called him Ronnie, so perhaps his name was Ronnie Mackintosh); I wanted to know about ' the interview ' and what sort of post he had got. Helen would have asked straight out, of course, but Helen was not shy and gauche. Helen was poised and beautiful. Helen knew how to talk to young men.

"Perhaps it would interest you to hear the history of the little brass knob," suggested Ronnie. "I asked Aunt Edith and she told me. It came off the end of her bed. It fell off this morning when she was turning the mattress and she hadn't time to screw it on, so she popped it into her bag for safety—so that she wouldn't lose it." His eyes were twinkling but his mouth was perfectly serious.

"Oh, that was it," I said. "I wondered . . ."

"Quite a simple explanation."

"Yes, of course."

"It's often the way," declared Ronnie. "I mean things that seem mysterious often have quite a simple explanation—when you know. Have you noticed that?"

"Yes, I have," I said.

"The button is still a mystery," continued Ronnie. "As a matter of fact I didn't like to ask about the button. You see Aunt Edith is a spinster—and rather proper—"

We were talking nonsense. We were wasting time. The clock in the corner of the room said it was half-past two and I knew I must go. Mr. Gow would be frantic if I were not at the bus to meet him at ten minutes to three.

"I ought to go," I said feebly.

"Go!" exclaimed Ronnie in dismay. "Oh no, you can't possibly go away and leave me alone amongst all these ladies. Please don't go."

"I ought to—really."

"Why ought you?"

"I've got to meet somebody at ten minutes to three. He'll be waiting for me."

"Let him wait," suggested Ronnie cheerfully.

"But I can't," I said desperately. "He'll be frightfully worried if I'm not there."

"Does it matter? Is he terribly important?"

"Not really," I said. "I mean he isn't important in himself—but I promised to be there. Promises are important, aren't they?"

Ronnie had been teasing me but now, suddenly, his face changed and he was quite serious. "Yes, promises are important," he agreed.

I hesitated for a moment and then I rose and held out my hand. "Good-bye," I said. "You understand, don't you? I really must go."

"If you must, you must," said Ronnie. "I shall hide behind a shiny magazine until Aunt Edith appears."

He rose and we shook hands.

A few minutes later I was running down the street to meet Mr. Gow and catch the bus.

Chapter Six

1

The morning after my expedition to Edinburgh I was awakened early by a loud gurgling sound and the splash of water. It was rainwater pouring off the steeply-sloping gable and running down the pipes. The roof was just over my head so it sounded very loud and the first time I heard it I had imagined that something queer had happened to the cistern and that the water was pouring into my room . . . but now I knew what it was so I did not worry. I lay and listened to it—gurgle, gurgle, splash, splash—and thought about all that had happened.

I thought about Ronnie. If I shut my eyes I could see Ronnie quite clearly; I could see his tall figure and his broad shoulders and his long legs. I could see his brown hair (which would have been wavy if he had not brushed it down so sternly) and his strong white teeth and twinkling eyes. Ronnie had wanted to be friendly—he had asked me to sit down and talk to him—but instead of meeting him half-way I had been gauche and stupid and tongue-tied. How differently Helen would have behaved!

I thought of all I might have said—it was easy to reconstruct the conversation. Instead of talking about brass knobs and buttons I should have said, 'You know I was sitting next you in the lounge before lunch and I couldn't help hearing what you were saying to your aunt about your new post. Do tell me about it.' Then he would have told me. He would have been glad to tell me. It would have been something worthwhile to talk about. Then I could have told him who I was and why it was so important for me to meet Mr. Gow. I could have explained it all in a few words and made a joke of it. I imagined myself saying, 'Oh yes, Mr. Gow is terribly important. He's our gardener. He came with me to Edinburgh in the bus. If I don't meet him at ten minutes to three he'll think I've got lost or been run over. He'll be simply frantic!' I imagined myself laughing—and Ronnie laughing.

It was too late now, of course. I had been an absolute idiot. The only thing to do was to put it out of my mind . . . but somehow I knew that it was going to be difficult.

2

It was surprising how quickly we had settled down to our new life; Helen and Rosalie swept and dusted and polished the furniture, and I helped Mother in the kitchen—or at least I tried to help her. Unfortunately I was clumsy and awkward; dishes slipped out of my hands and crashed on to the floor in the most astonishing manner and I took so long over the simplest task that Mother lost patience.

"Away with you!" she would cry. "Go out and dig the garden! You're all fingers and no thumbs! I can do it myself in half the time."

She could, too, for she was methodical and neat in everything she put her hand to. She cooked and cleaned and washed up dishes and scrubbed the kitchen floor . . . and actually she seemed to enjoy it and thrive upon it.

Soon after our arrival at Ryddelton Mother went to a sale and bought a second-hand bicycle. It was in very bad condition but she got it cheap and Mr. Gow cleaned it up and put it right. The bicycle was a strange-looking contraption with very high handle-bars and an upright seat; Helen refused to ride it but Rosalie and I were not so proud . . . indeed I found it extremely useful for going down to Ryddelton and doing the shopping.

As I was not much use in the kitchen the shopping became one of my duties and before long I got to know the little town well and made friends with some of its inhabitants. The people in the shops found time to chat and to ask how we were liking the cottage. They often added, "It'll be quiet after London. You'll notice the difference!"

Although I had become used to the habit of understatement and could take it in my stride this beat me completely. It meant something—I knew that—for several people said it and waited for an answer.

"Oh yes," I said solemnly. "I notice the difference." What else could I say?

One morning when I had done the shopping and was on my way home an old lady stepped off the path just in front of me. I swerved quickly but not quite quickly enough. The handle-bars caught her arm and she spun round, lost her balance and fell on the road. I fell off the bicycle and every-thing in the basket was scattered. It had happened so suddenly and unexpectedly that I was quite dazed but I scrambled to my feet and ran to the old lady.

"Oh goodness!" I cried. "I'm terribly sorry! Are you badly hurt?"

"It's my arm," she said.

I helped her to get up. She was very small and light, and if need be I could have carried her quite easily, but except for her arm she did not seem to be much the worse. Fortunately the accident had happened just outside her house; she had been crossing the road to go into her house when I knocked her over.

I helped her across the road and into her house and made her lie down upon the sofa. Her face was quite grey by this time and her wrist was swelling visibly, but although she was in pain she was perfectly calm and composed.

"You had better call Solda," she said. "Solda must ring up the doctor. It looks as if I had sprained my wrist."

Solda proved to be a tall angular Frenchwoman, dark and sallow, with a most unfriendly air. She was even less amiable when I told her what had happened. Thrusting me aside she rushed to the telephone and I could hear her demanding that Dr. Ferguson should come at once, and explaining that "Madame" had been knocked down in the road and nearly killed by a careless girl on a bicycle.

Meantime I returned to my victim. "I'm awfully sorry," I declared. "It's frightful! I don't know what to say—"

"You've said you're sorry," she pointed out.

"I know, but—but I wish I could *do* something."

"You'll find a bottle of whisky in the dining-room cup-board. Bring two glasses," she added.

I found the whisky and the glasses and brought them to her. The second glass was for me. I had never tasted whisky before and I thought it extremely nasty. It burnt my throat when I swallowed it. We were both drinking whisky when the doctor arrived.

"Your maid said you were nearly killed!" he exclaimed.

"Solda exaggerates," said the old lady tartly. "I've hurt my wrist, that's all. It was my own fault. I stepped off the path without looking."

This was true, of course, but it was decent of her to say it to the doctor. The accident had happened so suddenly that I had been wondering if she realised it was not my fault.

Dr. Ferguson glanced at me and said, "You're Miss Harcourt, aren't you? I've seen you in church."

I had never seen him before but I was so used to everybody knowing me that I was not surprised.

"Let's see the wrist," he added. "H'm. Looks to me like a fracture. We had better have it X-rayed."

"Couldn't you tie it up with a bandage?"

"I could, but I won't," he replied smiling. "I'll take you straight to the hospital. Can you walk to the car?"

"Walk to the car!" cried the old lady scornfully. "It isn't my leg that's broken! What's to prevent me walking to the car?"

There was plenty of courage in her but I noticed that when she stood up she was very tottery and was glad to lean on the doctor's arm.

It was not until they had driven away that I remembered the bicycle and the groceries which had been scattered all over the road, but I need not have worried. Somebody had picked up everything; had packed all the parcels into the basket and parked the bicycle against the fence. There was nobody in sight and I never knew who did it. Ryddelton is full of good neighbours.

3

I felt rather queer as I toiled up the hill. My eyes were blurred and there was a strange sort of rushing in my ears. Mother was waiting at the gate and the moment I saw her I began to cry like a baby. It was extraordinary—for I scarcely ever cried—and it was completely unexpected. I had not felt the least like crying until I saw her.

"Oh Jane!" exclaimed Mother. "I knew there was something the matter! I felt it in my bones! You fell off that horrible bicycle! I wish I had never bought it! Oh Jane, your poor knees!"

"That's nothing," I sobbed. As a matter of fact I had not even noticed that my knees were grazed. "That's nothing—my knees don't matter—I knocked her down—"

Mother had the same idea as the old lady. She seized my arm, dragged me into the house and brought me a glass.

"Drink that," said Mother firmly. "It will do you good."

I looked at it and hesitated. "I think I've had enough whisky," I said.

"It's brandy," declared Mother. "But if you've had whisky already—" and she snatched it away.

"I'll—try—it—if you like—"

"No, you won't," said Mother, gazing at me. "You're half tight already. What you need is blotting-paper."

"Blotting-paper!" I echoed. It seemed so funny that I began to laugh. Did Mother think I had been drinking ink?

She brought me two dry biscuits and made me eat them and they seemed to do me good. I stopped laughing and dried my eyes.

"Now, tell me," said Mother.

"I knocked her down," I said. "She stepped off the pavement—without looking. I couldn't help it. She said it wasn't my fault—and it wasn't—but her wrist is broken. The doctor took her to the hospital."

"Who is she?" demanded Mother. "Where does she live?"

I did not know who she was, but I described where she lived.

"The Corner House," nodded Mother. "I don't know who lives there now but I'll ring up Elspeth. Elspeth is sure to know all about her."

It was discovered that my victim was a Mrs. Millard who had come to Ryddelton two years ago and bought The Corner House.

"She's not really old," declared Mother. "Elspeth thinks she's about sixty-five."

Sixty-five seemed 'really old' to me.

"Does Mrs. Hunter know her?" Helen inquired.

"Not at all well," replied Mother. "Nobody in Ryddelton seems to know much about her. She's not a friendly sort of person, she keeps herself to herself. She brought an old servant with her—a Frenchwoman—so she doesn't need a daily."

Helen smiled rather nastily and said, "That's why nobody knows much about her."

It was true, in a way, for if you had a daily woman to help in the house Ryddelton soon heard all about you, but there was no need for Helen to sneer. What did it matter who knew about you unless you had something to hide?

"Perhaps she *has* something to hide," suggested Rosalie.

4

The next morning Mother said I must call upon Mrs. Millard and take her some flowers.

"You needn't go in," said Mother. "Just ask how she is."

"Must I?"

"Of course you must," said Mother firmly. "It's your duty to go. It's only polite."

I would have avoided the duty if possible; I had been told that Mrs. Millard was 'not a friendly sort of person', and even if I did not go in and see her I should have to speak to the French maid (who was very unfriendly indeed) but Mother would listen to no excuses; she picked the flowers herself and arranged them in a posy and sent me off as if I had been ten years old.

Mrs. Millard was at home and before I could explain that I did not want to see her I was ushered into the sitting-room and found her lying on the sofa with her arm in a sling.

"How kind of you to call!" she said pleasantly.

"I just came to ask how you are. I'm awfully sorry—" I began.

"You've said that before," she declared. She had an incisive manner of speaking which was slightly alarming. "There's no need to keep on saying you're sorry. Of course you're sorry. If you weren't sorry you'd be a fiend—and you appear to be a kind-hearted young woman—and an artistic young woman," she added with a glance at the flowers.

"Oh, Mother did that," I said hastily.

"A young woman of integrity!" exclaimed Mrs. Millard.

I could feel myself blushing.

"A modest young woman," added Mrs. Millard smiling.

Of course she was making fun of me, but I did not really mind. "How is your wrist?" I asked. "I hope it isn't very painful."

As I said the words it occurred to me that it was almost the same as saying I was sorry and I wondered if she would reply that I must be a fiend if such was not my hope. I believe she thought it, but fortunately she did not say it. She just explained that a small bone was fractured but it had been set and put it plaster and would soon mend. "It wouldn't matter if it were my left wrist," she added.

I began to say that of course one's right hand was much more useful, but she interrupted me.

"I'm writing a book," said Mrs. Millard. "And I can't write with my left hand. That's the trouble. I'm writing the biography of a naughty lady," she added with a smile.

"A real book! How wonderful!"

"There's nothing wonderful about it. Writing a biography is hard work, that's all. If you've got the material you can go ahead, and I've got plenty of material—in fact rather too much. There's no need for you to gaze at me as if I were Charlotte Brontë and Jane Austen rolled into one. It's a job—just like any other job—and I do it for money."

I still thought it was wonderful—and clever.

"This isn't my first attempt," she continued. "I've done several biographies. It's an odd feature of modern life that respectable families should allow a complete stranger to browse amongst their family-papers and concoct a story about an ancestress who was no better than she should be. Don't you think so, Miss Harcourt?"

"Yes," I said. "At least—I don't know. Perhaps it might be rather amusing."

"Oh, it's amusing," said Mrs. Millard with a wicked smile. "The adventures of Lady Esmeralda Pie make *very* amusing reading. She was a baggage; there's no other word for her. I was just beginning to get things sorted out—and now *this* has happened."

I very nearly said again that I was sorry, but remembered in time to choke back the words.

"What were you going to say, Miss Harcourt?" inquired Mrs. Millard sweetly.

"It was just—I wondered—couldn't you get a secretary?"

She shook her head. "Solda would be as jealous as hell and there would be rows. I can't stand rows. If I could get somebody to come in for a couple of hours in the morning it might work out, but there's no hope of that in Ryddelton. No, I'm afraid Lady Esmeralda will have to wait until my wrist is mended."

"Would I be any good?" I asked. I felt I had to offer, for although the accident was not my fault I felt responsible, but my offer was very half-hearted and I was extremely glad when it was refused.

"I don't think I could bear it," said Mrs. Millard, looking at me thoughtfully. "I tried a secretary once before. I thought it would save time. She really was wonderful. She wrote shorthand faster than I could speak, so she was always waiting for me to continue—waiting patiently with her pencil poised and her large earnest brown eyes fixed upon my face. I think she must have given me an inferiority complex or something. I know she nearly drove me mad."

"How awful!" I said, smiling. And then I rose and said I must go.

"Can you do shorthand?" asked Mrs. Millard.

"Oh no! I can't write shorthand. I can't do anything that proper secretaries do. I've never had any training."

I had said good-bye and was half-way to the door when Mrs. Millard called me back. "We might try," she said. "If I found you were driving me mad we could stop before I was raving and biting pieces out of the carpet."

It was a joke of course. I could see that by her face. I thought it was a poor joke but I laughed and said, "It was silly of me to offer. Of course I wouldn't be any use at all. It was just that I was . . ."

"Sorry?" suggested Mrs. Millard.

I could hear her laughing as I went down the path.

5

Never before had I met anybody the least like Mrs. Millard, so I could not help thinking about her and wondering about her book. If she wrote as she talked the book would be unusual to say the least of it. I did the shopping and walked home. It was pleasant to live on a hill because of the view and because of the joyous feeling of rushing downhill on a bicycle with the breeze whistling in your ears, but it was not so pleasant to toil home with a heavy basket on your handlebars.

Mother was in the kitchen making scones.

"There you are!" she exclaimed. "If you'd been here a few minutes sooner you could have answered the telephone yourself. She left a message to say you're to go at ten on Monday."

"Who?"

"Mrs. Millard, of course. I thought it was all arranged. She said you'd offered to go to her as secretary."

I lifted the basket on to the table and gazed at Mother in consternation.

"Didn't you offer?" asked Mother.

"No—I mean yes, but I didn't mean it."

"She thinks you did," said Mother, squeezing the dough off her hands and taking up the rolling-pin.

"Are you sure it wasn't—a joke?"

"Of course it wasn't a joke. Half a crown an hour, she said. It isn't much, but you're not trained so I don't suppose you could expect more." Mother sighed and added, "We could have Mrs. Gow twice a week, couldn't we? But don't go if you don't want to, darling."

I was not sure whether I wanted to or not. There was something very exciting about Mrs. Millard—but a little frightening as well. I said, "But she wouldn't keep me, you know. She said if she found I was driving her mad it would stop."

"Driving her mad!" echoed Mother in amazement.

I decided that I could not take the job. I had no idea what she would want me to do, but whatever she wanted me to do I was sure I was incapable of doing it . . . and then she would be cross. The mere idea of Mrs. Millard being cross was terrifying. I explained this to Mother.

"She sounds mad already," said Mother. "She sounds absolutely crazy. You had better ring her up and say you can't manage it after all. Say you're sorry," added Mother.

I could not help smiling as I went to the telephone, but my smile faded when I tried to make up my mind what to say.

The telephone receiver was sticky with dough and as I wiped it off I thought of all that Mother did in the house: making scones and washing the dishes and scrubbing the floor. I was no use to her—and I had an uncomfortable feeling that I never would be any use—I seemed incapable of learning. How nice it would be if I could pay Mrs. Gow myself! I stood and looked at the telephone—and wondered. Well, why not? I thought. If Mrs. Millard found me hopelessly incompetent she could sack me. There was no harm in trying.

Chapter Seven

1

It was exactly ten o'clock when I rang the bell of The Corner House on Monday morning. (The clock on the tower of the Town Hall was beginning to chime); the door was opened immediately.

"Oh, it is you!" said Solda without enthusiasm. "*Enfin*, it is stupid to ring the bell and take me from my work. You can walk up the stairs to the study."

There were several doors on the top landing but fortunately I chose the right one and looked in. The room was large and sparsely furnished with a roll-top desk, a typewriter and a bookcase filled with reference books; a chest stood upon the floor near the fireplace.

Mrs. Millard was sitting at a large solid kitchen-table covered with piles of papers and letters. She looked up and said, "A punctual young woman! Take off your jacket and hang it on the door. Have you got a pen?"

I had brought my fountain-pen and a scribbling-pad as well, so I sat down in the chair opposite to my employer and waited for orders.

"These are the letters," Mrs. Millard explained. "There are more in that chest—hundreds of them. Some are from Esmeralda to her friends and some are from friends to Esmeralda. There are letters from enemies as well—but you'll see as we go along. Here's a sheaf of them for you to clip together in chronological order."

There was nothing difficult about that, so my spirits rose and I tackled the job cheerfully. For a time we worked in silence. Mrs. Millard was reading the letters and sorting them into three separate piles. Presently she said, "Some of these letters are useless; some have passages which I can use; some I must have in full." She chuckled and added, "Here's one I must have in full. Can you read it?"

The question was by no means superfluous, for the letter was written in thin spidery writing which would have disgraced a child of eight years old.

"That's a specimen of the Lady Esmeralda's calligraphy," said Mrs. Millard. "She was an indifferent penwoman and her spelling leaves much to be desired but she made up in quantity what she lacked in quality. When she was excited her writing deteriorated and became even more illegible. Obviously she was excited when she wrote *that*. See what you can make of it, Miss Harcourt."

"It would be easier if you called me Jane."

"Very much easier," agreed Mrs. Millard promptly. "Here you are, Jane. You can take the letter and copy it out clearly. I want it exactly as it is, with all the abbreviations and peculiar spelling. Sit over there at the desk."

"Just—copy it out?" I asked.

"That's what I said," declared Mrs. Millard impatiently.

It took some time to decipher the letter (at first glance it seemed an impossible task) but I had a feeling that this was a sort of test and if I failed my engagement would come to an abrupt conclusion—so I struggled on. After a bit I began to get more used to the scrawl and except for a word here and there—which stumped me completely—I made a clear transcript.

No wonder Lady Esmeralda had been excited when she sat down at her 'booreau' to pen the letter to her 'dearest Emily' (most young women would have been too excited and upset to write at all) for it contained news of a 'fearce jewel' which had taken place at dawn between two of her ladyship's admirers, both of whom had been 'woonded in the fray.' Lady Esmeralda had been present in person, hiding in the 'shrubary', and obviously had enjoyed the fun. To see the 'bludde' flowing, and to be aware that it was shed for her, had given her the most delicious sensations which she described in full. She explained to dearest Emily that it was not a mere whim which had lured her from her comfortable bed at such an unwonted hour; it had been essential to see the contest with her own eyes so that she might determine which of the contestants she liked best.

I took the letter and my transcript to Mrs. Millard and showed them to her.

"Very neat—just what I wanted," she said. "It's taken you a long time but you'll get used to her scrawl. That word is *étonnant*. You've left a space for it. Don't you understand French?"

"I didn't realise it was a French word," I said. "I see it now, of course."

"Esmeralda used quite a lot of French words to describe her sensations. It's an interesting letter, isn't it, Jane."

"Is it true, Mrs. Millard?"

"It depends what you mean by true. The letter is authentic—I mean it was written by Esmeralda to her friend—but whether it is a veracious account of what happened or merely a charming fairy-tale—"

"A fairy-tale!"

"To amuse dearest Emily, to make her heart beat faster and give her shivers up her spine," explained Mrs. Millard with a wicked smile. "Here's another letter," she continued. "Not quite so lurid. I only want the passages I have marked."

"I can type," I told her. "Not very fast, I'm afraid, but it would be neater than—"

"The chatter of a typewriter!" cried Mrs. Millard with a shudder. "My dear Jane, do you want to drive me mad?"

I said no more, for the last thing I wanted was to drive her mad. I was getting interested in Lady Esmeralda and I wanted to keep my job.

2

That first morning is very clear in my memory, perhaps because I was all keyed up and anxious to do well. After that we worked every morning for two hours and on Saturday I was able to give Mother thirty shillings. She took half—to pay Mrs. Gow—and made me keep the rest and I must admit that it was a pleasant feeling to have fifteen shillings in my pocket—fifteen shillings which I had earned myself.

I had wondered whether Mrs. Millard would sack me when her wrist was better but her wrist mended and nothing was said. We went on working together and I knew I was useful. From the first I had been fascinated by Lady Esmeralda and as the weeks went past her personality emerged more and more clearly and took a firm hold upon my imagination.

One day when I went into Mrs. Millard's study there was a little miniature lying on the table amongst the papers.

"There she is," said Mrs. Millard. "That's the lady. They've sent me the picture to be reproduced as a frontispiece to my book."

She was exactly as I had imagined, with a long white neck and dark curls and a mischievous twinkle in her emerald-green eyes.

"It's exactly like her!" I cried.

"How do you know?" asked Mrs. Millard teasingly. "How can you possibly know? The artist had to make her beautiful or he wouldn't have got paid for his work."

"I know—because it matches the letters!"

"You're besotted with the creature," declared Mrs. Millard. "It's all the more strange because if you met her in real life you would dislike her intensely."

I stood there, wondering.

"It's true, isn't it?" said Mrs. Millard. "You would be terrified of Esmeralda . . . but never mind, you're not likely to meet the lady. She's been dead for nearly three hundred years—so you can hang her on the wall over the chimney-piece and go on worshipping at her shrine."

I hung her over the chimney-piece and, although I did not worship her, it gave me a great deal of pleasure to look at her picture and to marvel at the strange anomalies of her character. She could be kind and generous; she was often cruel. She was reckless to the point of insanity. It amused her to have half a dozen admirers and to play them off—one against the other—like a juggler playing with coloured balls. Occasionally she met a gentleman and found him 'inchanting' and wrote detailed accounts of his perfections to her dearest Emily. Then suddenly, and for no apparent reason, she would tire of him or find somebody more attractive, and the unfortunate gentleman was thrown aside like a worn shoe. She possessed a peculiar sense of humour and one of her chief pleasures was to play practical jokes upon her friends:

jokes which were the scandal of the town and frequently got her into trouble.

The letters received by Lady Esmeralda were almost as revealing as those she wrote and almost as ill-spelt. As we ploughed through the contents of the oak-chest we discovered scores of love-letters and invitations to routs. There were bills for dresses and mantles and shawls ... and one day I found an anonymous letter demanding money. It was quite short and very much to the point and was written upon a dirty piece of paper.

"Look at that!" I exclaimed, passing it to Mrs. Millard.

"Blackmail!" cried Mrs. Millard in delight. "It isn't surprising! No woman could live that sort of life without laying herself open to blackmail—but how lucky that she kept the letter and didn't burn it!"

"Shall I copy it?" I asked.

"Of course! Use your brains, child, and don't ask superfluous questions."

Mrs. Millard was always telling me to use my brains and the consequence was I had begun to use them. It was good for me.

Lady Esmeralda's background was no less interesting than herself; it was a colourful picture of luxury and squalor. Armies of servants thronged the great houses; coaches rumbled up to the doors. Huge meals were eaten at tables laden with silver and lit by candles; there was drinking and gambling and duelling. Highwaymen frequented lonely roads and footpads lurked in the streets. Thieves were hanged and crowds gathered to see the grisly entertainment.

The picture of life in those far-off days became so real and clear that I felt as if I had lived in them myself. It was almost as if I remembered them. Sometimes I returned to them in my dreams (which was not always enjoyable) and occasionally I found myself using words and phrases which occurred in the letters.

Perhaps this was why Mother suggested that I should 'give it up'.

We were all having tea together in the sitting-room. It was a wild stormy afternoon; we could hear the wind howling in the chimney, but inside the cottage it was warm and cosy. Rosalie was making hot-buttered-toast.

Helen had been teasing me about something I had said. "You'll be saying 'odds bodikins' next!" she declared.

Then Mother said, "Don't you think you ought to give it up, Jane? You only went temporarily to oblige her while her wrist was in plaster."

"Oh no, it's fascinating. I couldn't possibly give it up."

"You could help me in the house—"

"Mrs. Gow is far more help than I was."

"It's changing you," said Helen.

"I'm growing up, that's all. You ought to be pleased. You always said I was too young for my age. I'm learning things—"

"What sort of things?" asked Mother anxiously.

"I'm learning about the world. I'm learning how to write a book. I'm learning history far better than I ever learnt it at school."

"How to write a book!" exclaimed Helen scornfully. "That will be useful! I suppose you intend to write a book yourself."

I said nothing. I knew I was no match for Helen in this sort of argument.

"Honestly, Jane, I wish you would give it up," repeated Mother. "We know nothing about Mrs. Millard—or at least very little."

It was obvious that Mother had heard something about her— something not to her credit—but I did not care. I was absolutely determined not to give up my post as long as Mrs. Millard would keep me. I had told Mother that I was growing up and learning about the world and this was true, but my daily contact with Mrs. Millard was teaching me more than that. It was teaching me how to talk to people and not be frightened. It was giving me confidence in myself.

3

There were various changes in the family arrangements during the winter. Cousin Margaret asked Helen to stay for a few days and go to some parties. Of course Cousin Margaret knew scores of people in Edinburgh so Helen had a very good time. She went to a ball with her host and hostess and danced all night with handsome young men in kilts and enjoyed herself tremendously. I gathered that Cousin Margaret had enjoyed it too and had looked quite marvellous in black velvet and diamonds. It would have been interesting to know if Helen had met Ronnie—the young man with the brown hair—but she did not mention him and I could not ask. For one thing I did not know his name and for another I had no wish to be questioned about him. Helen would have wanted to know where I had met him and what he was like, and she would have given me no peace until she had got the whole story out of me.

In addition to the ball at the Assembly Rooms (which had been the high-light of her visit to Edinburgh) Helen had been to a cocktail party and a very amusing play. It had all been so enjoyable and everybody she met had been so friendly that she wanted us all to move to Edinburgh forthwith . . . She did her best to persuade Mother to sell Timble Cottage and buy a little house in Murrayfield which happened to be for sale at the time.

There was a great deal of argument about it (if you can call it an argument when one person talks incessantly and the other says, "No, Helen," in gentle accents) but at last Helen saw it was hopeless and gave it up.

Soon after that Helen found herself a job in Edinburgh—and off she went. The job was that of a receptionist at a big hotel and it suited Helen admirably; she arranged the flowers and received the guests and made herself generally useful. Occasionally she came down for a week-end to Timble Cottage and we heard all about her doings—about the dances she had been to and the friends she had made. Mother was a little worried for she was afraid Helen would find it much too tiring, but she assured Mother that she never felt better in her life. "Edinburgh is so bracing," she declared. "Edinburgh suits me."

Timble Cottage felt quite different when Helen had gone. Helen had been cross and miserable and had done nothing but grumble about everything from morning to night. It felt as if a cloud had lifted when she went away.

When Rosalie heard about all the gay parties she thought that she would like a job in Edinburgh. She talked about it a lot but took no steps to find one—which was just like Rosalie. Mother said nothing, either for or against.

"Why don't you want Rosalie to get a job?" I asked her.

"I *do* want Rosalie to get a job—she would be much happier with something to do—but I don't want her to go to Edinburgh with Helen," replied Mother.

I thought I saw what Mother meant; Helen was such a strong character that she dominated Rosalie. It had always been the same: when Helen was absent Rosalie was herself—sweet and kind and helpful—but when Helen was there she seemed a different person. Curiously enough their attitude to each other varied; sometimes Rosalie did what Helen told her without demur and at other times she would assert herself and argue stubbornly about things that did not matter at all. I had often wondered why this should be so but had never found a satisfactory solution to the problem.

"I want Rosalie to have a life of her own," continued Mother. "She has suffered all her life from being 'like Helen'. Even when she was four years old people used to say, 'She's like Helen, of course, but not so pretty.' That's a dreadful thing, Jane. It would be better if Rosalie were not pretty at all than just a not-quite-so-pretty copy of Helen."

"But Rosalie is a very pretty girl!"

"Yes, she's a very pretty girl—until you see Helen," said Mother. "And that's the reason I don't want her to go to Edinburgh—with Helen."

Mother's ideas and mine were almost the same but she had given me one new idea to think about. I had often wished I were like my elder sister, with fair hair and blue eyes and a rose-petal complexion, but according to Mother I ought to be thankful that I was not; according to Mother it was better to be 'not pretty at all' than to be a 'not-quite-so-pretty' copy of someone else.

Having said that Rosalie would be 'much happier with something to do' Mother proceeded to make inquiries about a job in Ryddelton and discovered that Mrs. Ferguson, the doctor's wife, wanted somebody to go to her daily and help her in the house and look after the children. Rosalie was fond of children and very good at managing them so it sounded just the thing. At first Rosalie refused to consider it and said it was not the sort of job she wanted and she would rather go to Edinburgh, but Mother persuaded her to try it and see how she got on. Fortunately it was a great success; the Fergusons were so kind that she soon made friends with them and became devoted to the children. Indeed we heard so much about Deb and Sally that we began to get a little bored with them—or at least I did. Mother was much more patient. Mother was delighted with the success of her experiment and was willing to listen for hours while Rosalie held forth about the amusing things they did and said. One afternoon we had Deb and Sally to tea at Timble Cottage and they certainly were dear little creatures. Then we had the Fergusons to supper.

I had met Dr. Ferguson several times when he came to The Corner House to see Mrs. Millard about her wrist. He was thirty-five—big and friendly with fair hair and blue eyes. He was very popular in Ryddelton; his patients said you had only to look at Dr. Ferguson and you felt better. I could well believe it. Mrs. Ferguson was small and dark with bright brown eyes—not exactly pretty but attractive and amusing.

The supper party was a great success. It was one of those happy occasions when everything goes right. Rosalie was at her best, I had never seen her look so happy. By this time she knew the Fergusons well and called them Kenneth and Jean, so it seemed natural for us all to do the same. They stayed quite late, sitting round the fire and chatting about one thing and another, and before they left they invited us to go and have supper with them.

Kenneth was busy of course; it was not easy for him to get away, and quite often he was called out to an urgent case in the middle of a meal, but in spite of this we saw a great deal of the Fergusons, it was the beginning of a very pleasant friendship for us all.

Chapter Eight

1

Mrs. Millard spared no pains to have every smallest detail of her book correct. She had said it was just a job and she did it for money but it was much more to her than that. In February she suddenly decided that she must go to London and do some research at the British Museum which meant that I had a holiday until she returned.

Unfortunately my holiday coincided with Mother's visit to Murrayfield Gardens; it had been arranged weeks before that she would stay with Cousin Margaret and Cousin Andrew in February and go to a series of concerts which were taking place in the Usher Hall. She had been looking forward to it, I knew, and when she said she would put it off I refused to let her. There was no object in putting it off. Rosalie came home every evening and I did not mind being in the house alone.

For the first few days I enjoyed my holiday immensely. I made sandwiches and put them in my pocket and walked miles over the hills. It was a pleasant feeling to be free to do as I wanted—a feeling I had never experienced before. I remember one day particularly. There had been frost in the night and there was rime on every twig of faded heather like diamonds glittering in the bright morning sun. In every little burn there were icicles hanging from the rocks. The sky was blue and cloudless and there was not a breath of wind. It seemed wonderful to me. I walked along slowly, enjoying every moment. I enjoyed the beauty, I enjoyed breathing the still, cold air, but most of all I enjoyed the silence. The silence was absolute, not a sound broke it, even the burns had ceased to prattle over their stony beds . . . and I realised what R. L. S. had been thinking of when he wrote of the essential silence that 'chills and blesses' in the lulls of his home. The silence blessed me so beautifully that every unworthy thought was banished and I felt happy and at peace with all the world.

After that marvellous day the weather broke and it was wet and unpleasant and stormy so I could not go out on the hills. There was very little to do in the house and I missed my work with Mrs. Millard. I thought of her quite a lot and wondered how she was getting on—and when she would come back. I had not realised before how much I liked Mrs. Millard.

It was so tedious doing nothing that I decided to try my hand at writing a story just for my own pleasure and to while away the time (as a matter of fact the idea would never have occurred to me if Helen had not put it into my head) so I bought a large exercise-book in the town and started off.

Needless to say the story was set in a bygone age; I was so steeped in the days when Esmeralda was alive that the background was filled in already—or perhaps it would be more true to say that the stage was set and the scenery in place—all I needed was the plot and the characters. I went to sleep thinking about it and woke in the morning with my mind full of ideas. My heroine was not Esmeralda but her opposite in every way, she was a gentle little creature caught up in the tangle of the plot—not brave by nature but capable of courage in defence of the man she loved. Esmeralda had been fickle and ruthless, Agnes was faithful and kind.

At the time I was perfectly certain that my conception of Agnes owed nothing whatever to Esmeralda, but now I see that it owed her a great deal for I had merely taken the naughty lady and, turning her inside out, had produced my paragon—but that is by the way and does not matter except to show how little we understand the workings of our subconscious minds.

The story took shape as it went along and when Mrs. Millard returned I was in the throes of it. Mother returned too, looking very much the better for her holiday. Of course I was delighted to see her but it meant I had very little time to write. I was determined to say nothing about the story until it was finished and perhaps not even then. It all depended upon whether I was satisfied with what I had done. This being so, the only time to write was at night and the only place was my queer little bedroom with the sloping roof. I wrote by the light of an oil-lamp but this was no handicap, for an oil-lamp was the right sort of light for the story, and the shadows it threw in the corners of the strangely-shaped attic stirred my imagination. My wallpaper-birds kept me company; sometimes when I looked up from my work they seemed to be hopping about and peeping at me as they had done the first morning.

2

Mrs. Millard was away much longer than she expected; she had browsed in the manuscript room of the British Museum and had found all sorts of curious documents connected with the period, which linked up with passages in the letters and clarified them. She was delighted, of course, but it meant that parts of the book which already were written had to be altered and rearranged. I had a feeling that if this went on the book would never be finished at all—but it was no business of mine. My business was to sort out Mrs. Millard's notes and copy them and there was so much to do that sometimes I stayed and had lunch with Mrs. Millard and we worked all the afternoon.

In addition to the notes Mrs. Millard had brought a box of jewellery which had been in the bank. One morning when I went in she had opened it and was examining its contents; there were brooches and bracelets and a necklace of emeralds and diamonds and a string of curious-looking grey beads.

"I had almost forgotten these," she said. "What shall I do with them? They're no use to me."

"You could sell them. Mother got a lot of money for her jewellery."

"Yes, that would be the sensible thing to do. I'm not likely to wear them again."

I wondered when and where she had worn all those glittering ornaments. I still knew nothing about her past.

"You can't see me wearing them, can you?" she said, smiling (one of the odd things about her was that she seemed to be able to read my thoughts).

"Oh, I don't know—" I began uncomfortably.

She took up the necklace and fastened it round her neck over her grey woollen frock. "There," she said. "Shall I wear it like that when I walk down Ryddelton High Street? People here think I'm mad already so it wouldn't make much difference. Mad and bad—that's what they say, isn't it, Jane?"

"Not to me," I told her. "I wouldn't believe it if they did."

She looked at me with a curious expression and said, "No, I don't think you would. Oh well, I wasn't as gay and naughty as Esmeralda but some of my experiences would shock you considerably."

"Shock me!"

"But I'm not going to tell you about them because Mother wouldn't like it," said Mrs. Millard, laughing.

(So far Mother and Mrs. Millard had never met. I wanted them to meet because I was sure they would appreciate each other and I had tried to bring it about. After a great deal of persuasion Mother had asked Mrs. Millard to tea—but Mrs. Millard refused. "You've made her ask me," Mrs. Millard said. "Fortunately I've got more sense than to go. Tell Mrs. Harcourt that I am desolated but I have a previous engagement of long standing.")

All this passed through my mind in a flash and I said, "You're wrong about Mother. I wish you could meet her. I know you'd like each other—"

"The conviction does more credit to your heart than your head," said Mrs. Millard dryly.

I had no idea what she meant, but when she spoke like that I knew it was no use asking.

She was still wearing the diamond necklace (she had for-gotten it of course) and it looked so odd over her grey woollen frock that I reminded her about it.

"Oh yes, of course," she said, and she took it off and put it on the table. "I shall sell it," she added. "I shall sell everything except the pearls."

"Pearls!" I exclaimed in surprise. I saw no pearls amongst the collection of jewellery.

"The poor things are sick," said Mrs. Millard, taking up the string of grey beads and looking at it sadly. "Pearls go sick if you shut them up for years in a little box; that's why they look so queer."

They looked so queer that I could hardly believe they were pearls. I wondered why she had shut them up for years and let them get like that. I wondered why she did not wear them.

"Shall I tell you about it?" she asked. "I've never told anybody—not a creature. It's a story about old unhappy far-off things and battles long ago. You see, Jane, these pearls were given to me by someone I was very fond of. He wanted to give me something beautiful and valuable, something that I could wear always, so he bought the string of pearls. He couldn't afford them for he was young and hadn't much money but he didn't care. It was a sort of—a sort of gesture. In giving me the pearls he was giving me everything he possessed. He fastened them round my neck and said, 'with all my worldly goods I thee endow'. Then he went away and I never saw him again. He was killed at Mons."

I was silent. There was nothing I could say.

"Of course I meant to wear them always—night and day—but after a few months they began to lose their colour, they began to look dull and lifeless, so I took them to a jeweller and asked what was the matter with them and he said they were sick. He said I ought never to wear pearls. He said pearls should be worn on a soft moist skin—my skin is dry and acid—he said if I continued to wear them they would be completely spoiled. I didn't believe him, it sounded like nonsense, but I went to another jeweller—a man who specialised in pearls—and he said exactly the same. Pearls like a soft warm skin and fresh air and sunshine and they like to be steeped in sea-water every now and then."

"You couldn't wear them! You couldn't do as he wanted! How dreadful!" I exclaimed.

She nodded. "Yes. That was the trouble. That was what made me so miserable. I couldn't do as he wanted." She was silent for a few moments and then she continued in a different tone of voice. "I ought to have sold them. The jeweller advised me to sell them. It was sensible advice, but I didn't feel like being sensible just then. I couldn't wear them and I didn't want to sell them so I put them away in a box—and they went from bad to worse. It's a silly story, isn't it, Jane?"

"No, not silly," I murmured.

"I believe you're as silly as I am," said Mrs. Millard smiling rather sadly. "You're a sentimental young woman, I'm afraid. You mustn't be sentimental; it's a sure road to a broken heart. It's ever so much better to be tough and callous—and a little bit selfish."

I thought of Helen—it was dreadful of me to think of Helen but I could not help it—Helen was like that: tough and callous and a little bit selfish and she sailed through life very comfortably.

"What shall I do with them?" asked Mrs. Millard. "Tell me what to do. Shall I put them back in prison or take them to a jeweller and see if he'll give me anything for them. I don't suppose he would give me very much."

"Can't they be cured?" I asked.

"The only way to cure sick pearls is for somebody to wear them," she replied. Then she said, "Will you wear them for me, Jane?"

"Me!" I exclaimed. "Oh no, I couldn't!"

"Why couldn't you?"

"Because—because they're valuable. I might lose them—it would be awful if I lost them!"

"I don't see how you could lose them, but if you did I wouldn't mind."

"You wouldn't mind!"

"Not really," she said thoughtfully. "I know it sounds strange, but I would rather they were lost than shut up in prison."

"Mrs. Millard, I couldn't! Besides you don't mean it! You wouldn't like me to wear them!"

"Do I ever say things I don't mean?"

She didn't, of course. I hesitated—for I knew Mother would not like it—and then, for some strange reason I thought of Ronnie. Supposing Ronnie had fastened a string of pearls round my neck—and had gone away—and never come back! The thought of Ronnie made it all seem more real and tragic. How could I refuse?

When I went home I was wearing the string of pearls round my neck; I put them inside my jumper so that neither mother nor anybody else should see them.

Chapter Nine

1

My story was finished. I had decided to call it *The Lamb and The Wolf*, so I wrote the name on the title page: THE LAMB AND THE WOLF by Jane Harcourt. It looked rather good. It was three o'clock in the morning, for the last two chapters had raced along like mad; they had practically written themselves and I had not been able to stop.

The whole thing was written in fat red exercise-books; I had started to write it in this form and had just gone on getting one book after another as I went along. Now that it was finished I gathered the books together and put them away in a drawer. Some day I would read it over and perhaps I might show it to Mother but meantime I buried it under a pile of stockings.

The next day I felt sleepy and relaxed. I had been working at the story for weeks—sometimes quickly and easily but at other times plodding along with nothing but a fixed determination to keep me going—now I had completed the thing and put it away and I was not going to give it another thought. To-night I could creep into bed at ten o'clock and sleep solidly till morning.

"Jane, you're wool-gathering!" exclaimed Mrs. Millard. "Have you been burning the midnight oil?"

The question took me by surprise. I gazed at her stupidly. "How—how did you—know?" I stammered.

"I didn't know, but I know now."

"About the oil-lamp?"

"That was merely a *façon de parler*. You look tired and your eyes are owlish and I've spoken to you twice without getting a reply."

"It was just a story," I said hastily. "I'm sorry I was inattentive but I finished it last night, so—"

"A story about Esmeralda?"

"No, of course not! It wouldn't be right! Esmeralda belongs to you. It's just a story, Mrs. Millard. The people aren't real—besides nobody will ever read it."

"How long is it?"

"How long is it!" I echoed in surprise.

"How many words?"

"But—but I couldn't count the words. I just started at the beginning and went on until it was finished."

"An admirable method!"

"It's quite long, really," I told her. "About as long as a novel, I should think."

"And about as wide as a carpet, I suppose?"

She was teasing me of course, so I played up to her. "It's wider than a stair carpet," I said solemnly.

"You're learning, Jane," declared Mrs. Millard smiling. "But there's no need to be cheeky."

"You taught me to be cheeky," I said.

"Goodness!" she exclaimed. "I thought I was being so careful to teach you nothing you shouldn't know! Well, never mind about that," she added. "You can bring the story to-morrow. Now, for heaven's sake let's get on with the job."

The last thing I had intended was to tell Mrs. Millard about my story, but sometimes it seemed as if she could see through a window into my brain. Mother was good at this, too, but she was not a patch on Mrs. Millard, and it was a different kind of seeing. She did not pounce on you suddenly and surprise you into saying something you had meant to keep to yourself.

Mrs. Millard said no more about the story and as I went home I decided that she had forgotten all about it—and anyhow I was not going to take it to her to-morrow and let her read it. That was out of the question. That was definite. I thought about it several times during the day—and I thought about it as I crept into bed at ten o'clock that night. Quite definitely I was not going to show the story to Mrs. Millard.

Next morning my feeling was not so definite. I disinterred the pile of red exercise-books from the bottom drawer and hesitated with it in my hands. Should I or should I not let Mrs. Millard read it? Of course she would laugh and tease me about the story, but would that matter? The point was, did I want her opinion? It would be a perfectly frank opinion—and an expert opinion—and therefore worth having.

It was time to go to The Corner House and I had not made up my mind so I decided to take the story with me and leave it in the shed with the bicycle. Then, if she remembered . . . but she would not remember, of course.

"Where is the novel?" demanded Mrs. Millard when I walked in.

She did not read it at once (we were busy with Esmeralda's affairs) but she made me leave it with her for the week-end. When she saw the pile of exercise-books she raised her eyebrows and remarked, "No wonder you couldn't count the words!"

"It isn't as long as it looks," I assured her. "And it isn't really very messy—and the books are all numbered."

"That, at least, is something to be thankful for," said Mrs. Millard dryly.

2

I was quite frightened to go to The Corner House on Monday morning. Mrs. Millard would laugh; or perhaps she would be kind, which would be almost worse; or perhaps she would be angry, which would be worst of all. When I had put away the bicycle I hung about in the garden for a few minutes trying to pluck up enough courage to go in.

Suddenly the window of the study was flung open and Mrs. Millard's head appeared.

"Interesting spectacle of an author suffering from cold feet!" she exclaimed.

I looked up and smiled feebly.

"Come in," she said. "You'll get a cold in your nose as well if you hang about out there."

The pile of exercise-books was lying on the table in the study.

"Oh yes, I read it," said Mrs. Millard in answer to my question. "You kept me awake till half-past one. Oh yes, I finished it. Yes, it interested me—but I'm not sure whether it would have interested me quite so much if someone else had written it. There's a lot of Jane in it."

"Then it's no good—"

"Did I say so? For heaven's sake give me a chance to speak! Love Stories are not in my line, and if someone else had written it I wouldn't have read it—that's all I meant."

"You're not angry?"

"Why should I be angry?"

"Because—because you taught me—all that. I mean I just thought—afterwards—that you might be—annoyed."

"Calm yourself," she replied. "If you become any redder in the face you will have a fit. Let me assure you that I am not angry—not even annoyed. Certainly you learnt the background of your story from Esmeralda, but what does that matter? You could have learnt it from other sources if you had wanted."

"Not so well."

"Perhaps not, but if you're going to write about a bygone age it's better to have an authentic source of information—and why should I deny it to you? It's rather interesting," added Mrs. Millard, looking at me with a piercing stare. "You've got the atmosphere. The story isn't just a story staged in the period, with cardboard scenery . . . and as a matter of fact there are quite a number of little touches that you couldn't have learnt from the letters."

"Perhaps I dreamt them," I said.

"So you dream of Esmeralda? How strange!"

It did not seem strange to me. If you work for hours every day with papers and letters written long ago by a vital colourful personality it would be strange if she did not haunt your dreams . . . but she did not haunt Mrs. Millard, that was obvious.

"I wonder where we should send it," said Mrs. Millard thoughtfully.

"Send it!" I cried. "But I only wrote it for fun! I started because I was bored—the idea came to me—and then I couldn't stop. It went on—unrolling—if you see what I mean."

"Unrolling," said Mrs. Millard nodding. "Yes, of course. That's why the beginning is dull and sticky. The beginning very nearly put me off. You'll have to alter the beginning, Jane."

"It's a sort of build up. You have to describe—"

"You don't build up this sort of story. You don't describe the scenery and the characters. This sort of story is an entertainment for people who can't be bothered with long and detailed explanations. You must plunge straight into the middle of the story on the very first page." She smiled and added, "Here am I telling you how to write a novel . . . and I couldn't write a novel to save my life."

All the same she was right. The beginning was too heavy and it was not until Chapter Four that the story began to get going.

"Tell me more," I said eagerly.

Mrs. Millard was clever—I had always known that—but it was not until she began to discuss my story that I realised what a brilliant brain she had. The whole plot and all the characters were clearly in her mind and she put her finger on the weak points with unerring judgment.

"You've given away the secret a bit too soon," she declared. "You should keep it up your sleeve—and you could do that quite easily if you cut out the highwayman's visit to the inn. That gives the show away completely. Then there's Giles. You changed your mind about Giles half-way through—he's too black at the beginning and too white at the end—and you don't make it clear what changed him."

"It was his wound," I explained. "He had never been ill in his life and he thought he was dying."

"But you don't say so," she pointed out. "You'll have to make more of Giles's sudden conversion. I'm not a believer in sudden conversions, but that's neither here nor there."

"I wondered about Ralph?"

"Don't touch Ralph. I believed in Ralph. As a matter of fact I fell for him, good and hard—Ralph is a darling."

"I'm glad you like Ralph," I said.

"He's real, isn't he?" asked Mrs. Millard. "He's a flesh and blood young man—with his long legs and his broad shoulders and his twinkling eyes. Where did you meet him, Jane?"

"In Edinburgh," I said—I could feel myself blushing. "But I don't know him—properly. I don't know his name—or anything— and I don't suppose I shall ever see him again."

I thought perhaps she would tease me about it but instead of that she sighed and said, "What a pity! I like the sound of Ralph."

For a moment I hesitated. It would have been a relief to tell Mrs. Millard the whole story, and I had a feeling she would understand, but while I was still trying to make up my mind about it she changed the subject and the opportunity was lost.

"You haven't been so successful with your heroine," declared Mrs. Millard. "Agnes isn't human; she's much too good to be true."

"But I didn't want her to be like Esmeralda!"

"You've gone to the other extreme! You must do some-thing about Agnes. Give her some ideas! Put some life into the creature!"

"Perhaps I could—"

"Of course you could! Some of the minor characters are very good—Ralph's father for instance. I think you could make a lot more of Ralph's father. Fill in the sketch and give him more to say . . ."

She went on talking about my story, praising this and criticising that. I had intended to make notes of her suggestions, but there was no need for notes. I saw it all clearly; I saw exactly how to alter it and improve it. I was quite breathless with excitement by the time she had finished; my fingers were itching to get hold of a pencil and begin the task.

"Take it and go away," said Mrs. Millard at last. "Do it now, at once, while your eyes are blazing, and don't come back until it's done."

"But your book—"

"My book can wait. I shall take a few days' holiday. Solda and I can get on with the Spring-cleaning."

"But if I go back now—" I began, hesitating at the door.

"It's a secret!" cried Mrs. Millard in delight. "It's a secret—even from Mother! And of course if you go back now, in the middle of the morning, Mother will want to know why—and you'll have to tell her all about it—and that will spoil everything."

It was true, of course, but Mrs. Millard had twisted it round and made it sound a little unpleasant—as she always did when she spoke of Mother. I stood there wondering how I could explain.

"But it's quite easy," continued Mrs. Millard nodding. "You must work here."

"That would be marvellous," I said eagerly. "If I could work here—if I wouldn't be in your way. Perhaps you've got an attic—or a cellar—"

"Alas, I have neither," said Mrs. Millard. "Neither an attic nor a cellar. The Corner House is sadly lacking in amenities. All I can offer is a very prosaic spare bedroom."

"I can write anywhere!" I cried.

She laughed—and I laughed too, for I saw she was pulling my leg.

3

Mrs. Millard's spare bedroom was a marvellous place to write. There was a solid table in it and when I had moved the table near the window and found a suitable chair I had all that I wanted. Nobody came near me, nothing disturbed me, and I could work in peace. In three days I had made all the alterations suggested by Mrs. Millard and several others that I thought of myself. When it was done I showed it to Mrs. Millard and she was pleased.

"You've improved it," she said. "It's better in every way, but I don't like the title. *The Lamb and the Wolf*—no, Jane, it won't do."

"Agnes and Giles," I pointed out. "She's the lamb and he's the—"

"Oh yes, that's obvious, but you need a title that will catch the eye and be easily remembered—a title that will describe the book. What about *Highwayman's Halt*, or *The Mulberry Coach* or—"

"*The Mulberry Coach!*" I cried.

There were a few other mistakes (small details about clothes, and the terms I had used in describing the duel between Ralph and Giles); in several places my critic objected to the phraseology and made me alter it. By the time we had done all this the manuscript was in a frightful mess and I said I would rewrite the whole thing.

"Indeed you won't!" declared Mrs. Millard. "Give it to me at once. If you rewrite the story you'll change the wording and take out all the freshness and spontaneity. You aren't experienced enough to leave well alone. We'll pack it up here and now and send it to be typed."

"Nobody will be able to read it."

"My woman in London will. She gets worse messes than this to decipher."

Mrs. Millard made up the parcel, sealed it and sent Solda to the post office without more ado . . . and the moment it had gone I thought of all sorts of improvements which I should have made.

"Put it out of your head," cried Mrs. Millard in exasperation. "We've wasted nearly a week over your wretched novel. We shall have to work double time to make up."

Chapter Ten

1

"Where did you get those beads, Janie?"

I had been thinking about *The Mulberry Coach* (and wondering how long Mrs. Millard's 'woman in London' would take to finish the typescript) and before I could answer Mother's question Helen chipped in. Helen had come down to Timble Cottage for the week-end and this was Sunday morning.

"She got them at Woolworth's, I should think," declared Helen, helping herself to marmalade as she spoke.

"There isn't a Woolworth's in Ryddelton," Rosalie pointed out.

"Well then, she got them at that little shop in the High Street; the shop that sells cheap sweets and tin trumpets and packets of balloons."

"I think it's a nice little shop," said Rosalie. "And the woman is awfully nice. She has very good oranges and they're a penny cheaper than McBain's."

They began to argue about the shop—Helen's voice with its contralto note and Rosalie's lighter treble. The argument spread and became heated and illogical, as it always did when they argued, and they forgot about the pearls. Presently when nobody was looking I slipped them inside my jumper and heaved a sigh of relief.

As a matter of fact I had been wearing the pearls for a month. I wore them next my skin, night and day, and only when I went for a walk on the hill did they see the sun. It was impossible to soak them in sea-water—we were miles from the sea—but that could not be helped. Already there was a slight difference in their condition (although they were still a bad colour they were not so dull and lifeless) but I had not shown them to Mrs. Millard. We had been working very hard and her mind was engaged with Esmeralda's affairs so she might have forgotten about the pearls.

Mother came upstairs when I was making my bed. She said, "Jane, darling, I wouldn't wear those beads if I were you. They're not very pretty and they look—they look rather cheap. I don't like artificial pearls very much, and—"

"But they're not artificial," I said.

"My dear lamb, of course they are! Real pearls cost the earth! You couldn't buy a string of real pearls in a little shop in Ryddelton."

"I didn't, Mother."

"But you said—"

"Helen said it, and they were so busy arguing—"

Mother smiled. "Well anyway I wouldn't wear them, darling."

"You don't mind if I wear them inside my jumper, do you?"

"But why wear them at all?"

I saw she would have to know so I took them off and dropped them into her hand and told her about them; I told her all that was necessary. It would not have been right to tell her about the boy who was killed at Mons for that was Mrs. Millard's secret and not mine to tell.

Mother listened without interrupting and then she said, "Yes, of course I've heard of pearls going sick—and they certainly look very strange—but she had no right to ask you to wear them and you'll have to take them back to her."

"Oh Mother, why?"

"It's much too dangerous."

"Dangerous!" I cried.

"Yes, dangerous," said Mother firmly. "I won't have you wearing them. You might be robbed—or the house might be burgled."

"Burgled for the pearls!"

"They're valuable, Jane."

"Oh I know they're valuable. I suppose they must be worth about fifty pounds—" I began.

"Darling goose!" exclaimed Mother. "If they're real—which I suppose they are—five hundred is more like it."

I could not believe it. Five hundred pounds for that little string of beads; it was fantastic!

"Probably more," said Mother, examining them carefully. "I don't know much about pearls but these are beautifully graded and that makes the string much more valuable. Supposing you were to lose them, Jane?"

"I asked Mrs. Millard and she said it didn't matter."

"Didn't matter!" echoed Mother in amazement.

"She would rather I lost them than keep them shut up in a box—that's what she said, and she meant it. You see she's an unusual sort of person. She doesn't value *things*, she values *ideas*. The pearls have been shut up for years. They've been in prison; they're sick and miserable. She said it made her miserable to see them. Don't you understand?"

"Yes, I can understand that," said Mother reluctantly. "But you'll have to take them back. We don't even know if they're properly insured."

They were not insured. I had asked Mrs. Millard and she had replied that she could see no object in paying a lot of money to insure things you were fond of, because it did not prevent them from being lost. Houses and furniture were different—she could take the insurance money and replace them—but she could not replace the pearls except by buying another string which would not be the same. I saw what she meant of course, but I could not explain it to Mother without telling her the whole story, so I just said they were not insured—and left it at that.

"Not insured!" cried Mother in dismay. "Goodness! You must take them back at once. I won't have them in the house another minute. Put on your coat and—"

"Mother, listen—"

"No," said Mother. "No, Jane. It's all very well for Mrs. Millard to say she wouldn't mind if they were lost, but I should mind—and so would you. Just think how frightful it would be if they were lost—or stolen!"

"But I'll wear them all the time under my jumper. How could I lose them? And how could they be stolen when nobody knows they're here? Nobody will know. Even if people see me wearing them it won't matter. People will think they're artificial—you thought so, yourself. That makes it safe."

"It makes it safer," Mother agreed. "But all the same you must take them back. I can't accept the responsibility."

I wanted to wear the pearls. At first I had agreed to do it because I was sorry for Mrs. Millard (though she would not have liked me to say so) and because she had done so much for me that it seemed ungrateful to refuse. Now there was yet another reason; I had become fond of the pearls themselves and I wanted to cure them. It seemed a worthwhile thing to do. So I went on persuading Mother as hard as I could, and at last I saw she was weakening.

"Mother, look at them," I said. "I've been wearing them for a month and they're better already—honestly they are. If I take them back they'll be shut up in a horrid little box. You don't want to send them to prison, do you? You wouldn't like to think of the poor things shut up in prison, getting uglier and more miserable every day."

"Oh Jane, you are awful!"

When she said *that* I knew the battle was won.

"You are awful," she repeated. "It's quite wrong . . . It's absolutely crazy . . . Andrew would be horrified . . ."

I hugged her and said, "Thank you, thank you! I *do* want to cure them."

"But I must write to Mrs. Millard," declared Mother. "I must make it clear that I can take no responsibility at all. If she wants you to wear the pearls the responsibility must be hers."

"She won't mind."

"And another thing," added Mother. "Remember this, Jane; nobody must know—not Helen, not Rosalie, not anybody."

"But if they ask me?"

"You must tell them a lie, that's all."

It was so amazing to hear Mother saying I must tell a lie that I was speechless.

"Yes," said Mother, nodding. "You must say—if necessary—that you bought them from Mrs. Struthers for three and elevenpence."

I suppose my face looked funny for she began to laugh and the next moment we were both laughing uncontrollably.

"I don't know why I've given in," declared Mother when at last she could speak. "You've twisted me round your finger. You've persuaded me against my better judgment. You're far too clever for me, Jane."

She was wrong about that and I told her so. It was impossible to work with Mrs. Millard for six months without knowing one's limitations.

"Oh yes, you are," said Mother. "You're the only one of the family with brains. I suppose you must have got them from your father. You ought to have gone to Oxford. I should have managed somehow. I could have borrowed the money from Leonard if I hadn't been too proud."

She looked so sad all of a sudden that I kissed her and said it didn't matter and I was much happier here.

Mother shook her head. "That's nonsense," she declared. "And I never gave you permission to tell lies indiscriminately—only about the pearls."

"Come on," I said. "Don't let's talk about it any more. Let's go and peel the potatoes. That'll cheer us up."

We often peeled the potatoes together and it always cheered us up; Mother's theory was that potatoes were like people—some big and important, others timid and insignificant. Their eyes were set differently in their heads; their noses were of different shapes and some of them had mouths. Sometimes Mother cheated a little and cut a mouth just where she wanted it and held up the potato and said 'Who's that?' It was silly and childish but it was fun.

To-day we were especially lucky; Mother got Mrs. Struthers with her fat bulging cheeks and her smiling mouth and I got Aunt Thelma with her eyes close together and her knobbly forehead. Mother cut a round piece of peel and stuck it on the back of her head and we both giggled.

It took longer when we peeled the potatoes together but time is not important in Ryddelton. It is not like London where everybody lives with one eye on the clock.

Chapter Eleven

1

The next day Rosalie returned from the Fergusons' full of excitement.

"They're all going to Ayr for the Easter holidays," she said. "And they've asked me to go with them. Jean says it will give them much more freedom if I'm there to look after the children. The only thing is . . ."

"Clothes!" exclaimed Mother.

Clothes were becoming a big problem. We had brought all our clothes with us and although they were not exactly the sort of garments to wear in Ryddelton we had managed to make them do. Now they were getting threadbare and shabby and there was no money to replace them.

"We'll manage," said Mother after a moment's thought. "We must put off painting the house, that's all. Andrew said we ought to have the outside woodwork painted, but it will have to wait."

Rosalie and Mother went to Edinburgh for the day; they went early and did their shopping and lunched with the cousins at Murrayfield Gardens. It was a very successful expedition and they both enjoyed it. Rosalie was delighted with her new coat and skirt, it was soft bluish-grey tweed and suited her admirably, and she had got a felt hat to match. They had bought nylon shirts and stockings and brown leather shoes and a blue silk frock for the evening. Altogether it was quite a trousseau. I had been a little doubtful as to whether it was right to put off painting Timble Cottage (for the paint on the windows was peeling off and the wood was showing) but Rosalie was so happy about her new clothes, and Mother was so happy when she saw Rosalie wearing them, that I changed my mind.

It was curious that when we had been able to buy new clothes whenever we wanted we had never really appreciated them nor enjoyed them. You have to be in the position of needing things very badly indeed before you can appreciate possessing them.

So Rosalie went to Ayr with Kenneth and Jean and the children. They were all going to stay with Kenneth's brother; he, too, was a doctor and although he was a good deal younger than Kenneth they were tremendous friends and we had heard quite a lot about him. He had taken a temporary post at Ayr while one of the local doctors was on holiday and was living in the doctor's house.

"It's a big house," said Rosalie. "There will be plenty of room for the whole family. Jean says there's a lovely garden for the children to play in. I think it will be fun."

When they had gone Mother and I were alone at Timble Cottage and to tell the truth it was very pleasant indeed. We decided that as we could not go away for a holiday we would have one at home, so we neglected the house a little and when I came back from my morning's work with Mrs. Millard we went out together and walked for miles. Mother knew the country well, she had ridden over the moors when she was a girl, and she was able to show me paths and tracks which I had not found in my solitary wanderings. One day she took me to see Mount Charles which had belonged to her parents; it was a beautiful old house embowered in trees with stables and greenhouses and a fine old garden, sheltered by a high stone wall. We were standing at the gate, rather sadly, when the gardener saw us and asked if we wanted to come in.

Mother explained that she had lived here when she was a child so she was interested in the place but she did not know the present owner. We were just turning away when the gardener came after us and said he was sure Sir Edward Fisher would like to see us.

"Why should he?" asked Mother in surprise.

"Because he's a nice friendly sort of gentleman. That's why."

This seemed an insufficient reason for the intrusion of two complete strangers and we were still arguing with the hospitable gardener when the gentleman himself appeared. He was short and rather tubby with sandy hair and a round cheerful face and spectacles; I liked him at once.

"Here's Sir Edward," said the gardener—and he added, "I was just telling the leddies to come in. They used to live at Mount Charles and I thought they'd like to see the garden."

"Of course they must come in!" exclaimed Sir Edward. "They must see the house as well." He bowed to Mother in a politely old-fashioned manner and invited us to come in and have tea.

I could see that Mother was not anxious to accept the invitation but Sir Edward was so insistent, so kind, and so eager to entertain us that it was impossible to refuse . . . and soon we were sitting in the drawing-room of Mother's old home having tea with its new owner. Mother was not quite as cheerful as usual—which did not surprise me—but Sir Edward was a talkative little man so there were no uncomfortable silences. First he talked about the house, and how much he liked it, and he detailed a few improvements he had made, and then he told us that he was a widower with three children. He told us that he was very lonely when the children were away at school but when they came home in the holidays it was delightful. ("This old house likes children," he said). The children were at home now, for their Easter Holidays, but they had all gone over to Dunnian to spend the day.

When Mother heard that he knew the Dunnes she cheered up a little and they chatted about various other people in the neighbourhood. He knew the Fergusons too. They were old friends (and very good friends, said Sir Edward); it was Jean Ferguson who had told him Mount Charles was for sale and it was partly because he liked Kenneth so much that he had decided to live at Ryddelton. When Mother told him that Rosalie was with the Fergusons, helping to look after the children, he was quite excited.

It struck me, as I watched them talking, that it would be a very good arrangement if Mother were to marry Sir Edward and return to Mount Charles as its chatelaine; it was the sort of thing that happened in story books. Sir Edward was younger than Mother but he was one of those people who seem older than their years, and Mother seemed younger—so that would not matter. I was just arranging it all comfortably, and had begun to wonder what Rosalie and I would do, when Mother rose and said we must go home.

"But you must stay to dinner!" cried Sir Edward. "I want you to see the children—they'll be home any minute now. Do stay, Mrs. Harcourt! Stay to dinner and I'll send you home afterwards in the car."

He really wanted us to stay and was so persuasive that it was difficult to get away without being unkind but we managed it at last.

"It was rather—painful," said Mother as we walked down the avenue. "I mean seeing the dear old house. Of course it's well cared for; he's fond of it, you can see that." She sighed and added, "I ought to be glad that it hasn't been turned into a hotel, like Tocher, or a Rehabilitation Centre for Displaced Persons—that would be a lot worse."

"It's still a home," I agreed.

When we got to the gate a large Bentley passed us; it was driven by a chauffeur in uniform and there were three children in it—two boys and a girl—they all had round chubby faces and one of them had spectacles. There was no doubt whatever about their parentage.

"Just like Daddy!" exclaimed Mother. "No wonder he's proud of them."

"I thought he was awfully nice, didn't you?"

"Awfully nice describes him admirably, but I don't think I want an awfully nice husband, Jane. Oh yes, I saw you marrying me off to the poor little man. You decided it would be 'awfully nice' for me to go back to Mount Charles and live happily ever after in the home of my childhood. Really Jane, you ought to know better at your age."

I laughed rather uncomfortably.

"Did you notice his silly little feet?" asked Mother. "They weren't much bigger than mine."

"I liked him," I said stubbornly. "I thought he was nice."

"No, Jane," said Mother laughing. "I like my men tall and dark with enormous hands and feet; but there's no need for you to find one for me, I'm perfectly happy as I am, strange as it may appear."

2

We had several other expeditions while Rosalie was away. The weather was wonderful for the time of year, dry and warm and sunny. One especially fine morning I rang up Mrs. Millard and asked for a day off and we took the bus to St. Mary's Loch. I had heard about the loch and had read Wordsworth's poem but it was even more beautiful than I had expected, and a great deal bigger. It lay surrounded by hills and it was so clear and so still that every tree and rock was reflected in the water. There was nobody to be seen. The only living creatures besides ourselves were the sheep and the birds; the only sounds were the gentle lapping of the water on the shore and the trickle of the numerous little burns.

"It's all for us," I said to Mother as we sat down together on a fallen tree and took out our sandwiches. "All this beauty and peacefulness is just for us. It seems queer, doesn't it?"

Mother smiled and said, "Yes, I know what you mean, but perhaps it's partly for the sheep and the birds. You should write a poem about it, Jane."

"I've written a novel," I told her.

As a matter of fact I had been trying to tell her about *The Mulberry Coach* but had never been able to make up my mind to do it. I had felt rather guilty about keeping the secret and the longer I put off telling her the harder it seemed.

"You've written a novel!" she exclaimed in amazement.

"It's just a story," I said. "I started it for fun—to see if I could do it—and then it went on. I couldn't stop, you see. I never thought of it being published or anything like that, but Mrs. Millard thinks it might be."

"Mrs. Millard," said Mother in an odd sort of voice.

"Yes, she knows about books of course."

"Of course," agreed Mother.

"You're pleased, aren't you?" I said.

"Yes, of course I'm pleased," said Mother but somehow her words did not ring true.

"Why aren't you pleased?" I asked her.

"Of course I'm pleased," she repeated. "I am—really. It's frightfully clever of you, Jane. I suppose that's what you were doing in the evening, after you went up to bed. I knew you were writing something but I thought it was extra work for Mrs. Millard. Silly of me, wasn't it?"

"No, of course it wasn't silly. How could you know?"

Mother was silent.

There was peace all round us, but not inside. My heart had begun to thump in a most uncomfortable manner and my mouth was dry. "Mother," I said, "I thought you'd be—pleased. If it's published we may get some money. We might get enough to have the house painted. That would be nice, wouldn't it?"

"Oh Janie, don't," said Mother in a shaky voice. "Don't talk about money—as if that were all that mattered."

"What do you mean? I don't understand!"

"I don't understand—myself," said Mother rather pitifully. "Of course I'm pleased—it's wonderful—it's frightfully clever of you, darling . . . but I wish you'd told me. I know I can't help you like she does. I can't share things with you—I'm not clever—but I could have given you peace to write—if you'd told me. I could have done that."

"Mother, listen—"

"It's just that you seem to be drifting away."

"But that's nonsense!"

"That's what I feel. Ever since you went to work for her you've been—drifting away. Sometimes I've felt rather—miserable about it. I suppose I'm jealous—or something. It's horrible, isn't it? Quite horrible. Don't let's talk about it, Jane."

"We *must* talk about it!" I cried. "It's a different sort of thing. Of course I'm fond of Mrs. Millard and terribly grateful to her for all she's done. She's absolutely wonderful in her own way. She's brilliant and you can't help admiring her, but she isn't the sort of person you can love."

We were sitting there, looking at each other. It was frightful. It was terrifying. I did not know how to go on. I took her arm and shook her. "You're you!" I said desperately. "There's nobody like you—nobody at all! You *must* understand. You can if you try."

"Oh Janie!" said Mother, but she said it in a different tone of voice and I saw she had begun to understand.

"If you knew her you wouldn't be so silly about her and she wouldn't be so silly about you," I declared.

"Is she silly about me?"

I hesitated and then I said, "Yes."

"Oh," said Mother thoughtfully.

3

It was time to go back to the inn and catch the bus so we collected all the litter and buried it in a deserted rabbit hole. I did not know whether to say any more about Mrs. Millard or leave it alone. Mother seemed quite cheerful and more like herself and I was afraid of saying the wrong thing.

"Tell me about the novel," said Mother, slipping her hand through my arm as we walked along. "I'm sorry I was so silly about it, but you'll let me read it, won't you?"

So it was all right!

"Of course you must read it," I said.

"What is the book about?"

"Oh—just people," I said vaguely.

"People in Ryddelton?" asked Mother with some anxiety.

"Oh goodness no! It's about highwaymen—and duels—and—and things like that."

Mother laughed and said she was glad. "We might have had to leave Ryddelton in a hurry," she explained. "I once read a book about a woman who wrote a book about her neighbours and they weren't at all pleased. She had to fly for her life."

"We shan't have to leave Ryddelton," I assured her.

Chapter Twelve

1

When we got back to Timble Cottage there was a car standing outside the door. It was Cousin Andrew's car but there was no sign of its owner.

"We've missed him! What a pity!" exclaimed Mother in dismay.

"We haven't missed him. He must be here somewhere."

"But Jane—"

"But Mother," I said laughing. "He couldn't have gone back to Edinburgh without his car."

"He must have gone for a walk," said Mother, vaguely.

This was the only explanation, for we had locked up the cottage and as usual had left the key of the front door hanging on a nail under the bird-table. The key was of iron and so large and heavy that it was uncomfortable to carry about. Mrs. Gow knew the secret, so she could get in if she wanted—and several other people knew about it too.

We were still gazing round, looking for our unexpected visitor, when the window of the sitting-room was opened and he looked out.

"I've been waiting for hours!" he exclaimed. "I wondered where on earth you had gone! I was beginning to get alarmed."

His voice sounded a little cross which was unusual, for Cousin Andrew was the most good-natured man in the world.

"Oh poor Andrew!" cried Mother. "How horrid for you to find the door locked! If only we had known you were coming—"

"How did you get in?" I asked.

"Climbed on to the shed and through the bathroom window," he replied, even more crossly. "Really, Anna, you should have more sense! Anybody could get in without the slightest trouble. It isn't safe. I suppose the bathroom window is left open all night?"

"Who would want to get in?" asked Mother evading the question.

"Burglars," replied Cousin Andrew threateningly. "Burglars could get in."

"There aren't any burglars in Ryddelton—and anyway there's nothing for them to—" She hesitated and I knew what she was thinking.

"Don't you ever read the papers?" asked Cousin Andrew. "Don't you realise that scarcely a day passes but some old woman gets murdered in her bed for a five pound note?"

"But Andrew, I haven't got a five pound note," declared Mother smiling at him sweetly.

By this time I had unlocked the front door and was hurrying into the kitchen, for it was nearly seven o'clock and we must feed our guest before he returned to Edinburgh. Fortunately there was cold beef—enough for us all—and there was a bowl of soup. There was cheese and biscuits and I could make coffee. It was not a luxurious repast but it would have to do.

The sitting-room door was open and I could hear them talking as I made the preparations for the meal.

"Yes, Andrew," Mother was saying. "Of course I meant to have the painters but I put them off. Rosalie had to have clothes to go to Ayr with the Fergusons. You see that, don't you?"

"I told you I would pay for the house to be painted."

"But I can't let you . . ."

The door was shut after that.

By the time supper was ready Cousin Andrew had quite recovered his temper and was his usual cheerful self. He asked about our day at St. Mary's Loch and recalled a fishing expedition to the loch which had taken place over twenty years ago.

"You were there, Anna," he said. "Do you remember?"

"Yes," said Mother smiling. "You caught a trout and I lost it for you. I tried to net it and I knocked the hook out of its mouth. It was the biggest trout we saw that day—I nearly wept."

"Nonsense!" he exclaimed. "It was quite small, and not well-hooked. I'd have lost it anyway."

"Oh Andrew, what a lie!" cried Mother.

They both laughed, and I laughed too—though quite honestly I could not see anything very funny about it.

"Have you met the fellow who's bought Mount Charles?" asked Cousin Andrew.

Mother nodded. "He seems very nice," she said. "Jane and I were peering in at the gate and he came out and asked us to tea."

"Very civil of him," remarked Cousin Andrew.

"Yes, wasn't it? Jane liked him a lot. Didn't you Jane?"

I knew she was teasing but I did not care. "Yes, I thought he was very nice," I said.

"He's a good chap," agreed Cousin Andrew. "I know him fairly well. I'm straightening out some of his tangles for him and he's extremely pleasant to deal with. Lady Fisher was an absolute tartar."

"Was she?" asked Mother with interest. "Do tell us about it, Andrew."

But of course he would not be drawn. He smiled and said he had told us too much already. *"De mortuis nil nisi bonum,"* said Cousin Andrew, and he added, "You ought to know better than to ask a solicitor to give away his clients' secrets."

By this time it was getting late and it was time for him to go, but before he went he took out his penknife and stabbed it into the woodwork of the sitting-room window.

"Look at that, Anna," he said. "Just look at it!"

"I know," agreed Mother regretfully. "But she had to have a decent coat and skirt."

"I've told you—"

"I know," repeated Mother. "But I must stand on my own feet."

"You're an awful trial."

"I know," said Mother for the third time.

He got into his car and drove away.

2

The next morning when I went to Mrs. Millard at the usual time there was a neatly typed manuscript lying on the table.

"It came yesterday," she said. "I know I shouldn't have opened it but the temptation was irresistible. Yes, it's *The Mulberry Coach* at last."

"Joy!" I cried pouncing upon it. "Oh joy! Have you read it, Mrs. Millard?"

"Yes, I've read it again. The amount of time I've wasted reading your simple little tale is deplorable."

"Is it any good? Does it read better in typescript?"

"It reads a great deal better in typescript. I've been trying to decide what publishing firm shall have the felicity of putting it on the market."

"I don't suppose any of them will take it."

"You suppose wrongly. *The Mulberry Coach* is a publisher's dream. It's a natural."

"You mean it's really good!"

"It depends what you mean by 'really good'," said Mrs. Millard thoughtfully. "If you mean is it a work of art which will enrol you in the annals of fame it isn't good at all. Alas, my poor Jane, you will never see your sculptured bust displayed on a marble column in the British Museum—or wherever it is that they display sculptured busts of the famous—but, unless I am very much mistaken, you will see a great many copies of *The Mulberry Coach* on the shelves of libraries and the counters of bookstalls all over the country—and probably in America as well if you have the temerity to cross the Atlantic Ocean. You see, my dear Jane, *The Mulberry Coach* provides an escape from the drabness of the modern world."

She took a long breath and continued, "Housewives will leave piles of unwashed dishes in the sink and revel in the richness and prodigality of the banquets which you have provided; miserable little clerks in lawyers' offices will neglect their dusty duties and be transported to a wider life and more colourful surroundings; girls will imagine themselves swept off their feet by the wooing of your masterful hero; fashionable ladies will say to each other, 'My dee-ar! You *don't* mean to say you haven't read *The Mulberry Coach*, by Jane Harcourt? It's abso-lootly thrilling! *Everyone's* talking about it!' Young men will choose it for Aunt Fanny's birthday and read it with avidity before despatching it by post with a suitable card . . . and of course people who haven't got twelve and sixpence to spare will rush to the nearest Public Library and clamour loudly for a copy of *The Mulberry Coach*."

She paused and looked at me. There was a wicked gleam in her eyes.

"That *will* be fun," I said. "But if I could possibly make a little money—just enough to have the house painted—it would be marvellous."

"Why not have the house pulled down and rebuilt," suggested Mrs. Millard. "Of course I haven't seen Timble Cottage—my own fault, I know—but it doesn't sound a very desirable residence for a popular novelist."

"It's a lot more desirable than it sounds."

"Well then, take Mother for a trip to the South Seas."

"I don't believe she'd go."

"How tiresome of her!" exclaimed Mrs. Millard. "And how tiresome you are! Here am I trying to help you to spend a fortune—"

"I haven't got it yet," I reminded her.

"If you don't make a small fortune out of *The Mulberry Coach* I'll eat my—I'll eat Esmeralda's letters!" cried Mrs. Millard and she gestured to the pile of letters which lay on the desk.

I did not believe it—not really—and I was not sure whether she believed it either. I said, "Well, of course it would be marvellous if I got enough money to—"

"Don't say it! You know perfectly well that it annoys me when you keep on saying the same thing over and over again."

"Yes," I said meekly.

Suddenly she was perfectly serious and in quite a different voice she said, "Listen, child, if you want fifty pounds to paint your revolting little house I'll lend it to you here and now. You can pay it back when *The Mulberry Coach* arrives."

She did believe it.

"Well?" asked Mrs. Millard. "Do you want fifty pounds or not? You can have it to-morrow if you want it."

"No," I said breathlessly. "I mean yes of course I want it, and it's frightfully kind, but I can't take it—honestly."

"Mother wouldn't like it."

I shook my head.

"Oh well, I don't blame her," said Mrs. Millard.

Chapter Thirteen

1

When Rosalie returned from Ayr I knew something had happened to her; she looked different—prettier and more alive. At supper that evening she had a lot to say about all she had done and the people she had met and how much the children had enjoyed their holiday . . . but I had a feeling that there was something she did not tell.

Helen had come down for the week-end and I saw her looking at Rosalie in surprise, and presently she said, "Couldn't we change the subject? I think children are boring."

"Boring!" cried Rosalie. "Deb and Sally are *terribly* interesting. They say the most amusing things."

"Why don't you tell us some of the amusing things—"

"But I have! I've just told you—"

"Helen is teasing you," said Mother quickly, and she added with unusual asperity, "For goodness' sake don't start quarrelling the moment Rosalie arrives."

After I had gone to bed and was lying, comfortably tucked in and reading, there was a little sound at the door and Rosalie appeared.

"Are you sleepy?" she whispered—and then, not waiting for an answer she came in and sat on my bed.

It reminded me of the night Helen had come to tell me about 'the earthquake' but there were several important differences between that night and this: Helen had come in her evening frock, with a white face and blazing eyes; Rosalie was in her old blue flannel dressing-gown, her face was pink and her eyes were shining softly. Helen had come with bad news but Rosalie's news was good.

"Jane, I must tell you," whispered Rosalie. "It's a secret. You won't tell anybody, will you? You won't tell Mother—or Helen. I couldn't bear Helen to know. It's about Kenneth's brother."

"Kenneth's brother?"

"His name is Ronnie," said Rosalie as if it were the most wonderful name in the world.

I gazed at her. "Ronnie!" I echoed.

"It's a darling name, isn't it?"

"Yes," I said. "Yes, it's a very nice name."

For a moment I felt a little faint. There was a queer cold feeling in my heart . . . but of course it could not be the same. There are dozens of young men called Ronnie.

"Oh Jane, he's marvellous!" declared Rosalie. "He's very tall and—and awfully good-looking—with brown hair—and blue eyes. There's something absolutely thrilling about him. I couldn't help—liking him—and he likes me. I know he likes me, Jane."

"Rosalie, are you—in love?"

She blushed and nodded. "I couldn't help it. I mean the moment I saw him I just felt—I felt as if there was nobody else in the world! He never said anything but I'm sure he felt the same. There wasn't time to say anything; Kenneth and Jean were there, and he was terribly busy seeing patients, so we were scarcely ever alone; but one afternoon when the others were out he came into the garden and talked to me and played with the children. Ronnie loves children and he's so—so sweet with them, Jane. We like all the same things," said Rosalie dreamily. "We like children—and we like birds."

"It sounds—perfect," I said. My voice sounded queer to me but Rosalie did not seem to notice.

"It is perfect," she said happily. "It's the most wonderful thing that ever happened. You'll like him, Jane. You won't be able to help liking him. You'll see him to-morrow."

"To-morrow? Do you mean he's coming here?"

"Yes, I forgot to tell you. He has got to be back in Edinburgh to-morrow night and he's going to lunch with Kenneth and Jean on the way. He has got a little car so it's all quite easy. He's coming here to tea."

She paused and looked at me. I could see she thought I ought to be more excited at her news, but somehow I could not be excited. I knew now, without a doubt, that Rosalie's Ronnie was the young man with the thick brown hair . . . but why should I mind? I had seen him once for a few minutes, that was all. Probably he had forgotten all about me—or if he remembered me it would be as a plain, gawky girl who was dull and unfriendly.

"It will be all right, won't it?" asked Rosalie with a shade of anxiety. "I mean Mother won't mind? I asked him to tea—at least he asked himself, really. He said would I be in if he called in the afternoon—so what could I do but ask him to tea?"

"Mother won't mind. She'll be delighted. You'll tell Mother, won't you?"

"Yes," said Rosalie. "At least I'll tell her that a friend is coming to tea. It's too soon to—to tell her anything else. I mean there's nothing to tell—not really. I mean I'd rather—wait. It's too soon to say anything. You won't tell her, will you?"

"No, of course not," I assured her.

"I thought you'd be more excited—but you haven't seen him have you? Wait till you see how marvellous he is!" She hesitated and then added "I'll just tell Mother I've asked a friend to tea, that's all."

Personally I thought it would be better to tell Mother a little more, but Rosalie would not have it, and it was for her to say.

Rosalie went on talking about Ronnie; she said the same things over and over again. It was late by this time, nearly twelve o'clock, and my lamp was flickering.

"I don't know how you can bear that thing," exclaimed Rosalie looking at it in disgust.

"I like my lamp," I told her. "There's nothing the matter with it except that it needs filling."

"Oh well, I suppose I'd better go to bed," said Rosalie. "I shan't sleep a wink—I'm too excited—but I suppose I had better go and try."

2

Mother was pleased when she heard that Rosalie had asked a friend to tea, for she was of a hospitable nature and there was nothing she liked better than entertaining guests. She liked preparing for them too; and when I went into the kitchen on Saturday morning she was beating up eggs for a chocolate cake and looking as happy as a queen. I could not help wondering what some of her London friends would have thought if they could have seen her in her big blue overall, her hair tousled and her face red with her exertions.

"Oh, Jane!" she exclaimed. "Rosalie was rather mysterious about her friend. Is it somebody very special?"

I did not know what to say so I said nothing at all.

"Oh, I see," said Mother smiling. "Well, it's all right; you haven't told me anything; but you'd better make tracks before I ask any more uncomfortable questions."

After lunch Helen went out for a walk (she had not been told that a guest was expected); Mother and Rosalie and I were busy laying tea in the dining-room when the guest arrived.

I had known before of course, but all the same it gave me a shock of surprise when he walked in. He had looked tall and large at the club, but he looked even larger at Timble Cottage, and his whole personality seemed more vital. There was a glow of health and good spirits and friendliness radiating from him . . . Rosalie had said he was 'thrilling' and the word described him well.

Rosalie should have introduced him, but she was shy and embarrassed and mumbled inaudibly; it did not matter, of course, for Mother was equal to the occasion and after her initial surprise at the size of her guest she recovered her poise and greeted him cordially. I had remained in the background, but when Mother said, "And this is Jane!" I came forward.

"Hallo!" he exclaimed. "We've met before, haven't we?"

"You've met before!" exclaimed Rosalie in astonishment.

"We crawled about together picking up treasures—combs and brass knobs and safety-pins—" declared Ronnie smiling.

"What do you mean?" asked Rosalie.

I could see she did not appreciate the joke and I was not surprised. I said hastily, "It was at the club—the day I lunched with Cousin Margaret. Miss Mackintosh upset her bag on the floor and I helped to pick the things up."

"Why didn't you say you had met?" asked Rosalie.

"I didn't know," I told her. "I had no idea he was Kenneth's brother—"

"We weren't properly introduced," said Ronnie, chuckling. "We were thrown together by force of circumstances as you might say! Then, after lunch, our relations abandoned us and we had a little chat until Jane had to hurry away to meet somebody important."

They were all gazing at me—Mother and Rosalie with expressions of amazement—but I did not mind. As a matter of fact I had imagined a conversation just like this so the words were ready, on my lips. "Oh yes, Mr. Gow is terribly important," I said. "He's our gardener. We went up to Edinburgh together in the bus and I promised to meet him at ten minutes to three. If I hadn't been there on time he would have thought I had got lost or been run over. He would have been quite frantic!"

Mother said, "Of course he would have been frantic, poor little man. He had promised me he would 'see after Miss Jane'."

I glanced at Mother gratefully. You could depend upon Mother to say the right thing.

They were all smiling now.

"Come and sit down," suggested Mother. "Come and tell us what you've been doing . . ."

After that it was easy. Ronnie was quite pleased to talk about what he had been doing at Ayr and what he was going to do in Edinburgh, and—with a little encouragement—he proceeded to tell us about the post he had got as assistant to a professor of bacteriology at Eastringford.

"Where is Eastringford?" Mother wanted to know.

"It's quite a small place not far from Oxford. I'm going there at the end of July. I was to have gone in January—it was all arranged—but they're building a new laboratory and it isn't ready yet. They've been held up, you see. Of course it's a wonderful opportunity for me to work under a man like Professor Black—and to work in this new lab. with all the latest gadgets. We're going to carry out some experiments and research."

"What sort of experiments?" Mother inquired.

"Tropical diseases," he replied. "I'll tell you about it if it won't bore you. Most people are bored to death when I start talking about it."

We were not bored . . . and although it was all rather technical and none of us knew anything about bacteriology, it was easy enough to listen.

"That's really my line," explained Ronnie. "I've always been madly keen about bacteriology so I was terribly lucky to be selected—and I don't mind waiting for it. I mean it's quite easy to fill in the time with temporary work. The post isn't very well paid but it will be a wonderful experience and it's bound to lead to something better."

"The great thing is to start on the right track," suggested Mother.

"Yes, and this is the right track—for me. I'm looking forward to it tremendously."

Rosalie said very little—she was leaving it to Mother to carry on the conversation—so presently Mother suggested that there would be time for a walk before tea.

"It's such a lovely afternoon," said Mother. "Why not take Ronnie to see the spring. I'll have tea ready when you get back."

"Couldn't I help to get tea ready?" asked Ronnie.

"Jane will help me," said Mother looking at me.

"Yes, of course," I said.

They rose at once and went off together up the hill.

"Why does nobody tell me things!" exclaimed Mother, half laughing and half in earnest. "I was expecting a girl—and in walked a gigantic young man! Nobody told me who he was, nobody mentioned his name! Am I supposed to have second sight or what?"

"I didn't know if it was the same man—" I began.

"Oh, I gathered that—I groped through the fog—but it would have been a lot easier if somebody had had the sense to tell me."

I was silent.

"Well, never mind," said Mother. "I know now—and he's a delightful young man. So friendly and kind and so good to look at. Did you have a nice chat with him that day at the club?"

"No, I was an idiot," I said gruffly.

By this time we were in the kitchen. I filled the kettle and put it on to boil and Mother fetched her cake from the larder.

"What a good thing I made it!" said mother. "It looks nice doesn't it? I think I shall put one of these paper d'oylies under it. He won't notice it, of course (it will be completely wasted on him), but I like to see a cake sitting on a nice paper d'oylie."

3

We were having tea in the dining room, as we often did when we had visitors, and it was all ready when Ronnie and Rosalie returned from their walk.

"It's no good waiting for Helen," said Mother.

"Helen has no idea of time," agreed Rosalie.

"Did you have a nice walk?" I asked.

"It was grand," replied Ronnie.

"We saw a heron," said Rosalie. "It flew over the hill quite near us, flapping its wings." She smiled across the table at Ronnie and added, "Ronnie knows all about birds."

"Not 'all about' them," declared Ronnie laughing. "I like birds, it's fun watching them, but it would take a lifetime of study to learn all about them."

"Well, you know a lot," said Rosalie. "I wouldn't have known it was a heron if you hadn't told me."

"Herons are easy," said Ronnie. "Their flight is quite different from other birds. I tell you what, Rosalie, if you're interested I could send you a book about birds. Ken gave it to me for Christmas—"

"Of course I'm interested," declared Rosalie. "The heron was beautiful. I wish we had been able to find its nest." She turned to Mother and added, "Ronnie thinks it may have a nest near the spring but we didn't have much time to look."

"Perhaps another day," suggested Mother. "Ronnie might like to come to lunch—if he isn't too busy. It doesn't take long to come over from Edinburgh."

"I'd love to," declared Ronnie. "I could bring the book and my field glasses . . ."

They went on talking and making plans. The plans were necessarily vague, for Ronnie had taken a temporary post in Edinburgh and did not know when he would be free to come, but he said he would let us know if he could manage it.

"You can't work all the time!" Rosalie pointed out.

"You can—if you're assistant to a G.P.," replied Ronnie smiling somewhat ruefully . . . and he began to tell us some of his experiences in the last few months.

Ronnie was in the middle of an amusing story when the door opened and Helen came in. She came in like a breeze from the moor, with her golden curls blown by the wind, her sea-blue eyes sparkling and a wild rose bloom in her cheeks.

"Goodness, am I late?" she cried. "I went further than I meant—it was so heavenly. I ran home all the way!"

"This is Helen," said Mother, and she added, "Ronnie Ferguson—Kenneth's brother."

"Hallo!" said Helen smiling at him.

They were all looking at Helen except me. I glanced at Ronnie. He had not risen—as he should have done—but was sitting glued to his chair. He was staring at her with his mouth a little open and his face reddening beneath its tan. There was a dazed look about him as if he had been hit on the head and did not know what had hit him.

"Hallo!" repeated Helen. "I saw your car outside the door so I knew we had a visitor. It's a racing model, isn't it?"

Ronnie did not answer, but his silence did not worry Helen. She had the easy self-confidence of a girl who has been used to admiration all her life. She sat down in the empty chair and went on talking. She helped herself to a scone.

"Rosalie and Ronnie walked up to the spring," I said, trying to draw Rosalie into the conversation. "They saw a heron—"

"Did you really?" asked Helen. "They're very rare, aren't they? I saw a big bird with long legs standing on a rock in the middle of the burn. Could it have been a heron?"

By this time Ronnie was recovering and was able to reply; they began to talk about the bird Helen had seen and to discuss whether it had been a heron or some other kind of bird. Quite soon the two of them were talking and laughing as if they had known each other all their lives.

Rosalie sat with her eyes on her plate and said nothing. Her face was as white as a sheet. I looked at Mother—but even Mother seemed to have nothing to say.

For a few moments I was so angry with Ronnie that I could have shaken him—and then my rage subsided. It was not Ronnie's fault; Ronnie was not to blame; Ronnie had no idea what was happening, and even if he had known he could not have helped matters at all. Rosalie was completely silent, she was making no effort to join in the conversation, and Helen was making every effort to put him at his ease . . . and of course she was enchanting (even I saw that).

I was sorry for Ronnie; I was sorry for Rosalie. In a way I was sorry for Helen too. She was not using her charm consciously, she was just being her natural self. Here was a shy young man, sitting at her mother's table, and she was drawing him out and entertaining him. Probably she would not have bothered so much if he had not been an attractive young man—but you could hardly blame her for that.

You could not blame anybody, that was the trouble; they were all acting their parts according to their different characters. The thing that was happening before my eyes had the inevitability of a Greek tragedy.

After tea they all three went out to look at Ronnie's car while I helped Mother to wash the dishes. When I peeped out of the window the bonnet was open and Ronnie and Helen were looking at the engine while Rosalie stood by. Helen was really interested in cars (it was not 'put on') and she was taking in all that Ronnie told her and asking intelligent questions.

Ronnie had said he would take Rosalie out for a little spin before he went back to Edinburgh but apparently he had forgotten or changed his mind.

Presently Helen came in for a bucket and some cloths. "We're going to wash Ronnie's car," she said. "We'll just have time before he goes back to Edinburgh. Can I borrow the shammy?"

"He promised to take Rosalie for a drive," objected Mother.

"Oh, Rosalie doesn't mind."

"Are you sure?" asked Mother. "Helen listen—"

"Of course I'm sure," she declared. "Ronnie asked her and she said she didn't mind at all. Besides there isn't time." She took the chamois leather and added, "He says he'll give me a lift to Edinburgh, it will be far nicer than that horrid old bus."

"But Helen—"

"And it will save the fare," she added, clinching the matter.

Mother hesitated. "Helen," she began—but Helen was filling the bucket and did not listen.

"It's a marvellous little car," she declared. "He bought it second hand, quite cheap, and he's done it up and fitted a new carburettor and now it goes like the wind. He was showing me the engine—it was frightfully interesting."

She went out with the bucket and they proceeded to wash the car. There was a great deal of talk and laughter and 'ragging' over the business. Helen and Ronnie both seized the chamois leather at the same moment and this resulted in a tug of war.

"I want it!" cried Helen, laughing and pulling with all her might. "I want it for the windscreen!"

"I want it for the lamps!" declared Ronnie, pretending to pull.

"The windscreen is much more important. We want to see out of it, don't we? Do let me have it, you horribly strong creature—"

Presently Rosalie came in and went straight upstairs to her bedroom and I honestly believe that the others never noticed she had gone.

"Mother, can't we do something?" I said.

"No, Jane."

"But you're so good at—at doing things—and—and it's desperate!"

"I know it's desperate," she said.

"Mother—"

"No, Jane, it wouldn't be any use."

4

It was six o'clock when the car was finished and they were ready to start. Mother and I went to the door to see them off.

"Where's Rosalie?" asked Ronnie, looking round in a bewildered sort of way. "I haven't said good-bye to Rosalie."

"She had to go down to Ryddelton," said Mother promptly.

"How odd!" exclaimed Helen. "But look, there's the bicycle! She must have come back. We had better find her and say good-bye."

"She walked," I said quickly. "She hasn't come back."

"Oh well, perhaps we'll see her on the road," said Helen. "If not, be sure to give her my love."

"Mine, too," said Ronnie cheerfully.

They got in to the car and drove off.

When they had gone we turned and looked at each other. "You had better go to her," said Mother. "Yes, it had better be you."

I went up to her room. She was lying face downwards on the bed crying into her pillow.

"Rosalie!" I said.

She held out her hand and I took it and sat down beside her. The hand was hot and wet and limp.

"They've gone," I told her.

"I know," she said in a hoarse voice, broken by weeping. "I heard them. I heard every word. Oh Jane, I can't bear it. I can't *bear* it! He *did* like me—he did—he did! Oh Jane, he's so sweet and good—and kind. It isn't his fault. He couldn't help it. It's *her* fault, Jane! I hate her! Oh, I know it's wicked to hate her—but Ronnie was mine—my friend. What shall I do? Oh, what shall I do!"

"He's still your friend—"

"No, she's taken him. He never even said good-bye!"

"He said to give you his love—"

"Yes, I heard," she sobbed. "He said 'mine, too.' That's worth a lot, isn't it?"

I gave the limp hand a little squeeze.

"Oh Jane, I've never had a friend before—not like Ronnie. She's got lots of friends—he's just one of the crowd to her. I love Ronnie—it's awful but I can't help it—and he—liked me. He did really—"

"Of course he likes you—"

"Not now. He never looked at me after she came in."

"Why did you let her?" I said. I was almost crying myself. "Oh Rosalie, why didn't you—do something—say something—"

"I don't know—I couldn't—what was the use! He never even noticed I was there. He liked me—before—at Ayr. He did, really. He talked to me in the garden and we had fun together—with Deb and Sally—but now—he doesn't like me—any more—"

"Yes, he does," I said desperately. "It's only temporary—it will pass—it's only temporary."

She did not listen. "Oh Jane!" she cried. "Oh Jane, did you see his face—when he looked at her? He never—looked at me—like that!"

I had seen his face. It was no use saying that I hadn't. "It's temporary," I repeated. "Honestly it is. It's a sort of magic like the poppy dust in *Midsummer Night's Dream*."

"It isn't. You don't really think so. You're just—saying it."

"You know what she's like—"

"Oh yes, I know what she's like!" cried Rosalie wildly. "She'll take him and—and break his heart—and—and throw him away! Like she did to Basil—like she does to them all. Oh Jane, I can't bear it! If she does that to Ronnie—I shall die!"

I could do nothing for her, nothing at all except sit beside her and listen and squeeze her hand.

Presently Mother came in and we got her undressed and tucked her up in bed. She was quieter by that time and we tried to make her drink a cup of tea but she would not have it, so Mother gave her a little red pill and sat beside her until she went to sleep.

5

When at last we sat down to supper Mother and I were both exhausted. We had cooked bacon and eggs; but I don't know why we had bothered because neither of us was hungry.

"This day feels like a week," I said miserably—and so it did. I could hardly believe it was only that morning I had gone into the kitchen and seen Mother beating up eggs for the cake.

"I know," said Mother. "But don't worry too much."

"Not worry!" It was ridiculous for Mother to say 'don't worry'. She was worried to death.

"I said, 'not too much,'" she explained. "It's no use. We can't do anything about it."

"What are we going to do with her?" I asked. "That's what's worrying me more than anything."

"She'll carry on with her job."

"At the Fergusons'?"

"Yes, at the Fergusons'. We must make her do that, Jane. It suits her and there's no earthly reason why she should give it up." Mother smiled rather sadly and added, "'Men have died from time to time, and worms have eaten them, but not for love.'"

"It will take her ages to get over it."

"I don't think so—not really. She'll be better to-morrow because she's got it off her chest. You see, Jane there are two kinds of people: there are the people who weep and wail when they're in trouble and the people who shut it all up inside. People like Rosalie recover more quickly. It's better for themselves but harder on their friends. You're the kind that tholes in silence," she added.

I said nothing. There was nothing to say.

"All the same," continued Mother. "Even if you don't weep and wail there are occasions when it's quite a good thing to talk about things." She hesitated and looked at me.

For a moment I hesitated too, but only for a moment. "It's no use—talking," I said.

Chapter Fourteen

1

The next few weeks were very uncomfortable; Rosalie recovered and went about as usual but she looked pale and wretched and was liable to dissolve into tears at unexpected moments. Fortunately she never suggested giving up her job at the Fergusons'; I think she found comfort in the children.

Jean and Kenneth knew all about it. They were fond of Rosalie and had not been blind to what was happening at Ayr. Kenneth wanted to 'speak to Ronnie' but of course that would have been fatal, so Mother persuaded him to hold his peace.

Presently a letter arrived from Helen saying she was not coming down for the week-end as arranged because Ronnie had offered to take her to St. Andrews on Saturday to spend the day with some friends; and Ronnie's aunt, with whom he was staying, had invited her to lunch on Sunday. Kenneth had a letter from Ronnie containing the same news, but he had added in a hasty postscript that Helen was wonderful; he had never met anyone like Helen before.

Jean brought the letter and showed it to Mother and said that Kenneth was upset about the whole affair—and what were they to do? Again Mother persuaded them to do nothing, but it took a lot of persuasion.

All this was very difficult for Mother because Helen was her daughter—just as much as Rosalie—and if Helen and Ronnie were fond of each other it was nobody's business but their own. Mother saw quite clearly that Helen was not to blame for what had happened, nor Ronnie either for that matter, so the only thing to do was to make the best of it. Mother's time was spent soothing people and she found it extremely wearing. I might have been more help but I was particularly busy at Mrs. Millard's; Esmeralda's biography was nearing completion and the publishers had written asking when it would be finished.

Work at Mrs. Millard's and troubles at home kept me so busy that I scarcely had a moment to myself and when we heard that *The Mulberry Coach* had been accepted by a publisher without the slightest hesitation I was not as excited as might have been expected. I was pleased, but my pleasure was shadowed.

It was June by this time and we had not seen Helen for several weeks nor had we heard much from her; but one afternoon, when I went home after a whole day of work with Mrs. Millard, I found Jean Ferguson having tea with Mother. They both looked up when I went in and there was a moment's silence.

Then Mother said, "Jean has come to tell us that Helen and Ronnie are engaged. He rang up and told them at lunch-time. I expect Helen will ring up to-night."

"Oh!" I exclaimed—and then I added, "That's good news, isn't it? We all love Ronnie."

"Yes, of course," agreed Mother. "It will be lovely to have dear Ronnie as a son-in-law."

Jean said nothing but I could see from her face that she was angry, and I wondered why. Just lately she and Kenneth had been more resigned and had accepted the fact that if the engagement took place the only thing to do was to make the best of it. The situation was so difficult that I did not know what to say, but I had to say something.

"Oh well," I said, trying to speak lightly. "We've seen it coming, haven't we? I don't suppose they'll be married for some time—"

"Early next month," said Jean . . . and then she burst out, "I can't pretend to be pleased. Helen isn't the right girl! I don't want her for Ronnie! Oh, I know it's dreadful of me to talk like this but honestly I can't help it. Helen is completely selfish—she cares for nothing except herself—she'll ruin his whole life—that's what will happen. She's made him give up that post at Eastringford!"

"Oh no!" I cried.

"Oh yes, she has! I've just been telling your Mother about it. Ken is absolutely furious; I've never seen Ken so angry. Ken says it's madness to throw up the post. Ronnie is a brilliant bacteriologist, he only wants experience and this would have been the most marvellous experience for him. It was an honour for him to have been chosen—at his age—to work on these new experiments; he's not likely to get such a chance again . . . and Helen has made him give it up!"

Mother and I were silent.

"Oh, of course it's all glossed over," continued Jean bitterly. "Ronnie says it's his own choice and Helen has nothing to do with it—but we know better than that! He was looking forward to it tremendously; he could talk of little else. Ronnie knew it was his great opportunity and he kept on saying how extraordinarily lucky he had been. *Now* he says the salary wouldn't be enough and he could get a better-paid post at one of the London hospitals. Well, of course he could! We knew that from the beginning—but money isn't everything!"

"But that's dreadful!" I exclaimed. "Can't we do some-thing? Surely if we explained to Helen—perhaps Helen doesn't know."

"Helen!" cried Jean. "Helen knows as well as I do. She doesn't care a bit about his career. All Helen cares about is herself and her own comfort. Helen wants to live in London and have a good time . . . besides it's too late to alter it now. The thing's done. He's written and given it up." She rose and added, "I'm sorry. I shouldn't have said all that. I shouldn't have come here while I was in such a raging temper. I had better go home."

"I'm sorry," said Mother. What else could she say?

"Oh, I know," said Jean. "It isn't your fault—but it's all so miserable—the Eastringford post—and Rosalie—and everything." Her anger had gone and she was nearly in tears. "It's all so—miserable," she repeated. "And Ronnie is such a darling. I love Ronnie as if—as if he were my very own brother. Ken and I have always been so proud of him. If only it had been Rosalie! Rosalie would never have—made him—do this."

"Rosalie—" began Mother in sudden anxiety.

"I've told her," said Jean. "It was no good trying to hide it. She took it extraordinarily well. She just said she knew it would happen. I'll go back to the children and let her come home." Jean kissed Mother and added, "It won't make any difference—to us. Will it?"

"I hope not," said Mother. She was very fond of Jean.

2

Soon after this Helen gave up her work in Edinburgh and came home.

"There's a lot to do," she said. "We shall have to find a flat in London and I must get busy with my trousseau."

"Has Ronnie got a post in London?" asked Mother.

"Oh yes," replied Helen, but she did not tell us what it was.

Rosalie was now staying all day with the Fergusons (they were finding her very useful) so the two girls only met at breakfast. This was a great relief to Mother who had been wondering what she would do with them both in the house together, and what she would do when Ronnie came down from Edinburgh to spend the day. Rosalie could not always go to bed with a streaming cold, as she had done the first time the engaged couple came down from Edinburgh to lunch.

Helen's trousseau was a very elaborate affair, she had bought yards of peach-coloured nylon and was making frilly nightdresses and petticoats. She had always enjoyed making 'pretties' for herself, even before the 'earthquake'.

The wedding was to be in July; Helen wanted to have it in London, but Mother said no.

"It would cost far too much," explained Mother. "I simply haven't got the money. You can be married in Ryddelton and we'll have a small reception at Tocher House."

"And ask all your friends!" said Helen scornfully. "That *would* be nice for you. My friends happen to live in London."

Mother said nothing but her eyes filled with tears.

Of course it was true, but there was no need to say it so unkindly. (The fact was the atmosphere at Timble Cottage was like tinder and only required a spark to set it ablaze. We were all living on our nerves and all, except Helen, knew the cause.)

A few days later Helen received a letter from Aunt Thelma; it arrived when we were at breakfast and when she had read it she passed it round the table without saying a word. There was a look of triumph on her face which made me feel uneasy so I got up and read it over Mother's shoulder.

Aunt Thelma said that she and Uncle Leonard were glad to hear Helen was to be married soon as they did not believe in long engagements. They had talked over Helen's suggestion and would be very pleased to have the reception in their house. They would give it to Helen as a wedding present. It was natural that Helen should want to be married in London and ask all her own friends but the reception must be limited. Fifty guests would be as many as they could manage. Aunt Thelma added that they would be very pleased to have Helen to stay (and she had better come at least ten days before the wedding and help with the preparations) but there would not be room for us all so perhaps the rest of the family could stay with friends or make other arrangements.

"Very kind of them," said Mother, and went on eating her breakfast.

I could see she was upset and I was not surprised. There were all sorts of reasons why she should be upset. For one thing she did not like Helen asking Aunt Thelma to have the reception at her house; for another the whole affair had been taken out of her hands and she would only be a guest at her daughter's wedding; last but not least it would be hard for Mother to go back to London and meet all the people she had known before and to be aware that they were pitying her for her changed conditions.

Having got her own way Helen became cheerful and pleasant and at once began to talk about which of her friends should be asked to the reception.

"Only fifty!" she said. "It will be terribly difficult. I'm sure we could have more if Aunt Thelma moved all the furniture out of the drawing-room and opened those double-doors. I can see about that when I'm staying with her. Rosalie must be my bridesmaid, of course. I shall only have one—or perhaps I had better have Vera as well."

Rosalie said nothing. She was staring at her plate.

"I would rather you didn't have Rosalie," said Mother.

"Not have Rosalie!" exclaimed Helen in amazement.

"No, not Rosalie," repeated Mother. She took up the spoon to help herself to marmalade and I saw that her hand was shaking.

"But of course Rosalie must be my bridesmaid!" cried Helen. "She's the obvious choice! She's my sister!"

"You can have Jane—" began Mother.

"Really, Mother, I think you're mad!" cried Helen. "Rosalie would be just right. She and Vera would look charming together. Jane would be quite wrong. She's far too tall and gawky." She turned to me and added, "You wouldn't enjoy it a bit, would you?"

"No, I shouldn't," I replied firmly. It was not my line at all. The mere idea of mincing up the aisle decked out in garments of Helen's choosing gave me the shudders. Carrying a bouquet! Wearing a wreath of roses on my hair!

"I wouldn't enjoy it either," said Rosalie in a low voice.

"You wouldn't enjoy it either! Why ever not?"

"I don't think I can come at all," said Rosalie desperately. "I mean the children would miss me. I mean Jean really needs me to—to look after them—and—and—"

"Surely Jean would let you off to go to your sister's wedding!"

"But they'll want to go," I said. "Kenneth is Ronnie's brother. It's Ronnie's wedding just as much as yours."

"Jane is right," declared Mother. "Ronnie is sure to want Kenneth and Jean to come to the wedding so Rosalie will have to stay and look after Deb and Sally."

"Oh, really!" exclaimed Helen. "So Rosalie can't come to my wedding because of those horrible children! And what about you, Jane? I suppose you can't come either?"

"It will be difficult," I said. "Mrs. Millard is terribly busy, but I expect she would let me off for two or three days."

"I've got a funny sort of family!" cried Helen furiously. "None of you think of *me*! You're jealous because I'm going to have a proper wedding in London! Yes, you're jealous, that's what it is! You sit there as glum as owls and pour cold water on the whole thing! But I don't care. If you don't want to come to the wedding you can stay away—all of you. If neither of my sisters wants to be my bridesmaid I can ask someone else. There are lots of girls who will jump at it."

She pushed back her chair violently and got up and left the room banging the door behind her.

"She's angry—" exclaimed Rosalie, bursting into tears.

"Poor Helen," said Mother sadly.

Another person might have said *poor Rosalie* but Mother was always sorry for people with blinkers.

Chapter Fifteen

1

I DID not want to go to Helen's wedding any more than Rosalie but I could not let Mother go by herself. At first Jean and Kenneth decided that they would come too, and Rosalie was to stay with the children, but these arrangements were upset at the last minute by Deb developing measles. Jean refused to leave her and Kenneth seized the excuse to remain at home himself. He was still angry with Helen—and almost more angry with Ronnie—so any excuse for not going to the wedding was better than none. Of course the change of plan meant that Rosalie could have come to the wedding, but this was never mentioned.

When I told Mrs. Millard about the wedding she offered me a week's holiday—and then withdrew the offer. I suppose she saw in her usual perspicacious way that I was not very enthusiastic about it.

"I can't spare you," she declared. "I'm a selfish old woman."

"I think I shall have to go," I said doubtfully.

"Three days then," said Mrs. Millard. "You'll get three days' holiday—no more and no less. If you don't report for duty on Friday morning you'll get the sack."

"Oh, thank you. That will be marvellous!" I exclaimed. "We can go on Tuesday and come back on Thursday and miss the party."

"The party would be intolerable?"

"It's a question of clothes," I said. "I mean we couldn't wear the same clothes as we're going to wear at the wedding—"

"Jane," interrupted Mrs. Millard. "There's no need to pretend to me. For one thing it's useless, I know you too well, and for another thing I know all about it. Oh I'm not a witch! You see I've met your future brother-in-law (Dr. Ferguson introduced him to me) and of course I recognised him at once. Dr. Ferguson said his name was Ronnie, but I knew better."

"I don't know what you mean!"

"His name is Ralph."

I said hastily, "It was just—dreams. There was nothing—"

"Just dreams," said Mrs. Millard with a sigh. "Oh well, I've had dreams too. The best thing to banish a dream is to fill your life full of hard work." She hesitated for a moment and then added, "You may not believe me but hard work brings its own reward. It's a good second-best."

She said no more and neither did I.

Rosalie came to the station to see us off. She had been in better spirits since Helen had gone to London, but as the train drew off she dissolved into tears and we left her standing weeping upon the platform. Mother, herself, was not very far from tears and sat gazing out of the window with a face of tragedy.

"Anyone would think we were going to a funeral," I said crossly.

"Anyone would," agreed Mother with a faint smile. "You're quite right, Jane. I'll cheer up in a minute or two. It's just that I'm so worried about Rosalie. When I think of the future I wonder what will happen to her. Will she ever be able to stand on her own feet? Life bears hardly on people like Rosalie."

I was still a bit cross so I said, "Yes, it's better to be tough and callous and selfish."

"Oh Jane, what a dreadful thing to say! It isn't like you!" She hesitated and then asked, "Was it Mrs. Millard?"

"But she didn't mean it," I said hastily. "She says things like that—things that she doesn't really mean. It's a sort of joke."

"A horrible sort of joke!"

"Well, anyway," I said bitterly. "It's worked in Helen's case, hasn't it. Helen has got exactly what she wanted by being tough—and callous—and selfish."

Mother was silent but she looked so miserable that I wished the words unsaid.

We had had several invitations to stay with friends in London, but as neither of us felt sociably inclined we had refused them. We took a double room in a small hotel in Bloomsbury. It had the advantage of being cheap, but no other advantage that I could see; it was noisy and over-crowded, the beds were uncomfortable, the food was poor and we had to share a bathroom with innumerable other people.

Mrs. Millard's 'selfishness' meant that we could stay in London for two nights only and it meant that we could not attend the large tea-party the day before the wedding and be shown the presents. We could have travelled south by night, I suppose, but Mother never suggested it and neither did I.

Our wedding garments presented no difficulties, for Mother had kept two of her smart London frocks and altered them for the occasion. One of them was cherry-coloured and had been altered to fit me; the other, which she was wearing herself, was soft dove-grey with lavender embroidery and she had a hat made of lavender feathers with a diamante ornament at one side. She had sold all her good jewellery, but she still had an old necklace of Irish paste and a bracelet to match. My hat had not cost a penny! Mother had made a crochet cap out of some white wool, which she happened to have in her work basket, and she had got a whole bag of little white feathers from old Mrs. Gow's hens. The feathers had been washed and then sewn on to the cap, covering it completely. I had never possessed a more becoming little hat in all my life.

2

The room in the hotel was so small that there was scarcely enough space for the two beds—let alone anything else—so it was difficult to get dressed but we managed it somehow and the results were remarkably good.

"Will I do, Jane?" asked Mother anxiously. "I can't see what I look like in that spotty little mirror."

"You look beautiful," I told her. "Really beautiful. Nobody could possibly pity you for a poor miserable exile from the delights of the great metropolis."

"You're too clever by half," declared Mother laughing. "As a matter of fact you don't look bad, yourself. That colour suits you, Jane, and the hat is a great success. Wait a moment while I arrange it for you." She did so and then added, "I see you're wearing the pearls."

"Why not? The poor things will enjoy the party, and nobody will think they're real."

"They look real—now. I wonder if it's wise."

Wise or not I was determined to wear the pearls, for they were beautiful—and valuable—and I felt they would give me the confidence which I so badly needed. I was sure Mrs. Millard would not mind; she would think that it would be nice for them to have a little outing and to be admired. By this time the pearls were almost back to normal, but not quite, for although they had regained their lovely pearly colour they were not yet as glossy as they should have been. Soon I should have to take them back to their rightful owner but I wanted them to be absolutely cured before I returned them.

In spite of my assurances Mother was still a trifle anxious about her appearance.

"Are you sure I'm all right?" she asked. "It's so long since I dressed up like this. If only I could see myself properly . . ."

"You're marvellous," I told her. "Do come, Mother. We'll be late if we don't go now."

As I followed Mother down the narrow dingy staircase we met a young man coming up; he was one of the inhabitants of the hotel; I had met him that very morning going into the bathroom. He was whistling gaily, but the whistling ceased when he saw us and he fell back and clutched the banisters and gazed at us with his eyes like saucers and his mouth agape. (I suppose we were rather an unusual sight in those sordid surroundings.)

"Good afternoon," said Mother sweetly and swept past him with a swish of her silken skirts.

Poor young man! I never saw him again but I owe him a debt of gratitude. We were both giggling feebly when we climbed into the waiting taxi.

3

Aunt Thelma had not asked us to go to the house before the wedding so we drove straight to the church and found it spread with red carpets, decorated with flowers and full of guests. I saw dozens of people I knew—all Helen's friends—and amongst them Basil Romford and his mother. We were in the front pew with Aunt Thelma; she nodded to us as we went in—but without much enthusiasm—and I had a feeling that Helen had been complaining about us.

Ronnie was there already. He looked splendid in his wedding garments, but his face wore the somewhat anxious expression not unusual in the circumstances. It brightened a little when he saw us and he smiled wanly. His best man was almost as tall as himself and he, too, looked anxious; his fingers kept straying to his waistcoat pocket to make certain he had not mislaid the ring.

The bride was late, which did not surprise me, it was ten minutes past the appointed hour (and everyone had begun to get restless) when at last she appeared, leaning upon Uncle Leonard's arm and followed by four bridesmaids. I had always known Helen was beautiful but to-day she was more beautiful than ever before; no wonder Ronnie had fallen in love with her. There was magic in her triumphant smile.

The wedding followed its appointed course. I was too upset to listen very intently but when it came to those strange and solemn and rather terrifying vows 'to love and to cherish . . . to have and to hold till death us do part.' I noticed that the bridegroom made his promises in a low tone and stumbled over the words but the bride's voice was clearly audible and contained no trace of emotion.

There were far more than fifty guests at the church and all went on to the reception. The furniture in Aunt Thelma's drawing-room had been moved and the double-doors opened but even so it was slightly overcrowded. There was champagne and a large cake and all the usual etceteras . . . the bride and bridegroom stood in the large bay window and received the congratulations of their friends.

When I kissed Helen she murmured, "Isn't this lovely, Jane? I'm so happy I could fly over the moon."

Ronnie seized my hands and said, "Jane, my dear! It's wonderful to see somebody I know! Stay and talk to me for a few minutes for goodness' sake."

Of course I could not stay and talk to him for people were crowding round and Helen was introducing him to everybody and they were all telling him how lucky he was to have got such a beautiful wife.

Mother was having her own little success in another part of the room; she was surrounded by an admiring group which grew larger every moment. I heard someone say, "Anna is over there. Have you spoken to her? She's more amusing than ever—and prettier than ever." And someone else replied, "I know. Isn't it odd? Seems to suit her being buried in the wilds."

I knew nearly everyone in the room but quite a number of people seemed to have forgotten me. Basil Romford had not.

"Hallo Jane!" he said. "You seem to have grown up. I suppose it's porridge and haggis."

"I suppose it must be," I said laughing.

"How do you like your new brother-in-law?"

"Very much indeed."

"Didn't seem to know his lines, did he?" said Basil lightly.

I could not let that pass—and Basil was an old friend—so I said quite seriously, "They're awful promises, Basil. I think Ronnie was feeling *that* when he made them."

"And Helen was not?"

Fortunately there was no need to reply, for Uncle Leonard had begun to make his speech, and when he had finished and the healths had been proposed and drunk, Basil did not refer to it again.

Instead he said, "Jane, those are real pearls you're wearing."

"Do you think so?"

"I know they are. They're beautiful. You don't mind my saying so, do you?"

"They aren't mine," I told him. "I'm just wearing them for a friend."

After that it was all a whirl; Basil caught hold of several people—there was Ned Elton and Frances Wilmerton, Edgar Mowbray and others too numerous to mention.

"Look who's here!" cried Basil. "It's Jane! you know Jane Harcourt, don't you?" and all at once everybody seemed to remember me and they were all teasing and laughing and saying I had grown and put on weight and was much better looking. Basil kept on saying it was porridge and haggis, and somebody else said, "More like salmon and grouse—and whisky!"

They all roared with laughter, and I laughed too.

"But what do you *do* with yourself all day long?" asked Mrs. Romford in her affected voice which always annoyed me a little.

"I've written a novel," I said. Goodness knows what made me say it. I had no intention of mentioning it until I heard myself uttering the words.

"Not really!" they exclaimed.

"Not a real novel?"

"You don't mean it's going to be published?"

"What is it about?"

"Shall we be able to buy it in a shop?"

"What is it called?"

"Yes," I said laughing. "Yes, yes, yes! And of course you'll be able to buy it in a shop and it's called *The Mulberry Coach*."

"That's easy enough to remember," they said. "*The Mulberry Coach*! It sounds as if it were about highway robbers and haunted houses and things."

"It is," I said. "And it's about a duel and an elopement and a marriage at Gretna Green—"

"Gosh, it's got everything!" exclaimed Basil in amazement. "I shall have to buy it and give it to Mother."

"I suppose it's pure?" asked Ned Elton anxiously.

"Oh yes," I told him. "It's quite suitable for Aunt Fanny's birthday—but you should read it first yourself."

This seemed to everyone the soul of wit and they roared again.

The noise and the heat and the champagne and all the people crowding round and asking questions had begun to make me feel quite dizzy (I was 'a bit above myself' as old Mrs. Gow would have said); so perhaps it was just as well that at this moment one of the bridesmaids pushed her way through the throng and said that Helen was changing in her room and wanted to see me.

4

When the bride and bridegroom had vanished in the usual shower of confetti Aunt Thelma asked if Mother and I would stay to supper, but the invitation was somewhat half-hearted and it was easy to refuse.

"I'm sure you must be tired," said Mother. "I'm sure you should rest. Jane and I will just go back to the hotel."

"Well, I am a little tired," said Aunt Thelma.

So we thanked her for all she had done and went back to the hotel; and we took off our finery and lay down on our lumpy beds.

We were both suffering from reaction and I thought Mother needed a little cheering, so I said, "You were the success of the party."

"I didn't do badly," agreed Mother. "But you were the great success. I saw you chattering away to everybody. You've got over your shyness."

"It was partly the pearls," I said thoughtfully. "And partly the hat—I kept on remembering dear Mrs. Gow's hens—but most of all it was *The Mulberry Coach*. If you've done something worthwhile it gives you a certain amount of cheek and you don't feel such a worm."

There was a little silence after that, and then Mother murmured, "Four bridesmaids!"

"And they all matched," I agreed. "All fair, and of moderate size, and all pretty—but not as pretty as Helen."

"Don't, Jane," said Mother. "I can't bear it when you talk like that."

Chapter Sixteen

1

WHILE we were away Rosalie had been staying with the Fergusons and helping to nurse Deb; then Sally developed measles, which was only to be expected, and Jean also—which was totally unexpected because she had had the complaint before! The doctor's house was like a hospital and Rosalie had three patients on her hands. She could not come home and leave them so she stayed on and seemed happier than she had been for weeks. Kenneth said she was a born nurse.

After that there was an epidemic of measles amongst the children in Ryddelton and, as the Fergusons were better by this time, they 'lent' Rosalie to some of their friends. Jean told Mother that she and Kenneth thought it was so good for Rosalie that they wanted her to go. The Fisher children all got measles, one after the other, and their poor little father was in such a state that

Rosalie went to Mount Charles and helped to nurse them. Then she went to Dunnian on the same errand of mercy.

Needless to say everybody was delighted to see her. Even if she had not been 'good with children' she would have been welcome as another pair of hands, but Rosalie loved children and was willing to do anything for them, so she was as welcome as the flowers of spring.

In this curious haphazard way Rosalie became known to many people in the district and made friends with them all—and when she had time to come to Timble Cottage we noticed a new assurance in her manner. Nursing little children was Rosalie's 'Mulberry Coach': she had found something worthwhile to do and knew she could do it well.

All this time I had been working with Mrs. Millard and at last the book was finished. It was finished in October on a Friday afternoon; I helped Mrs. Millard to parcel up the manuscript and posted it off to London to be typed. Of course there was still a great deal to be done before the book would be ready for the publishers but my part in it was finished and I went home feeling miserable. What was I going to do? I must do something and I would never get a job like that again.

It had been so interesting—and Mrs. Millard herself was unique. I had become very fond of Mrs. Millard, and I had a feeling that she was fond of me. Of course I could still drop in and see her occasionally but it would not be the same as going there every morning. It was working with her that had been so fascinating—watching how she tackled her problems and knowing that I really was a help.

In my opinion *The Biography of Lady Esmeralda Pie* was quite outstanding—not that my opinion was worth very much.

Mrs. Millard had asked me to go on Monday morning to help to clear up the mess; there were papers to be collected and docketed and put away in the chest and several letters to be written—so I went down as usual. When I reached The Corner House I was surprised to find all the curtains had been taken down. Solda was on her knees, rolling up the hall carpet.

"We are going away to-morrow," said Solda, looking up and smiling. I had never seen her smile before in all the months I had known her; there was nothing pleasant about her smile.

"Going away to-morrow," she repeated loudly. "I am glad. We 'ave been 'ere too long."

I went on up the stairs without answering.

2

Mrs. Millard was in the study—and it was all tidy and bare. There was not a single paper or letter on the table. The chest which had contained the letters was roped up. The waste-paper-basket was bulging.

"You're going away!" I exclaimed. "I didn't know!"

"Neither did I," replied Mrs. Millard. "I made up my mind quite suddenly. Quite suddenly I realised that there was nothing to prevent us from leaving Ryddelton. We're going to Provence; Solda wants to see her mother. Provence in October is a dream of beauty—warmth and golden sunshine!"

"But you're coming back! I mean—it's just a holiday?"

"Coming back? I don't think so," she said vaguely. "I've always gone on—from one thing to another—never back. I've stayed here longer than most places and it's time to move. Life is like a bog. If you stand still too long your feet begin to sink into the mud."

"I shall miss you—frightfully!"

"That's the devil of it," she said in a low voice. "That's the bog. I've begun to sink. If you stand still too long you're stuck for ever."

"I don't understand—"

"You're young and you haven't been torn to pieces." She hesitated and then exclaimed, "I hate getting involved—emotionally. It's happened to me before and I've always said it shouldn't happen again. I must be free. I must be—free!"

I was a little frightened at her vehemence. I said, "It's been wonderful, Mrs. Millard. You've taught me so much. I'm very very grateful for all you've done. It's been—wonderful."

It was only now when she was going away that I began to realise what a wonderful experience it had been. My work with Mrs.

Millard had filled my life with colour: Esmeralda—the pearls—my own *Mulberry Coach*—The pearls! I took them off and held them out to her without speaking.

"Oh Jane, they're cured!" she cried in surprise.

"Nearly cured. I think they ought to be a little more shiny."

She had taken the pearls and was running them through her fingers. I could see she was pleased. "Nearly cured," she agreed. "They ought to be soaked in sea-water. That's what they need now. You had better keep them," she added, handing them to me.

I took them gladly for I had wanted them to be in perfect condition before I handed them back, and they were so nearly perfect that it seemed a pity not to complete the cure . . . besides I was fond of them; there is a strange sort of magic about pearls, and these pearls meant all the more to me because they had been sick and miserable and had recovered when I wore them round my neck.

"Yes," I said. "I'll go on wearing them until they're in perfect condition—perhaps I could manage to go to the sea for a day. If you give me your address I can post them to you. I could insure them to go through the post."

"Keep them," said Mrs. Millard.

"Keep them!" I echoed stupidly.

"Don't you understand English, Jane?"

"You don't mean—keep them—always?"

"Yes, of course."

"But, Mrs. Millard—"

"What else do you suggest I should do?"

"But I couldn't!" I cried. "Mrs. Millard, I couldn't possibly—"

"In that case you had better put them back in the box. You'll find it on the chimney-piece."

I opened the box—and hesitated with the pearls in my hand. Mrs. Millard was sitting at the table, her head was turned sideways and she was looking out of the window—not at me. I had always admired her tremendously but now, quite suddenly, I saw her in a different light: small and pathetic—and lonely. She had chosen loneliness because she hated 'getting involved emotionally'. She was afraid of getting hurt. Freedom was what she wanted but it seemed to me a poor substitute for affection.

I thought of all she had told me about the pearls; she couldn't wear them; she didn't want to sell them; she hated to shut them up in prison.

I should have liked to say, "Mrs. Millard, do you really mean it? Do you *want* me to keep the pearls?" but I knew it would have annoyed her. I stood there looking at her profile and trying to think of something to say, but I could find nothing.

"Have you put them back in the box?" asked Mrs. Millard.

"No, I can't," I said desperately. "May I change my mind, please?"

"Yes," she replied.

I fastened the string round my neck and went over to where she was sitting. "I suppose I can say thank you?" I asked doubtfully.

"I suppose you can—just once," she replied. She was smiling but her eyes were full of tears.

I kissed her and said, "Thank you, I shall wear them always—for you and for him."

"I'm afraid you're a sentimental young woman," said Mrs. Millard. She added, "Go away now—without saying good-bye."

I went at once—without saying good-bye.

3

Mother was not surprised at the news that Mrs. Millard was leaving.

"I expect she needs a holiday," said Mother cheerfully. "You need a holiday too. You're looking quite worn out. It would be a good plan for you to go to Edinburgh and stay with Andrew and Margaret—they've asked you several times. As for getting another job, you needn't worry about that. Look at all the money you're going to get when *The Mulberry Coach* is published!"

"That won't last for ever."

"But you can write another, can't you?"

"Yes, I suppose so," I said.

As a matter of fact I had been toying with the idea of writing a successor to *The Mulberry Coach*. Already I had several ideas in my head for a novel set in the same period and written in much the same style . . . but now that Mrs. Millard was leaving Ryddelton is seemed beyond my powers. I knew only too well how much I owed to Mrs. Millard's encouragement and constructive criticism.

"Of course you can," said Mother confidently. "You're tired now, and no wonder, but you'll feel a different creature after a week in Edinburgh and you'll have plenty of time to write."

"Perhaps Cousin Margaret won't want me—" I began.

"Of course they'll want you," declared Mother. "They're both very fond of you, Jane . . . Oh, and while I remember you're to call them Andrew and Margaret."

"Did they say so?"

"Yes," said Mother laughing. "They both said so quite definitely. They said now that you were all grown-up there was no need to cousin them! Rather a feeble jape, I thought, but it amused Andrew considerably."

Mother had said nothing about the pearls (perhaps it was because she was so used to seeing them round my neck that she had forgotten all about them) and now she had another much more important matter to occupy her thoughts: Helen wrote to say she was going to have a baby.

"Not until April of course," said Mother. "But it's lovely to think I shall be a grandmother." She added cheerfully, "Helen is feeling wretched. Her letter is one long moan; you would think nobody had ever been through it before."

Usually I was shown Helen's letters but apparently this one was not considered suitable for me to read.

Chapter Seventeen

1

The house in Murrayfield Gardens was a very pleasant place to stay; it was run in a free and easy manner and guests were not 'entertained' against their will. Instead of arranging parties for me, as she had done for Helen, Margaret took me to see the Castle and Holyrood Palace and the Royal Mile. She had read so much about the beautiful old city that her brain was stored with all sorts of facts and fancies: not Guide-Book information but the stuff of romance. Some of the people she talked about were real and others imaginary but Margaret made them all come alive to me. As we strolled up the West Bow she reminded me of David Balfour who had ridden in haste to rescue Catriona from prison . . . 'I was in the saddle again before the day, and the Edinburgh booths were just opening when I clattered in by the West Bow and drew up a smoking horse at my lord Advocate's door.'

Quite near was the dwelling of Deacon Brodie: a respectable cabinet-maker on weekdays; a Deacon of the Kirk on the Sabbath; by night, a thief 'pickeering among the closes', lantern in hand.

Margaret had queer little bits of information which never appear in guide-books and she told me that a chest of drawers in the nursery where Robert Louis Stevenson had spent his childhood had been made by the 'deacon' with his own hands. It held a curious fascination for the imaginative little boy and haunted his dreams. Later this childhood memory inspired him to write a play about the sinister character . . . and, more than likely, inspired the story about the double life of Dr. Jekyll and Mr. Hyde.

So we strolled and poked about and enjoyed ourselves hugely in our own peculiar way and Margaret discoursed with some of the inhabitants of The Tall Lands and afterwards translated their remarks into what she teasingly described as 'Oxford English'.

Sunday was a beautiful day, it was more like late August than early November, and at breakfast Andrew announced his intention of playing truant from church and taking me to Dirleton for lunch. Apparently this was a most unusual dereliction from the path of virtue, and Margaret did not altogether approve, but Andrew pointed out that ever since I came I had been 'craiking' to go to the seaside and build sand-castles—and this was the only chance he had of fulfilling my desire.

It was true that I wanted to go to the sea, but the sandcastles were Andrew's idea; he had been teasing me about them for days.

Andrew added that we would take sandwiches and a flask of coffee and picnic on the shore.

"But you haven't had a picnic for years!" exclaimed Margaret.

"Surely that's all the more reason to have it to-day," returned Andrew smiling, and he added, "It will please the child."

Margaret smiled too and hurried away to make the sandwiches, for of course if Andrew wanted a picnic he must have it. There was something delightful about their relationship. They appreciated each other's qualities and enjoyed each other's jokes.

2

The drive to Dirleton was very pleasant. We saw Dirleton Castle (a magnificent old ruin which had once belonged to a branch of the great family of Douglas); we passed through the picturesque little village with its triangular green and then turned sharply down a narrow lane which wound towards the shore. Andrew told me that in summer-time the place was crowded—but there was nobody here to-day. We left the car at the end of the lane and walked on past a little wood and over the grassy dunes to the sea.

It was beautiful and peaceful. The tide was half-way out and there were black rocks and yellow seaweed. Close inshore, separated from the mainland by a narrow strait, was the curiously-shaped island of Fidra. The sea was blue and the sun was golden and only the faintest breeze stirred the silvery green spikes of the bent grass.

"There," said Andrew. "It's all yours, Jane. Go and build your sand-castles," and he sat down with his back against a convenient rock and took out his pipe.

It was all mine. The words reminded me of the day at St. Mary's Loch when I had said the beauty was all for us, and Mother had replied that perhaps it was partly for the sheep and the birds. To-day I was sharing the beauty with the soaring gulls and the tiny crabs which lived beneath the seaweed and scuttled away as I approached. I noticed that the tide was going out—so it was safe—and finding a little pool quite near the edge of the lapping waves I put the pearls into it and sat down to dream.

Dreaming was easy. I could dream for hours—not thinking, not wondering, not conscious of the passing of time. I could dream at all times and in all places—and this place was made for dreams. I did not awake until Andrew's shadow fell across my knees.

"Where are the sand-castles, Jane?"

"They were castles in Spain," I replied, smiling up at him. "But the real reason I wanted to come to the sea was pearls. Pearls like sea-water and sunshine."

He stooped over the pool and said, "Not real pearls, surely!"

"Yes, Mrs. Millard gave them to me."

"Mrs. Millard gave them to you!"

"Yes."

Andrew was a philatelist and always carried a little magnifying-glass in his pocket, so now he lifted the pearls out of the water and examined them with his lens.

"They're beautiful!" he exclaimed. "I've never seen a more beautiful string of pearls . . . but you can't accept them from her."

"I have accepted them."

"You don't understand," he declared. "These pearls are too valuable. You can't accept a present worth hundreds of pounds from a woman like Mrs. Millard. Honestly, Jane, your Mother would be horrified. You must send them back."

I was silent.

"Your Mother doesn't know that Mrs. Millard gave them to you, does she?"

"No."

"You must send them back," declared Andrew. "We'll do them up and send them off to-morrow."

"I don't know her address," I said.

It was perfectly true. I had asked Mrs. Millard for her address but she had not given it to me, nor had she left it at the post office for letters to be forwarded. I had thought it a strange oversight on her part, but now I had a feeling that she had withheld her address on purpose so that I could not be induced to return the pearls. I had found on several occasions that if you wanted to know why Mrs. Millard did this—or did not do that—you had only to look at the results of her actions.

"You don't know her address!" exclaimed Andrew in amazement.

I shook my head.

"But Jane! What an extraordinary thing! You worked with her for months, didn't you? I thought you were devoted to the woman . . . and then suddenly she gives you a necklace fit for a queen and vanishes into the blue!"

"Yes."

"Didn't she want you to write to her?"

"No."

"Did you have a row with her, Jane?"

"No."

"Well, it beats me," he said with a sigh of bewilderment.

After a few moments he continued, "Of course she's a bit queer, isn't she? Your mother was very worried about your going there every day but I managed to soothe her down. I told her Augusta Millard wouldn't do you any harm."

"Do you know her?" I asked in surprise.

"I don't know her—but I know you," said Andrew smiling, at me in his charming way. He sat down beside me on the rock and went on talking. "I never met the lady but I knew Millard quite well."

"You knew—her husband!"

Andrew nodded. "He used to live in Edinburgh at one time—everybody knew him—so his marriage caused quite a sensation."

"Why should it?" I asked.

"Oh, because he was a staid old buffer and she had had such a queer sort of life. She was engaged to a boy who was killed in the war—the First War, of course—and some months after she had an illegitimate child. After that she went completely off the handle and got mixed up with some very undesirable people. There were all sorts of wild stories . . . Oh well, the least said about that the better. Then she met Millard and married him and he adopted her son. Millard was old and not in good health and people said she married him to give the boy a name but she was a good wife to the old man and looked after him until he died. The boy was killed at Alamein—but I suppose you know all that?"

"Most of it," I said, not altogether truthfully. And yet I did know most of it. I knew the most important part. I knew about the boy who had been killed at Mons; the boy who had said, "With all my worldly goods I thee endow," and had given her a string of pearls and a son.

I wondered why he had not given her his name—there must have been some reason—but to me it seemed that their marriage was more real than many marriages which take place in church.

Half-way through Andrew's story I had almost stopped him, but now I was glad I had heard it all. It was a bald bare story but I could fill in the details only too easily. My eyes were wet and I had to keep on blinking them for a few moments before I could see.

3

Andrew and I had lunch together, sitting in a grassy hollow amongst the dunes. The pearls were round my neck—all wet with sea-water. I saw Andrew glance at them from time to time but he said no more about them. We were friendly and companionable; I thought then that Andrew was one of the nicest people I had ever met and I have not changed my mind.

After a little he began to talk about Mother and to ask all sorts of questions about our life at Timble Cottage. He wanted to know whether it was a success and whether we were happy and what we did with ourselves all day.

"You don't think she misses London?" he inquired anxiously. "She had so many friends in London—and such a gay life—you don't think she finds it a little dull?"

"Mother is never dull," I told him. "And nobody could be dull living with Mother. She makes her own fun, you see. Even peeling potatoes is fun when we do it together."

"Peeling potatoes! That doesn't sound a very amusing occupation."

"It is—with Mother."

"There's nobody like Anna," he said.

For a few moments there was silence. I looked at him sitting on the grass, gazing away over the sea and munching a sandwich.

His large feet were stretched out towards me—like the feet in an amateur snapshot which often appear twice their normal size.

"Andrew!" I exclaimed. "Were you ever in love with Mother?"

"Well, of course," he replied, smiling rather sadly. "I've always been in love with Anna—all my life. When I was twenty-one I was crazy about her. You all talk about Helen being 'beautiful' but she's not a patch on Anna. Beauty isn't skin deep whatever they may say. Anna at eighteen was as lovely as an angel—and as good."

"Why didn't you marry her?"

"My dear girl, I hadn't a penny! I was an undergraduate reading law. How could I say a word? Then Harcourt appeared and walked off with her under my nose."

There was a vague look in his eyes. I think he had forgotten me for the moment and was just remembering byegone days.

"I only saw her twice after she was married," he continued. "Once when she came to Edinburgh for a wedding and once when I went to London on business. I called to see her in the morning and she was just going out, but she put off her engagement and I stayed to lunch. She was just the same as always—friendly and natural and kind—then Harcourt came in and she changed into a different person. I asked them to dinner at the Savoy but Harcourt thanked me politely and declined—without consulting Anna. Harcourt didn't like me and he made it pretty obvious. I suppose you couldn't blame him."

Andrew took out his pipe and filled it carefully. "I came home the next day," he said. "It was better to come straight home. If I had stayed in London I might have gone to Wintringham Square again—and what was the use? I was a fool to go and see her at all. I came home feeling as miserable as a sick jackdaw. It took me ages to get over it and settle down."

"Have you got over it?"

"No," said Andrew gruffly. He took out a match and lighted his pipe.

"Why don't you marry her—now?"

"For Heaven's sake!" he cried, gazing at me in amazement.

"Have you never thought of it?"

"Of course I've thought of it! I'd marry her to-morrow! Anna hasn't thought of it, that's the trouble. I'm perfectly certain the idea has never crossed her mind."

I was silent.

"Jane," he said. "Listen to me, you extraordinary child. If I plunge in and—and ask her she would think I'd gone off my head. And, don't you see, it would spoil everything. She treats me like a brother—and she needs me. She really does need me."

It was true.

"She would think I had gone off my head, wouldn't she?" repeated Andrew.

He was looking at me searchingly but I was determined not to say another word. Perhaps I had said too much already. I knew Mother liked him—immensely—but I did not know whether the idea of marrying him had ever crossed her mind.

It was not until I had noticed his enormous feet that the idea had crossed *my* mind.

We were rather silent on the way back to Edinburgh. Andrew was thinking—and so was I. As a matter of fact I was wondering what on earth had possessed me to rush in where angels might well have feared to tread . . . and I was wondering what I should do if Mother married Andrew.

Mother and I were happy together, we got on perfectly, there was no discordant note. I had never been so happy in my life as I was now, alone with Mother, at Timble Cottage. Perhaps I had started an avalanche—I could not tell—but if so, and if the avalanche wrecked my life, I should have nobody to blame but myself.

4

The next morning when I went down to breakfast Margaret was having the meal alone; she explained that Andrew had gone to Ryddelton on business.

"I expect it's something to do with having the house painted," she said as she poured out the coffee. "I suggested he should tell you he was going but he went off early and didn't want to disturb you. What would you like to do to-day?"

I said I did not mind.

It is written in my diary that Margaret and I took the bus to Linlithgow and saw the old palace, but to be quite honest I remember very little about it, which seems a pity considering how very interesting it must have been.

We saw nothing of Andrew all day but when I was getting ready for supper he knocked on my door and asked me to come out on to the landing.

"Come out on to the landing?" I echoed. "Hadn't you better come in if you want to talk to me?"

"It would be better if you came out," he replied uncomfortably.

I pulled him into the room and shut the door. I really could not wait a moment longer. "Well?" I asked anxiously.

"I've been to Ryddelton. It's no use; I didn't think it would be."

"That wasn't the right spirit to go in!"

"Perhaps not, but it wouldn't have made any difference," he replied.

He seemed perfectly calm and composed on the surface, but beneath the surface I could sense his unhappiness. It was as if some inner light had gone out . . . and it was all my fault. Why had I not left well alone?

"What happened?" I asked. "What did you do? What did you say?"

"We walked about in the garden and I explained."

"You shouldn't have explained. You should have kissed her."

"Good heavens, no! There was nothing like that! She gave me—no encouragement at all. She seemed—rather amused," said Andrew miserably. "She was very kind, of course—she always is—but she made me see it was quite ridiculous to think of such a thing at our age. She said we were both too old. She said she was going to be a grandmother before very long. She pointed out that we both have obligations."

"Obligations?"

"Yes, she's got you and Rosalie to look after and I've got Margaret... look, Jane," he added. "We had better go down. It's supper-time and Margaret will be wondering."

Margaret may have been wondering why we were late for supper, but most certainly she was wondering before the meal was finished, for she had lived with Andrew so long and was so close to him in spirit that she could not fail to notice his preoccupation. She made no comment, for it was not her way to pry into other people's business, but after supper when we were washing up the dishes together she suddenly turned to me and said, "Is something the matter, Jane? Don't tell me if you'd rather not."

"I've been putting my foot in it, that's all."

"Nobody is ill—or anything like that?" asked Margaret anxiously.

I had to tell her. As a matter of fact I thought she had a right to know. I was afraid she might be angry with me for interfering, but she was neither angry nor surprised.

"Well, of course," she said. "He's always loved Anna, that's why he never looked at anybody else. That's why I never managed my tour round thee world. I shall never manage it now," she added with a little sigh.

I looked at her for a moment and then flung down the dish-cloth and went back to the dining-room, where Andrew was still sitting with a stone-cold cup of coffee in front of him.

"Listen, Andrew!" I cried. "You didn't do it properly. You messed up the whole thing."

"I shouldn't have done it at all," said Andrew miserably. "I've been thinking. Anna was right. We're too old—and we've both got obligations. What on earth would Margaret do if I got married?"

"Go round the world."

"Go round the world!"

"A tour round the world—it's been her dream for years. You know how Margaret loves travel-books? Well, she wants to see all the places she's read about."

"What an extraordinary idea!"

"It's a gorgeous idea—not extraordinary at all. I only wish I could..." and then I stopped and gazed at him with an astonishment which matched his own. Why couldn't I? There was no reason at all why I should not go—with Margaret. Rosalie could come too, if she wanted. Thanks to *The Mulberry Coach* I had the money to pay for us both.

I began to laugh excitedly. "We'll do it!" I cried. "Your obligations will all go round the world together."

"Have you taken leave of your senses?" demanded Andrew.

I saw then that I had gone the wrong way about it—so much so that it took quite a long time to convince him that I was in earnest—but at last he was convinced.

"Oh well, if that's what you want there's nothing to prevent you," he admitted.

"Except our obligations," I said. "We couldn't possibly leave Mother alone at Ryddelton and Margaret wouldn't dream of leaving you alone here."

"I wish you'd be serious. I've told you I asked Anna to marry me and she refused."

"But you did it all wrong! You should have kissed her—passionately—"

"Really, Jane!" he exclaimed in horrified tones.

"Yes, you should," I declared. "You should have kissed her—and then explained. You should have told her that you had always loved her—that you had been faithful to her for twenty years. You should have said you had never looked at another woman and never would. You should have said you couldn't be happy without her."

"You're laughing at me—"

"No, I'm not."

"But it's all true—every word."

"Well, go and tell her," I said crossly, "How is she to know all that unless you tell her?"

Chapter Eighteen

1

The next morning Andrew set off to Ryddelton so early that neither Margaret nor I was out of bed. We came downstairs to find a note to say he had gone—and that was all.

"Without any breakfast! Oh dear!" exclaimed Margaret in dismay.

"He'll be there in time for breakfast," I told her. It was not Andrew's breakfast—or lack of breakfast—which was worrying me.

"Aren't you going to have any porridge, Jane?" asked my hostess.

"No thank you, I don't want anything except perhaps a cup of coffee. Oh Margaret, why was I such a fool! An interfering busybody! What have I started? Why didn't I leave things alone?"

"You did it for the best," said Margaret consolingly. "He's been in love with Anna all his life. Why shouldn't he have his chance to be happy? If it comes off we'll go for our tour, and if not there's no harm done."

I was not so sure about 'no harm done'.

Fortunately my agony did not last long; we had scarcely finished dallying with cups of coffee when the telephone rang and it was Andrew in a state of incoherent excitement saying he was a happy man. Then Mother snatched the receiver out of his hand and said Andrew was mad and nothing was settled and were we quite certain it was all right, because nothing would induce her to marry anybody and leave Jane in the lurch . . . and what was this hare-brained scheme about going round the world when we could all live together happily at Murrayfield Gardens?

Margaret spoke to them and so did I, but there was no sense to be got out of them. The truth was they were both in such a state of excitement that they did not know what they were saying.

"Well, I suppose it's all right," said Margaret when at last the line went dead and there was nothing more to be heard.

"It's perfectly all right," I said. "And if you don't mind we'll heat up those sausages because for some reason I'm frightfully hungry."

2

Margaret and I had imagined that we would be able to settle things quite quickly and start off on our travels early in the New Year but all sorts of things conspired to delay us. Mother declared that she must buy some clothes (not a trousseau of course, that would be silly at her age; but she had not a single garment fit to wear) and Andrew insisted on having the Murrayfield house redecorated from attic to cellar for his bride.

Rosalie said she would come with us on our tour—and was quite excited about it—and then for no apparent reason she cooled off and decided to stay with the Fergusons instead.

Then Helen became very ill and Mother abandoned all her preparations for the wedding and went off to London posthaste. Helen had been taken to hospital, so Mother stayed with Ronnie in their flat, looking after him and visiting Helen daily. At first it was thought that there was no hope for the baby but things improved a little and on the fourteenth of February Mother rang up to say that the baby had arrived.

He was a seven-months baby, very small and weak, but they had hopes that he would live.

Mother stayed in London until Helen and her little son were better and she was able to leave them in charge of a capable nurse. They had called the baby 'Valentine' after his patron saint, not 'Gerald' as Mother had wanted, but he had been christened in such a hurry that there had been no time for discussion about his name.

By this time Mother was so exhausted that she would have backed out of her marriage if she could. She declared that she felt a hundred years old—she was an old done woman, more fit for her grave than her wedding—but Andrew refused to listen, Andrew had waited patiently for months and would not wait a day longer and he was so forceful and confident that he swept all before him. There need be no junketings, declared Andrew, and Anna needed no clothes except those she stood up in, but they would be married on Monday and go off to Skye for a peaceful honeymoon.

"Monday!" exclaimed Mother in dismay.

"Monday," said Andrew firmly. "The whole thing is fixed and I've taken the rooms for three weeks."

"Oh well—" said Mother . . . and then she added,

"Perhaps you should take your rod, Andrew."

"Two rods," said Andrew with a smile.

3

It was the end of April when Margaret and I stepped out of the plane at Rome airport. Neither of us had flown before but after our first wild terror had worn off we had both enjoyed the experience of being airborne. We had agreed that our tour was to be leisurely; we had all the time in the world at our disposal. Certainly we had no intention of wandering round the globe for ever—like a couple of Flying Dutchwomen. Our intention was to return to Ryddelton and live at Timble Cottage . . . but that was far off, it was a tiny picture seen through the wrong end of a telescope.

Rome was our first choice, for there were a hundred things in Rome that both of us wanted to see. We prowled round the place with a guide-book, feasting our eyes upon old buildings and churches and pictures until the lovely old city became as hot as an oven and we could bear it no longer. We flew to Capetown after that, and from there took ship to Australia . . .

It would be tedious to write of our travels day by day or week by week. We just wandered—and having discovered that we both liked ships better than aeroplanes we did most of our travelling by water.

Margaret was a perfect travelling companion; she never fussed nor worried; she never interfered. She was not stimulating nor very amusing (like Mother and Mrs. Millard) but she was extremely restful. She never besought me to 'use my brain'—and if I chose to walk round the deck with a young man she did not jump to conclusions. (Mother would have been the soul of tact, but in her own secret thoughts she would have robed me in white satin and orange blossom).

I soon discovered that Margaret wore blinkers, but she wore them with a difference; they did not make her inconsiderate nor selfish, but they prevented her from interfering in other people's affairs. Occasionally they got her into trouble and she floundered into bogs that a more perspicacious woman would have avoided . . . as when she remarked to the ageing husband of a very young wife, "How pretty your daughter is! *All* the young men admire her."

I could rescue her from some of her indiscretions but not from that one.

It was when we were steaming across the Indian Ocean that we met a young American, Tony Meldrum, who possessed a small but very efficient telescope through which he surveyed the heavens every night. When he discovered quite by accident that to me the word 'star' connoted a celestial body and not the body of an actress upon the screen he was 'thrilled to bits' and invited me to join him. He was further delighted when he discovered that I could actually see through his telescope. He assured me that most young women of his acquaintance could not.

Tony and I spent hours gazing at the Southern Cross and examining the craters of the moon. Like most Americans he knew his subject and was delighted to talk about it to anyone who showed an intelligent interest, and as I was delighted to be instructed we got on exceedingly well.

Tony was an attractive young man, well set up, with a thin eager face and bright eyes. At first we talked about stars and planets and satellites, but after a bit we began to talk about other doings . . . and one night when the moon was full and its beams were shining across the tumbled water, Tony kissed me and asked me to marry him. I very nearly said yes.

I liked him so much, he was kind and considerate and earnest, and although we had not known each other long we had spent a great deal of time together and had got to know each other well. I very nearly said yes, but at the last moment I found I could not say it.

Sometimes I wondered whether Margaret suspected that there was anything more than astronomy in my friendship with Tony Meldrum but if she did she was unusually discreet.

Some of the places we visited were slightly disappointing—we had expected too much—but others exceeded our wildest dreams. The Taj Mahal, for instance, struck us dumb. We visited it by moonlight when it gleamed like a silvery palace in a vision. We stayed on at Agra for several days and saw it at sunrise blushing like a pink pearl. It was a perfect thing, perhaps the most beautiful thing that was ever built by the hands of men. It would be difficult to pick out the high-light of our tour, but if I were obliged to do so I think I should pick out the Taj Mahal.

4

Our wanderings were so haphazard that letters followed us from one place to another and we were apt to get large budgets of news at infrequent intervals (occasionally we cabled and received a cable in reply to say that all was well); but on our way home we stayed at Trinidad and found a bundle of mail waiting for us at the hotel. Margaret had the lion's share—she always did, for she corresponded faithfully with numerous friends in Edinburgh.

I had hoped for a letter from Mother, but although there was one from her in the bundle it was addressed to Margaret and not to me. There were no letters from Rosalie nor Helen (my share of the mail consisted of a few uninteresting letters which had been forwarded from Ryddelton) so after a decent interval I went along to Margaret's room to hear the news.

"Anna writes a very difficult hand," complained Margaret, looking up as I went in. "It's large and looks easy but the words are all joined together in a curious way. I think she must write very fast."

"She does," I said.

"I can't make out what she means," Margaret continued. "But she says you will have heard from Rosalie so I suppose you know all about it."

"Not a word!"

"Something is happening on the 14th. That's to-day, isn't it?"

"They aren't ill, are they?"

"I don't think it's that, but they want us to fly home at once."

"Give it to me for heaven's sake!" I cried seizing the letter out of her hand. Mother's writing had no terrors for me—compared with the writing of Lady Esmeralda Pie it was as plain as a pike-staff—so I read it aloud:

> Dearest Margaret,
>
> By this time Jane will have had Rosalie's letter so of course you will know all about it—I wonder what you will think!!! This is just a hasty scrawl to catch you at Trinidad if possible—Andrew is waiting to post it—we both think you should fly home if possible before the 14th. It would be *such* a help if you were here. Of course we don't want to spoil your fun but you have been away such a long time and surely you have had enough travelling. Andrew is a darling and gets nicer every day—I can only hope they will be as happy. Andrew says we must be *enthusiastic* about it or at least *pretend* to be—but it is not easy to be enthusiastic. Andrew says if I don't finish this letter at once he will have to run all the way to the post.
>
> Much love to you both
>
> ANNA
>
> P.S. It seems so queer—such a difference in age and *not* very attractive—such silly little feet!

"What does it mean?" asked Margaret in bewilderment.

I too had been absolutely bewildered . . . until I got to the postscript. Then I began to laugh helplessly. "It's all right," I gasped. "Rosalie is going to marry Sir Edward Fisher, that's all."

"Sir Edward Fisher? You mean the man who bought Mount Charles? But Anna doesn't mention him? Did you know about it before?"

"I never thought of it for a moment. As a matter of fact I thought it would be nice for Mother to marry him and go back to Mount Charles as its chatelaine—and I thought he rather liked Mother."

"But Jane—"

"It shows how silly I was, doesn't it?"

Margaret looked thoughtful. "Perhaps you were right," she said. "I mean Rosalie is like Anna, isn't she? Only not so pretty."

5

We could not be present at the wedding—even by flying—for presumably the wedding was taking place at that very moment. So I suggested we should show our enthusiasm by cabling our best wishes to the happy pair.

Margaret was a little reluctant. "But supposing it isn't," she objected. "I still don't understand how you can possibly know it's him."

"It is him," I replied, regardless of grammar. "We'll go down to the desk right now and send enthusiastic cables and blow the expense. Andrew says we are to show enthusiasm and there's no other way."

She rose at once and followed me downstairs.

Chapter Nineteen

1

The evening when Margaret and I came home to Timble Cottage was one of those perfect Spring evenings which often bless the Border Country after a day of intermittent rain. We had been delayed by a breakdown on the railway, and it had annoyed us both out of all proportion; for although we had wandered over the big world happily foot-loose for a year we were now suddenly impatient to be home.

It was nine o'clock when we arrived in the taxi with our bag and baggage; the light was fading slowly into lovely twilight with a tinge of green in the sky. The hedge had been trimmed, the garden was tidy and well-cared-for. I found the key hanging beneath the bird-table (the enormous iron key which was more like the key of a jail than a cottage) and pushed it into the door.

A note was lying on the hall table:

Couldent wait. Had to go home. Will be there early to-morrow. Tongue and sallad in the fridge. Botles in your beds. Yours respectably Elizabeth Gow.

"Nice," said Margaret smiling.

It was nice. It was especially nice because there was no flowery welcome. Mrs. Gow had merely scrubbed the little house and polished it until it shone, put 'botles' in our beds and left our supper ready. We were tired of flowery speeches and the bowings and scrapings of hotel managers and stewards and waiters. We had come home to people who showed their feelings by deeds, not words.

We did not say much ourselves but when we were sitting at supper Margaret broke the silence.

"I'm going to breed dogs, Jane," said Margaret suddenly. "Spaniels, I think; they're so soft and silky—and so kind. You'll have your writing of course, and I shall breed dogs. I've always wanted to. You don't mind, do you?"

Of course I did not mind! Dear Margaret, she could breed elephants if that would make her happy.

"I shall do all the housekeeping, of course," continued Margaret. "I like housekeeping; that will give you plenty of time to write, and to walk over the hills for inspiration."

"I'll exercise the dogs," I told her . . . and we both laughed.

2

Before we could settle down to the quiet life we had planned it was necessary to see our family. Murrayfield Gardens was our first visit and there we found all we had expected of peaceful happiness. Mother and Andrew were very pleased to see us and welcomed us warmly—but not rapturously. It was easy to see that they were everything to each other and that other people did not matter to them quite as much as before. As Margaret put it, they were 'almost stodgy'.

Margaret did not come with me when I went to see Rosalie at Mount Charles. Sir Edward sent the car for me so I went over in state and the whole family was waiting on the door-step to greet me. There was no red carpet visible, but I felt it was there. Rosalie flung herself into my arms and hugged me ecstatically; nice little Sir Edward kissed me in a brotherly manner, and the three children greeted me affectionately as 'Aunt Jane'.

There was plenty to talk about as we sat round the dining-room table having lunch. They told me about the wedding and I told them about our tour. The two boys wanted to know if I had seen any Red Indians (they were at the Fennimore Cooper stage) and fortunately I was able to tell them that I had seen and spoken to several with painted faces and feather head dresses. This raised me to the height of admiration. I noticed that their behaviour was exemplary; they were friendly and polite, they talked neither too much nor too little. In fact they were small editions of their father whose manners I had always admired.

Sir Edward beamed happily through his flashing spectacles and beamed especially happily upon his wife. She was the queen with four adoring subjects to anticipate her slightest wish; to shut the window in case she might feel a draught or to run and fetch her a handkerchief from the right-hand top drawer of her dressing-table. Quite honestly their solicitude would have driven me mad, but Rosalie seemed to enjoy it.

After lunch Sir Edward shepherded the children away and left us to chat—and Rosalie chattered in her usual uninhibited manner.

"Aren't they sweet, Jane?" said Rosalie. "They love me, you know. They all love me and it makes me feel safe. I've never felt really safe since we left Wintringham Square. They're pleased with all I do, so I don't do silly things any more. Helen used to make me feel all wrong—and nasty."

I nodded to show that I understood.

"It was the same with you," she added.

"The same with me?"

"You weren't very nice when Helen was there," said Rosalie frankly.

This was a new idea to me . . . but perhaps she was right.

"They think I'm nice—so I *am* nice," added Rosalie with a sigh of perfect bliss.

It was as simple as that.

"I'll tell you something very queer," continued Rosalie confidentially. "Lady Fisher—I mean Edward's first wife—wasn't very kind. She wasn't nice to Edward and she was quite horrid to the children. Edward told me himself and I could hardly believe it! Fancy anyone being unkind to *them*!"

"It seems queer," I admitted.

"Edward told me," repeated Rosalie, opening her eyes very wide. "I can't tell you about it, because Edward wouldn't like it—but she wasn't *kind*."

Rosalie was so devoted to the children that she was the ideal stepmother, the very person to become possessed of a ready-made family, but when I said something like this she contradicted me.

"It's only half-made," she declared. "Edward and I think it would be awfully nice for Ted and Billy and Alex to have some dear little brothers and sisters—three would be perfect. Anna and Gerald and Jane," added Rosalie with a dreamy smile.

"Nice of you to—" I began.

But Rosalie was not listening. "I think—" said Rosalie. "I have a sort of feeling that Anna may be here in time for Christmas. Wouldn't that be lovely?"

We went on talking and Rosalie told me that she had liked Edward for quite a long time—ever since she had come to nurse the children when they were stricken with measles—and he had liked her too but had not said a word because he thought he was too old.

"Poor darling, as if that mattered!" said Rosalie fondly.

It was not until he heard that she was making plans to go for a tour round the world that he had managed to summon up his courage to propose. "So that was why I changed my mind about going with you," she explained. "I mean he hadn't actually proposed *then*, but I knew he was going to. Kenneth and Jean were so kind about it and made it all so pleasant and easy . . . but I mustn't talk any more about myself, I want to hear about you."

There was not much to tell her about me for although I had travelled far I felt that Rosalie had travelled farther.

When it was time for me to go Sir Edward suggested sending me home in the car, but it was such a lovely evening that I preferred to walk. He walked with me to the gate.

"How do you think she is looking?" he asked anxiously.

I told him I had never seen her looking better.

"Good! Good!" he exclaimed. "I think she's a little fatter—and of course that means she's happy and contented."

Personally I thought she was putting on weight too quickly but who was I to say so? If he wanted his Rosalie to be fat it was none of my business.

"I was just a little afraid at first," he continued. "She's so young—so very much younger than I am—but I'm doing my best to think of things to please her. I've got her a little car for her birthday—she'll like that, I'm sure. I can easily teach her to drive. It will make her independent; she can go out when she likes. If you could possibly tell me of anything else she wants . . ." he gazed at me searchingly, and waited.

"She's got everything she wants," I told him. "She just wants to be loved."

There were tears in his eyes. "Nobody could help loving Rosalie," he said.

As I walked home over the hill I remembered how Mother had worried about Rosalie's future and had wished that Rosalie could learn to stand upon her own feet . . . but there was no need for Rosalie to stand upon her feet; she was cushioned upon a feather mattress.

3

Having seen Mother and Rosalie it seemed natural to visit Helen as well, and as I had business in London—connected with *The Mulberry Coach*—it was possible to kill two birds with one stone, so I wrote to Helen and said I was coming, expecting an invitation to stay at the flat. The invitation came but it was luke-warm. They could have me to stay if I did not mind roughing it but she and Ronnie thought I would be much more comfortable in a hotel. Of course they wanted to see me and they would arrange to have me to supper or meet me at a restaurant whichever I would rather . . . and perhaps I would like to go to a play.

The letter was a trifle damping, but I told myself firmly that I would much rather stay at a hotel, so I took a room in a moderately-priced but comfortable hotel, recommended by Mrs. Hunter. I wanted to see Helen, and she had said she wanted to see me, but when I rang up and tried to fix a meeting it seemed a little difficult.

"I'm so busy," complained Helen. "It would have been better if you could have come next week. To-morrow is hopeless; I'm having my hair set in the morning and I've got to go out to lunch and then on to a bridge-party. Wednesday is Nurse's day off. On Thursday Vera is coming up from the country and I'm taking her to a matinee. You see how difficult it is, Jane."

"I could look in and see you on Wednesday," I suggested.

"Oh no!" cried Helen. "Val is frightfully shy and tiresome. I can't possibly have you when Nurse is out. Friday *might* be possible. I've got an appointment with Madame Peridot in the morning and a cocktail party in the evening, but I think I could meet you somewhere for lunch. Would that do?"

I felt like saying not to bother but I swallowed my pride and said it would do.

The following day when I returned to the hotel after an afternoon's shopping I found Ronnie waiting for me in the lounge. I saw him before he saw me and I thought he looked sad and worried—which was unusual to say the least of it. Ronnie had always glowed with health and vigour; he had always seemed full of high spirits; his vitality had been one of his charms. Then he saw me and smiled and looked more like himself.

"Jane, how nice to see you!" he exclaimed. "It seems ages—it *is* ages of course. I haven't seen you since you became a famous author. I loved *The Mulberry Coach*!"

"I'm glad, Ronnie."

"It was very naughty of you not to come to us."

"Oh well, I've got business to see to—"

"But you could have come to us and done your business. You could have been perfectly free. You've never seen the flat, have you? It's a nice little flat and quite convenient for tubes and buses—and we've got a spare room and everything," said Ronnie earnestly. "Honestly, Jane, when I heard you were coming to London—and not to us—I felt quite hurt."

"I'm sorry. I just thought it would be easier—"

"Well, never mind. We'll fix up for you to come for a meal—lunch or tea or whatever suits you best. You must see Val, of course. He's rather a pet," said his father smiling fondly.

"Yes, I want to see Val."

"Fix it up with Helen," said Ronnie nodding.

"She seems to have a good many engagements—" I began.

Ronnie's face clouded. "Far too many," he declared. "She does far too much and it isn't good for her to get overtired. She's got caught up in a whirl and doesn't seem able to stop; last winter she was ill, off and on, for weeks."

"Ronnie, is she really delicate?"

"We're all delicate," declared Ronnie with a quizzical smile. "We've all got a weak spot—at least I never met anyone who hadn't. Helen's weak spot is her chest. Damp and cold and fog and all the late nights and rushing madly from place to place all day are the worst thing for her. If only she would take care of herself there would be no need to worry—but she doesn't take care of herself so the only thing to do is to leave London."

"Leave London!"

"Yes, didn't Helen tell you? The idea is to go abroad. You can have a better standard of living for much less expense; you can have a bungalow and a lovely garden and servants. We might manage to keep a car—which would be nice. Helen seems to think she would like it."

"Where is this earthly paradise?" I asked. Ronnie had spoken as if it were a real place and not just a dream.

Ronnie admitted that the place was real. There was a post vacant in a hospital in Kenya and he could have it if he wanted. He explained that in addition to the usual hospital work he would be expected to help in the laboratory where the doctor in charge was conducting bacteriological research.

"You would like that, Ronnie!"

"Yes, it would be interesting. Of course it's a leap in the dark; Helen might not like it. She thinks she would like it, but we can't tell what sort of place it is until we get there. The climate is good—and there would be no smog." He hesitated and then added, "And I might be able to save a little money for Val's education. We don't seem to be able to save a penny here."

I was not surprised. If Helen was getting clothes from Madame Peridot . . .

He rose and said he must go—it was later than he had thought—but when he was half-way to the door he turned and came back.

"I suppose Helen *did* ask you to stay at the flat?" he asked, looking at me searchingly.

"Oh yes," I said.

"But not very—enthusiastically, perhaps?"

I laughed and said, "Don't worry, Ronnie. I'm quite comfortable here and I don't like being a bother. Helen and I are going to meet on Friday and have lunch together."

"So you won't be coming to the flat at all?"

I did not answer.

"Oh well, it can't be helped," said Ronnie with a sigh. "And anyhow I'll see you at Ryddelton. We must all go to Ryddelton for a few days before we go to Kenya, to say good-bye to Ken and Jean and the children. I'll see you then, and you'll see Val. Ken will be pleased when he hears I'm going to do some bacteriological research. 'Bye Jane, I must fly . . ."

As I watched him cross the room on his way to the door I decided that it would be better if I did not see Ronnie again; better for me. When he and Helen came to Ryddelton I could go to Edinburgh . . . or somewhere.

4

Helen was late for our lunch appointment, but I had managed to reserve a table in the crowded restaurant and I was sitting waiting for her when she came in. She was as beautiful as ever, and her clothes were perfection, and as she made her way towards me between the tables a great many people turned their heads and gazed at her. She did not notice the stares for she was used to admiration; probably she would have noticed if people had not stared.

"Hallo, Jane!" she said, smiling in a friendly manner. "It's nice to see you—and you're looking very well. You'll never be pretty but you've got quite an air."

"Thank you for those kind words," I said, laughing.

Helen had set the note for our meeting and it continued in the same key. She told me about the move to Kenya and I did not say I had heard about it already. It was obvious that Ronnie had not mentioned his visit to me at the hotel.

"Just think, Jane!" said Helen. "A lovely bungalow and a garden and lots of servants! It will be delightful . . . and I believe Adruna is quite a fair-sized place so there will be plenty to do. I mean you can have a very good time in a place like that. Vera went out to Kenya last winter to stay with her sister and she says there were parties and picnics and amateur theatricals and all sorts of gaieties. Of course I must get a nurse for Val, but there will be no difficulty about that." She went on talking about it, and I listened. It was not until we had finished and I had paid the bill that she asked if I had seen Rosalie.

"That *was* a funny marriage!" said Helen, laughing. "I wonder how long it will last."

"For ever, I hope," I replied seriously. "They have taken each other for better for worse—and they're blissfully happy."

"Oh Jane, you are a queer old stick!" declared Helen. "Where are my gloves? I always lose my gloves."

The waiter handed them to her and was rewarded with a radiant smile.

"Well, good-bye, Jane," said Helen. "I'll write to you from Adruna and tell you all about it."

"Are you coming up to Ryddelton before you go?" I asked.

"Goodness, no! Why should we? There won't be time. I must get clothes, and things—" said Helen. She kissed me and added, "Thank you for the nice lunch."

The last I saw of her was her graceful figure threading its way to the door ... and the heads turning, and the eyes staring at her as she went.

5

Naturally I had been keeping an eye on publishers' lists for *The Biography of Lady Esmeralda Pie* but something must have delayed its publication, for Margaret and I had been home nearly a year when the advance notices appeared. Almost immediately afterwards I received a copy of the book, from the author, inscribed "J.H. from A.M." There was no letter and no address. Of course I could have written to Mrs. Millard care of her publishers but I decided not to, for if she had wanted a 'thank-you-letter' she would have enclosed her address.

I had known the book was good but I had been too near it to see it in proper perspective. I saw now that it was far better than I remembered. The background was colourful and bore the stamp of authenticity. Esmeralda herself was a four dimensional figure, human and somehow lovable despite her many sins. The style was pungent, witty and polished and ran so smoothly that one could not lay the book down; I was not surprised when it was received by the critics with a chorus of praise. The book was too expensive to be a popular success but it certainly was a *succès d'estime*.

Several reporters from daily newspapers found their way to Timble Cottage and endeavoured to pump me about the book and its author:

"We understand you were Mrs. Millard's secretary? It must have been a very interesting post."

"Our readers would like to know something about Mrs. Millard."

"Was she pleasant to work with?"

"Are the letters absolutely authentic?"

"Did Mrs. Millard do a great deal of research?"

"Where is Mrs. Millard now?"

"Is she writing another book?"

There was no end to the questions—some of them I could have answered and others I could not—but I refused to answer any of them.

It was quite by chance that I saw Mrs. Millard again. Margaret and I had gone to Venice for a holiday and were in the Piazza of St Mark watching some children feeding the pigeons. Suddenly I saw her ... and after a moment's hesitation I went over and spoke to her. She was just the same—she did not look a day older—and obviously she was pleased to see me. We chatted for a few minutes and I told her how much I had enjoyed her book.

"Esmeralda was fun, wasn't she?" said Mrs. Millard. "I'm doing another biography now: a Venetian lady who was as naughty as Esmeralda, but in a somewhat different way."

"You're staying in Venice?" I asked.

She nodded. "Yes, I've taken a flat in an old palace. I shall be here for six months, until I have polished off my Venetian harpy, and then I shall move on somewhere else."

"And Solda? Is she here?"

"Oh yes, Solda and I have taken each other for better for worse," replied Mrs. Millard, laughing.

She asked after *The Mulberry Coach* and I told her about it. I told her also that I was writing another story of the same *genre*.

"I'm a little worried about it," I said. "I haven't got you to vet it for me."

She looked at me piercingly and I thought she was going to offer—I think the idea crossed her mind but if so she rejected it—"Caroline Smith would do it," she said. "If you like I can give you her address. She's a funny little dried-up stick but she lives and moves and has her being in the seventeenth century."

I took down the address in my notebook.

"What's the new book called?" asked Mrs. Millard.

"*Highwayman's Halt*," I told her.

"I shall have to buy it, I suppose," complained Mrs. Millard. "I bought *The Mulberry Coach*. Really, Jane, the amount of time and money I've wasted on your book is phenomenal!"

"I should like to send you the new one," I said meekly.

"That will be delightful and it will save me twelve and six—or is it fifteen shillings? I shall expect it to be suitably inscribed: *To Augusta Millard without whose help and encouragement this book would not have been written*," suggested Mrs. Millard with her wicked smile.

"I can say that—and more," I replied seriously.

"Let us avoid redundancy," said Mrs. Millard.

She did not ask me to visit her flat, and when I asked if she would come and have lunch at our hotel she refused the invitation promptly. Perhaps she saw I was disappointed, for she added quite kindly, "You should know me better, child. I hate going out to lunch and meeting strangers—and your cousin would dislike me intensely. I've enjoyed seeing you, but I don't want to see you again."

Coming from any other person this would have sounded rude, but I understood Mrs. Millard and was not offended.

We shook hands—for the first and last time—and said goodbye, and I went back to Margaret who had been waiting for me.

"That was Mrs. Millard," I told her.

"Mrs. Millard! How extraordinary!" exclaimed Margaret.

It was only afterwards that I remembered I had not said a word about the pearls; of course she must have seen them round my neck but it was like her not to have mentioned them.

Later, when I sent her my new novel I inscribed it 'A.M. from J.H.' for she had said, 'Let us avoid redundancy' and she liked to be obeyed.

Chapter Twenty

1

The next few years were uneventful; the diary (which I still kept, more from habit than for any other reason) is concerned with matters which were of interest to ourselves but to nobody else. Some of the entries read:

> We went to Edinburgh and had lunch with Mother and Andrew.
> Mistral had a litter of six. The puppies are adorable and Margaret is delighted with them. She has promised one to the Gows.
> *Highwayman's Halt* published to-day. Sent off a copy to Mrs. Millard—through her publishers.
> Walked over to Mount Charles and saw the new baby. She is a dear little doll. No doubt she will be thoroughly spoilt by her half-brothers and sister and the adoration of her fond Papa.
> Mrs. Gow returned from her holiday—at Dunoon. What a joy to have her back! The first thing she did was to scrub the kitchen floor. It needed scrubbing!

During these years I continued to write regularly and published three novels all in the same period as *The Mulberry Coach* and written in much the same manner. The stories gave me a great deal of pleasure and a great many people seemed to enjoy reading them. My books did not have quite the rampaging success that Mrs. Millard had predicted, but they produced an amazing amount of money. I was able to have Timble Cottage done up and painted; I bought a car and built a garage, and every Spring Margaret and I took a holiday and spent it in France or Italy or Spain. In addition I was able to send an occasional cheque to Helen, for although Ronnie was making quite a good income Helen was often in difficulties over money. Adruna seemed to be more expensive than they had expected.

These years were extraordinarily peaceful. Our families were comfortably settled; we were comfortably settled ourselves and we looked forward to a comfortably settled future . . . and then quite suddenly everything was changed and our peace was shattered.

2

It was Margaret's birthday. She was fifty-nine, but she certainly did not look it as she sat at the breakfast-table opening presents and birthday cards, and exclaiming in rapturous surprise at the kindness of her friends. The postman had brought an enormous budget of mail to Timble Cottage and it was all for Margaret which did not surprise me at all.

"Oh, look Jane!" exclaimed Margaret. "Here's a letter for you. It had slipped inside one of my cards. It's from Kenya."

The letter was from Ronnie and as I took it and held it in my hand I had a horrible feeling of foreboding; something had happened; some terrible disaster. The feeling was so real and strong that my hand was shaking as I opened the airmail envelope.

Adruna
Kenya

Dear Jane,

Helen has left me. I don't know whether you will be surprised or not. Things have been very difficult lately. Perhaps she told you when she wrote to you that she had begun to hate this place. I have been very busy helping Dr. Orton with an experiment in the laboratory so I could not be with Helen as much as I should have liked. Of course I knew she was friendly with Dick Lancaster—he came over from Nairobi quite often—but I never realised how far things had gone. I am explaining this very badly but I feel a bit shattered as you can imagine. Val is here with me of course but I cannot keep him here. I am out all day and sometimes I have to go over to the hospital at night and it is impossible to leave him here alone with the servants. Dr. and Mrs. Orton are very kind and I can leave Val with Mrs. Orton, but that is only a temporary arrangement. It would not be fair to Mrs. Orton to expect her to go on with it for long. I shall have to find some way of sending Val home. He is seven now so he would have had to go home to school soon even if this had not happened. Perhaps you would tell your mother about it. I simply cannot write to her. It is too dreadful. When I found they had gone I went after them to Nairobi but they had only stayed one night and flown on to Rome so I was too late. I don't know what to do, Jane. I will write again when I have thought it all out properly but I felt I must write to you at once. I really don't know what to do. Perhaps in a day or two I shall be able to sort things out and find some way. I don't seem to be able to think things out. I shall have to send Val home. He cannot be left in the bungalow alone with the servants when I am over at the hospital. I seem to be writing the same thing over and over again so I had better stop.

Yours affectionately,
RONNIE

"Jane, what's the matter! You look like a ghost!" cried Margaret.

I felt like a ghost. I handed her the letter without speaking and went out into the garden and through the gate on to the hill. I went up the path to the little spring which bubbled out of the ground between two large boulders. I did not know why I had come there. I scarcely knew where I was. Coming up to this place was instinctive. My legs had brought me here and now my legs could take me no farther, so I sat down.

It was a damp misty morning; there were no definite clouds; the skies were grey all over. Which ever way I looked the skies were grey.

I had to think what to do to help Ronnie, but I could not think at all. My mind refused to think. All sorts of things strayed through my mind—things that had been forgotten for years. I remembered Rosalie saying, 'She'll take him—and break his heart—and throw him away'. The words went over and over in my head, 'She'll take him—and break his heart—and throw him away'.

Rosalie had found solace for her misery, but I could find none for mine.

I have no idea how long I sat there, it may have been a few minutes or it may have been an hour, but presently I saw Margaret coming up the hill towards me.

"I thought you'd be here," she said. "If you don't want me just say so and I'll go away. I could start your packing; that would save time, wouldn't it?"

"Yes," I said. "That would—save time."

"Which suitcase will you take? Would you like my grey one? It's nice and light for travelling by air."

"Yes, your grey one will be splendid."

"I think you'd better come," she said, looking at me doubt-fully. "You can put out what you want to take and I'll pack it for you."

"Yes, I'd better come," I said.

As we went down the hill together I saw that the mist was thinning and there was a faint glimmer in the air which had been dead and grey.

3

Now that I saw what to do (and of course it was the obvious thing) I was impatient of delay, but however urgent one's business it is impossible to step into the first plane and fly to one's objective. I was obliged to spend two days in Edinburgh while Andrew fixed things up—and it was only because Andrew was particularly good at fixing things up that it did not take longer.

Mother and Andrew were not as surprised as I had expected; they had received a letter from Helen quite recently ("An odd sort of letter," said Mother. "Nothing definite but just—odd"). They agreed that someone must fly to Adruna, and that I was the best person to go.

"You can bring the child home," said Andrew. "We can have him here and he can go to school. That will be the best plan."

Margaret and I had thought of having Val at Timble Cottage, but I let it pass. None of us had any idea what Val was like. None of us had seen him since he was an infant. There would be time enough when we saw him to decide what was best.

When all had been arranged Mother and Andrew drove me over to Turnhouse to see me into the London plane, and it was only then that Mother began to fuss.

"Such a long way to go alone!" said Mother anxiously. "You'll take care of yourself, won't you? You must cable when you arrive."

"It will all be quite easy," said Andrew soothingly. "She's got her passport and her travellers' cheques and her tickets and her seat reserved on the plane. She has to change planes at London Airport, that's all—and Ronnie will meet her at Nairobi. She can't go wrong."

Put like that it sounded foolproof and even Mother was pacified.

"I know," said Mother. "And of course Ronnie will be delighted to see her." She hesitated and then added, "But you won't stay with Ronnie, will you Jane? I mean there will be a hotel or something. You won't stay at the bungalow."

"I'll see when I get there," I said. "It all depends whether—"

"I wouldn't stay with Ronnie if I were you," said Mother with a worried frown. "I mean—it would be better not to."

I could not help smiling. Here we were in the middle of this horrible mess and Mother was worrying about 'the conventions'.

"Your Mother is right," declared Andrew. "It would be most unwise for you to stay at Ronnie's bungalow in case of future complications."

He pursed up his mouth when he had spoken, pursed it into a thin line as he always did when he was giving 'lawyers' advice'. I had never thought of 'future complications' and I did not know what on earth he meant.

I might have asked him, and got the matter clarified, but the plane was ready to start. There was just time to say good-bye and get in.

4

Andrew had cabled to Ronnie that I was on my way, so he was there to meet me at the airport. He was standing amongst a little crowd of people but he was so tall that I saw him at once as the plane taxied in. He looked tired and haggard and a little untidy—as if he had not bothered about his appearance for days—but when he saw me his expression brightened and he came towards me with outstretched hands.

"Oh Jane, how good of you! When I heard you were coming it seemed too good to be true!" For a moment he clung to my hands like a drowning man, and then he turned away.

If it had been a different kind of arrival I would have been interested in the strange medley of people, white and black and brown, who were meeting and greeting each other all round us, but I was too anxious about Ronnie to be interested in anyone else. He looked distraught. His eyes were sunk in his head and glittered as if he had fever. He scarcely seemed to know what he was doing and I had to ask him twice to carry my suitcase before he understood what I meant.

"I'm sorry," he said. "I'm a bit—stupid, as if I had been knocked on the head. I haven't been sleeping—very much lately. It's awful, isn't it?" he added. "Is your mother very angry with me, Jane?"

"Angry with you? No, of course not."

"It's my fault. Helen was bored, you see. If she hadn't been bored she wouldn't have—gone."

We were sitting in the car by this time. He turned to me and asked, "Are you tired, Jane? Would you like to spend the night at the hotel? It's two hours' drive to Adruna—so if you're tired—but I must go back. I must go straight back *now* because of Val. Mrs. Orton is sitting with him, but he won't go to sleep unless I'm there. He's afraid that I'll go away and leave him, that's why. I've tried to explain, but he's only seven so he doesn't—quite—understand. If you're tired—and of course you must be tired—"

"Ronnie, don't worry; I'm not a bit tired. We'll go straight back to Val."

"But you'd like some dinner, wouldn't you? It's nearly eight now, so we wouldn't be back at Adruna till ten." He looked at me anxiously.

"We'll go straight back to Val," I repeated.

"You're sure you don't mind?"

"I'd much rather go back."

"You ought to have a meal—"

"I had a meal on the plane," I said firmly.

"Oh, well then . . ." said Ronnie with a sigh of relief. Perhaps if I had known what was in store I would not have been quite so anxious to embark upon the drive to Adruna. It was a nightmare drive. The sky was dark, there was no moon, and the road was hilly and winding. I had the uncomfortable feeling that Ronnie was in no fit condition to drive a car; he had said himself that he felt as if something had hit him on the head. Sometimes he put on speed and drove like a madman . . . and then he would remember his passenger and slow down. We rushed up hill and down with the headlights piercing the darkness. I kept on reminding myself that he knew the road. But knowing the road would not help if we met an animal, and we met several animals; one of them looked like a sheep and Ronnie avoided it only by a hairsbreadth.

"I'm sorry, Jane," he said, slowing down a little. "It's just thinking about Val. Mrs. Orton is sitting with him but he won't go to sleep until I come. The Ortons have been terribly kind, but I can't go on taking advantage of their kindness. It will be all right now that you're here."

"I can't stay long, Ronnie."

"No, but you can stay for a bit, can't you? Then we'll see. It's quite a nice bungalow. Helen liked it at first until she got bored. You see the work we're doing now—Orton and I—means that you've got to stick into it pretty closely. You can't keep regular hours at all. Sometimes Orton and I work most of the night, and there's the hospital work in addition. That was why Helen got bored. Helen had no use for any of the other women at Adruna—she couldn't stand Mrs. Orton—and she kept on complaining it was dull. She went and stayed at Nairobi now and then; she stayed with friends and had a gay time . . . and bought clothes. I don't know where she got the money but she seemed to manage."

I knew where she had got the money.

"Then she met Lancaster," said Ronnie. "She met him at Nairobi and asked him to come over and spend the day. He came several times after that. He had hired a Bentley—a beautiful car—and sometimes he took her for a spin. Helen likes cars and knows a good deal about them, so she liked the Bentley." He sighed and added, "I was a perfect fool."

It was difficult to know what to say.

"I was a perfect fool," repeated Ronnie. "Of course I saw that he amused her but I was so busy, so wrapped up in the work, that I was quite glad she had somebody amusing to take her out occasionally. I had no idea he came so often—it was not until afterwards that I discovered how often he came—and I had no idea there was anything wrong. That's why I said it was my fault. I ought to have known. I ought to have done something about it instead of sitting back and being pleased because Helen seemed more cheerful."

Chapter Twenty-One

1

The drive was very long, it seemed to go on for ever, but at last we arrived at the bungalow—a long low building with a wide veranda. There were lights in some of the windows and, as we drove up, the door opened and Mrs. Orton came out. She was older than I had expected, short and stout with smooth grey hair.

"He isn't asleep," she said with a worried frown. "I've been reading to him, but he heard the car."

Ronnie ran up the steps and disappeared.

"I'm glad you've come," said Mrs. Orton to me, and she added, "Just leave your suitcase, one of the boys will bring it in."

I followed Mrs. Orton into the drawing-room; it was a delightful room, large and airy with three big windows, and coloured rugs on the parquet floor. It was curious to see some of Helen's possessions here in these alien surroundings; the lovely old desk which Mother and I had given her as a wedding present (we had found it in an antique shop in Ryddelton and had had it cleaned and polished and done up). On the desk stood a little wooden dwarf which had been broken by me when I was dusting the sitting-room at Timble Cottage—I had knocked it off the chimney-piece. Helen had made a fuss and said it was her mascot, and old Tom Gow had taken it home and mended it so skilfully that you could hardly see the join.

It was a long way from Timble Cottage to Adruna and suddenly I felt most horribly homesick.

"I'm glad you've come," repeated Mrs. Orton. "We've done what we could of course, but it isn't much. Val is the problem. I don't mind having him in the daytime, he's no trouble at all, but it's difficult at night. He won't go to sleep unless his father is here. I don't know much about children, we never had any of our own. I've done my best to get him to go to sleep but it's no use. He lies and stares—it frightens me—so now I just sit and read to him until his father comes. He'll go to sleep now," she added with a sigh.

"Ronnie told me how kind you have been."

"We've done what we could," repeated Mrs. Orton. "Of course it has been a frightful shock to us all. Ronnie looks ill, doesn't he?"

"Desperately ill."

"I could kill that girl," declared Mrs. Orton. "Oh of course I shouldn't say it to you—you're her sister—but I feel very strongly about it. All this business has interrupted the work. Helen never considered the work—never. She was no help at all."

"Could she have helped?" I asked.

"Yes, of course. She could have helped by making him comfortable at home. The work they're doing is tremendously important. It's a privilege to serve people who are doing work like that; just to be there when you're wanted; to have a meal ready; to see that things run smoothly and they aren't worried by petty details that don't matter at all. Sometimes it isn't easy," admitted Mrs. Orton. "If you expect your husband to dinner and he doesn't come back until midnight—or after—it's apt to be a little annoying, but that can't be avoided because it's impossible to leave an experiment in the middle and go home to dinner. If you marry a man you've got to take that in your stride. You've got to stand by and help him all you can. It's no use whining."

"Yes," I said. Obviously Mrs. Orton did not whine. I admired her for it but I could see Helen might have found it difficult to live up to her standard.

"Of course he'll have to divorce her," continued Mrs. Orton. "Tom says there's nothing else to do . . . but Ronnie will be telling you all about it."

"Yes, I expect so," I said. Somehow I had never thought of that.

"You must be tired after your long journey," said Mrs. Orton briskly. "You'd probably like to have a bath and go straight to bed. Your supper will be ready in about twenty minutes, so you had better have it in bed."

"That sounds heavenly," I said, and I meant it, for I was absolutely exhausted.

Mrs. Orton looked at me searchingly. "You aren't a bit like your sister," she declared.

These words had been said to me before, quite often, but always in pitying tones. Mrs. Orton said them differently and she added, "Tom and I never liked Helen from the very beginning. She was very pretty, but good looks aren't everything."

I noticed that Mrs. Orton was speaking of Helen in the past tense—as if she were dead.

2

My room was bare but comfortable and the bed was very comfortable indeed. It was delightful to stretch out my legs and relax . . . and then, quite suddenly, I remembered what Mother had said, and I remembered Andrew's cryptic statement that it would be unwise to stay in Ronnie's bungalow 'in case of future complications', and I realised what Andrew had meant. Andrew had been thinking of divorce proceedings when he had spoken in his legal manner of 'future complications'.

I sat up and wondered what to do. Here I was, snugly in bed in Ronnie's bungalow, and Mrs. Orton had gone home. Well, what *could* I do? Should I get up instantly and make a fuss? Should I explain to Ronnie and ask for a bed at the Ortons' or demand that Mrs. Orton should come back? It was impossible (or at least it was impossible to me) I simply could not do it . . . and, anyhow, who was to know? Adruna was a long way from civilisation. Who was to know I was here? And Ronnie had so many troubles already that I was loth to add even a little trouble to the pile.

I had just made up my mind to say nothing whatever about it when the door opened and Ronnie came in followed by a large black man with a tray.

"Here's your supper, Jane," said Ronnie. He said it cheerfully, more in his usual manner, and busied himself with arrangements for my comfort. Two pillows were piled behind my back and a bed-table was fixed across my knees in the correct position. When all was in order the black servant went away and Ronnie sat down on the end of my bed.

It seemed a little strange to have Ronnie sitting on my bed, but I reflected that he was a doctor and therefore quite used to seeing people in bed—and, whatever I might feel, he obviously saw nothing strange in it.

"I can't believe it," declared Ronnie with a fleeting smile. "I can't believe you're really here. You've no idea what I've been through—wondering what to do and trying to find some way out of the tangle. Just having you here to talk to has made me feel more human. I couldn't talk to anybody else, you see. The Ortons are infinitely kind, but I couldn't *talk* to them—so it has all been bottled up inside me for days and days. I hope I'm not wearing you out; I've done nothing but talk since you arrived."

"I want to hear all about it, Ronnie."

"Well, eat your supper before it gets cold, and I'll tell you . . ."

He went on talking, first about Helen and then about Val (who had gone to sleep quite peacefully).

"Val isn't like her," said Ronnie. "He's thin and pale and his hair is—sort of mousy. He's—rather an ugly little boy. You'll see him to-morrow but I'm just warning you in case you're disappointed. Of course I think he's grand," said Val's father apologetically. "But even I can see he isn't—good-looking. Helen always says . . ." he paused and amended. "Helen used to say she couldn't understand how she could have such an ugly child."

Helen *would* say that! I thought. Aloud I said, "I'm sure I shall love Val."

"I hope Val will love you," said Ronnie seriously. "We'd better not tell him that you're going to take him home—at least not at first—not until he gets used to you."

"Don't worry, Ronnie," I said. All the same I was worried about it myself. It had been so easy to say I would fly out to Adruna and bring Val home, but Val was not a parcel. From what I had heard he was a sensitive human being and could not—or would not—go to sleep unless his father was there.

"It's not knowing what to do," declared Ronnie, rising and beginning to pace up and down the room. "That's what worries me. You can't tell me what to do—I've got to decide for myself—but just letting me tell you about it helps. I've thought and thought until my head goes round and round, but I can't make up my mind what's right. There are three things, you see. There's the work here: we're on the track of a virus which causes a great deal of trouble amongst the natives. It's no good bothering you with technicalities but now, at last, after prolonged research and experiments—and several failures—we seem to be making progress."

"It's important?" I asked.

He nodded gravely. "Yes, it's important. If Orton's idea is right, and we succeed, it will save a lot of suffering. That's the fact in plain language. There's still a good deal to do before we can be sure, but in another three or four months we'll know definitely whether or not we're on the right track."

Ronnie paused and looked at me and I nodded to show that I understood.

"Should I throw it all up?" said Ronnie. "If I throw it all up and take Val home it will hinder Orton a good deal. We've worked together and I know his ways. If I leave Adruna he will have to get somebody else, somebody who hasn't any idea what we're doing. It wouldn't stop him—nothing will stop Orton—but it would put him back several months.

"Then there's Helen. Should I throw it all up and go after Helen? I might be able to get her to come back. You see, Jane, I promised to take her for better for worse . . . 'to have and to hold till death us do part'."

"To have and to hold," he repeated. "I promised that—and I haven't done it. I've let her slip out of my grasp. Perhaps you think it's silly and old-fashioned to worry about that?"

"I'm old-fashioned, too. I think one should keep one's promises."

"Yes, I know you do. That very first day when we met at Aunt Edith's club you said 'Promises are important'."

"Fancy your remembering!"

"I remember all about that day. I tried to talk to you, but you weren't having any nonsense—"

"Oh Ronnie, it wasn't that! I wanted to be friendly but I was too shy. I was an absolute idiot!"

"I thought you disliked me," said Ronnie.

He thought I disliked him!

There was a little silence and then Ronnie said, "Oh well, it's a long time ago. Things that are past are past and it's no good thinking about them. We've got to think about the future. I've got to make up my mind what to do."

"What is he like?" I asked.

"You mean Dick Lancaster?"

"Yes, who is he? Has he got money?"

"Money?" said Ronnie vaguely. "Yes, he must be pretty well off. He was here with a party. It was one of those luxury tours—camping and shooting—you can't do that for nothing. He's about forty, or perhaps a little older. He's travelled a lot and talks well—drinks a bit too much. I told you I didn't like him—neither I do—but you can't help being interested and amused in his conversation."

"He sounds horrible!"

"No, he's not horrible. If I've made him sound horrible I've given you a wrong impression. He's rather attractive in his own way—but he's an egotist. Quite honestly I don't believe he ever thinks of anybody but himself."

"Helen won't be happy with a man like that."

"No, I don't think she will be happy. At least I think she may be happy for a few months—and then miserable. What will happen then?"

"Is that your responsibility—" I began.

"Yes," said Ronnie firmly. Obviously he had no doubts about that. "Yes, it's my responsibility—because I promised. If she's miserable—or if he takes a fancy to someone else—"

"Oh Ronnie!"

"He might," declared Ronnie. "He's that sort of chap."

I thought it over for a minute and then I said, "What does Helen want?"

Ronnie took a crumpled piece of paper from his pocket. "This is her letter," he said. "Parts of it are rather—odd. I'll just read you this bit: 'I can't stand it any longer. I am going away with Dick. We will stay at the usual hotel in Nairobi and you can get the evidence there. I want you to divorce me so that Dick and I can be married. You must divorce me—please Ronnie—Dick and I love each other. It's real this time—"

"This time!" I echoed.

"Yes—well—it *did* happen before—in London," said Ronnie miserably. "I got her to come back," he added.

"Oh, Ronnie!"

"Honestly, Jane, I feel like putting a bullet through my head. That would solve everything."

"Nonsense!" I exclaimed, trying to smile and speak lightly. "What about Dr. Orton? What about Val?"

He smiled back wanly and replied, "Yes, a bullet would only solve one of my difficulties."

We talked for a little while longer and I asked if Dr. Orton had given him any advice.

"Yes," said Ronnie. "Orton's advice is: do one thing or the other. Go after her and get her back or else start proceedings at once. But that's what he's like, you see. He's one of the Do Something Brigade."

"What do you mean?"

"The opposite of the Wait and See Brigade. He's like that in everything. He's like that at the hospital. It's his nature. I admire him tremendously but—but sometimes he's wrong. Sometimes it's quite a good plan to wait and see.

"You'll like him, Jane," continued Ronnie. "He's got a sense of humour, and a brilliant brain. It's a pleasure to work with him and he's taught me a great deal. That's why I should hate to let him down."

"You mustn't let him down," I said impulsively.

"You really think I should stick on here?"

Ronnie had said he must decide for himself, and this was true, but it could do no harm to offer him my advice.

"I think you should," I said. "That's my opinion for what it's worth."

"But I want to," said Ronnie doubtfully. "I want to stay on and see the thing through. I want it so much that I feel it must be wrong. Does that sound crazy?"

It did not sound crazy to me for I suffered from the same complex: if two courses were open to me and I particularly wanted to take one of them the other must be right. I explained this to Ronnie and added that it was illogical. It was allowing one's feelings to cloud one's judgment.

"Yes," agreed Ronnie. "Yes, I see that. To make a right decision one should have no feelings at all . . . but how can any human being do that?"

"No human being can," I replied, smiling at him. "And anyhow it's far too late at night to start discussing psychology. You had better go to bed, Ronnie. Go to bed—and go to sleep. Can't you take a pill or something?"

"I believe I shall sleep to-night," he said, stretching his arms and yawning. "I feel—more peaceful. It's having you here, Jane."

When Ronnie had gone I decided to lie and think about things for a few minutes and then get up and wash my teeth . . . but the next thing I knew was the sun shining into my room through the open window.

It was morning—and the enormous black man whom I had seen last night was standing beside my bed with a tray in his hands.

Chapter Twenty-Two

1

I HAD nearly finished my breakfast when Val came in. He stood at the door and looked at me without speaking.

Val was not in the least like Helen, nor was he like Ronnie. He was not good-looking—except for his eyes. His eyes were beautiful, large and clear and hazel, they seemed ridiculously large for his small thin face.

It was important to make the 'right approach' to Val and I had thought about it a great deal. I knew very little about children (as a matter of fact I had never taken much interest in them). What was the mental age of a child of seven? I had tried to think of myself as a child, and I remembered how much I disliked being patronised and 'talked down to'. I preferred people who spoke to me as an equal, even if I could not always understand what they meant. When I saw Val standing there gazing at me with his huge eyes I realised that it was going to be difficult to treat him as if he were grown-up. He looked so very young and defenceless.

"Hallo, Val!" I said cheerfully. "I suppose you've had your breakfast."

"I have it with Daddy at half-past seven," he replied.

I had smiled at him but there was no answering smile—just that unblinking and somewhat embarrassing stare. I had made up my mind not to rush him, and not to ask questions (questions and answers are not conversation) so I said no more but went on eating toast and marmalade.

Presently Val said, "You aren't like—like what I expected."

"People often say that," I told him. I saw him considering the matter so I added, "They usually say it in a disappointed sort of way."

"They do that to me, too," said Val. He removed his gaze from me and stared out of the window. "I don't care what I look like," he added with a defiant air.

"I would rather look like myself," I said. This was perfectly true. At one time I would have given a lot to have golden hair and a skin of milk and roses, but I had got over that long ago.

Val was silent for a few moments and I thought he had not understood, but at last he said, "You mean you would rather not be like—someone else—even if they were very pretty?"

"Yes, that's what I meant."

He turned and went away without another word.

It had been a very odd conversation. I wondered if I had said the right thing or not.

I had got up and dressed and was brushing my hair when Val came back. He said, "Daddy told me to ask you if you wanted anything, and I forgot. Do you want anything?"

"I don't think so."

"You had better tell me," said Val. "Daddy has gone to the hospital and the boys don't understand English—at least they pretend they don't."

"They pretend they don't!" I echoed in surprise.

"Do you want anything?"

"Well, perhaps I had better write a letter."

"There's writing-paper in the desk in the drawing-room. Ebra will bring you coffee at eleven—or would you rather have tea? Daddy said to ask you."

"Coffee, please," I said meekly.

"Well, if you don't want anything else I'll go out," said Val, and vanished forthwith.

2

When Val had gone I went into the drawing-room and began a letter to Mother but I did not get on very fast. It was an odd feeling to be alone in the bungalow with an unknown number of large black servants whose language I could not speak . . . and not at all reassuring to know that if I spoke to them in English they would pretend not to understand. Why would they pretend not to understand? There was something a little sinister about it—or so it seemed to me.

I told myself that I was a perfect fool to be nervous for I had travelled in many strange countries . . . but of course I had never been alone in a quiet bungalow in the wilds of Africa. It was very quiet indeed. Not a sound broke the stillness. I found myself glancing over my shoulder at the door . . . for although it was quiet it was not peaceful and I knew there were people about, moving stealthily. If something happened I should be helpless. Ronnie was at the hospital; he was probably quite near, but I did not know where.

Somehow I could not concentrate on the letter, and it required a good deal of concentration for Mother would want to know all I could tell her—and I must give her the impression that Mrs. Orton was staying here in the bungalow without actually telling a lie. I would tell her everything when I got home—and she would understand—but meantime it was no use worrying her.

Suddenly a tray was placed upon the desk beside me by a pair of large black hands. It was Ebra, of course, and he was bringing me my coffee, but he had moved so quietly that I had not heard a sound. I managed to murmur *thank you* and he moved away as noiselessly as he had come.

There were two cups on the tray and I was just wondering whom I might expect when Ronnie's face appeared at the window.

"Ah, coffee!" he exclaimed. "That's good. I just came back to see how you were getting on."

"All right. Only it is a little—queer."

"Africa is a queer place; you can imagine all sorts of queer things in Africa—if you're an imaginative person."

Ronnie came in and sat down and poured out the coffee. "Jane," he said. "I've something to tell you. It's something rather stupid. Orton says you shouldn't be here—at the bungalow."

"In case of future complications," I suggested.

"Oh, you know about it," said Ronnie with a sigh of relief. "Well, there it is. It's the silliest thing I ever heard of, but Orton says it's the sort of thing that might complicate divorce proceedings—if I'm going to take divorce proceedings."

"Are you going to, Ronnie?"

"I might have to," said Ronnie. "If they really want to be married it's the only thing to do . . . but I'm not going to do it straight off; I'm going to wait and see." He stirred his cup and added, "I suppose you had better go and stay with the Ortons."

"But I'm no good to you if I stay with the Ortons. Unless I'm here at night with Val I'm no good at all. I've been here one night so it won't make any difference if I stay a little longer—if I stay till Monday and then fly home and take Val."

"He wouldn't go with you!"

"He'll have to. There's no other way."

"I don't know what would happen," said Ronnie uneasily. "Val clings to me. He might be ill if I sent him away. If he knew you well it would be different, but you're a stranger to him."

"There's no other way," I repeated. I had thought about it myself but I could see no other way, for if Ronnie happened to be working at night or was called out at night to an urgent case at the hospital, Val could not be left alone in the bungalow. (I saw this even more clearly now that I had been frightened myself.) For the last week Dr. Orton had been doing all the night-work but obviously that could not go on.

While we were discussing the matter Ebra came in and removed the tray, but Ronnie went on talking. Probably Ronnie was so used to large black shadows that he did not notice Ebra was there.

"He understands English," I said, when Ebra had gone.

"Not a word," declared Ronnie. "None of them do. I wouldn't keep a boy that understood English. Listen, Jane, my plan was for you to stay here several weeks and make friends with Val, then he would have gone with you quite happily . . . but if you've got to go on Monday there isn't much time." He sighed and added, "We had better wait till Sunday night before telling Val."

"But you've made up your mind he is to come?"

"I suppose so," said Ronnie miserably.

3

That was Friday, so I had two days to 'make friends with Val' and I felt pretty hopeless. If Rosalie had been in my place she could have done it; she was used to children and 'had a way with them', but I did not know how to begin. I was just as miserable as Ronnie and was sitting in the drawing-room brooding about it, with my half-written letter in front of me, when the door opened and Val burst in like a whirlwind.

His face was red and his breath was coming in gasps. "Do you tell lies?" he demanded.

"Tell lies!" I echoed indignantly. "No, of course not!" . . . and then I hesitated, for of course it was not true. "Listen, Val," I said.

"Sometimes people have to—sometimes it's absolutely necessary—but I don't like telling lies and I don't do it often."

"Mrs. Orton tells lies—often!"

It seemed unlikely.

"Oh yes, she does!" cried Val. "Ebra tells lies too of course, but that's different. I mean you can tell by his face—and if you keep on trying you can make him tell you the truth—but you can't tell by Mrs. Orton's face whether she's telling lies or not. For instance last night Mrs. Orton said Daddy was over at the hospital. 'Detained at the hospital'—that was what she said. And of course it wasn't true. Daddy went to meet you at Nairobi."

He paused for breath and glared at me defiantly.

I wondered if I should try to explain why Mrs. Orton had thought the lie expedient, but it seemed too difficult. The woman had my sympathy but it was a silly lie.

"Val," I said solemnly. "I promise never to tell lies to you."

"Is it a real promise—cross your heart?"

"Yes, Val, cross my heart."

"Well then, have I got to go to England with you?"

"Yes," I said. "I'm afraid you'll have to."

His face had been red but now all the colour drained out of it and it was grey. "Without—Daddy?" he whispered.

"Yes. You know Daddy can't come. Listen, Val, you must be brave and sensible," I said desperately . . . and I explained the whole matter plainly, making sure that he understood. "You see, don't you?" I said. "Daddy doesn't want you to go, but there's no other way."

"I don't know how I'm going to bear it," said Val with quivering lips. "But I suppose I'll have to bear it—somehow. Anyhow I *know*. It's not *knowing* things. It's being treated like a baby that's so—sickening."

There was a pathetic dignity in Val's demeanour: it tore my heart. I tried to comfort him by saying that it would not be as bad as he thought; we would be friends and take care of each other till Daddy came.

"How long?" he asked.

"Four or five months—or perhaps six. He'll come as soon as he can."

"It's a long time," said Val. His tears were flowing now and he took a small grubby handkerchief out of his pocket to mop them up. "It's all right, I'm not crying," he declared. "At least I am, really, but I can't help it. Ebra told me I was going to England and I didn't know if it was true. That's all."

This was a strange way of beginning to make friends with Val but at least he trusted me, which was something.

When Ronnie returned from the hospital and heard my story he was first incredulous and then horrified.

"Get Ebra and ask him," I said. "Keep on asking until he tells you the truth. Val says that's the way to get to the bottom of Ebra—keep on asking."

"I'll get to the bottom of Ebra," declared Ronnie grimly. "If I had known he understood English I never would have taken him. Good lord, I wonder what else he heard—and retailed to Val!"

"You mean—about Helen?"

Ronnie nodded. "Yes, about Helen. Mrs. Orton told Val that she had gone to England for a holiday and would soon be back. As a matter of fact I thought at the time it was rather a thin sort of story (Val is no fool). But what could I do? How could I tell him the truth? If Ebra understands English—"

"He does," I said. "Go and ask him."

Ebra had told Val everything. Moving silently about the house and listening to the conversation he had heard the whole story and passed it on to Val. He was fond of Val in his own peculiar way—there was no malice in him, he was just an inveterate gossip—but clearly he was no fit companion for the child.

All this and other things showed quite clearly that Val must come home with me.

"Val has been here too long," said Ronnie miserably. "He has been neglected. Helen didn't bother about him; she left him to his own devices—and I was busy. It's my fault, of course. I ought to have sent Val home long ago. He must go with you whatever happens. He must go even if it makes him ill."

"Do you think it's likely to make him ill?" I asked anxiously.

"I don't know," replied Ronnie. "But there's no other way."

4

It was a dark cloudy night when we set out upon our journey. The plane taxied to the end of the airstrip and halted for a few minutes, testing its powerful engines; then suddenly it made up its mind that all was well—and we were off. To me this was always a terrifying experience (I never could really believe that the clumsy-looking contraption would leave the ground and soar like a bird) and to-night I was even more alarmed than usual for my nerves were all to pieces.

Val had been remarkably brave until we reached the airport and saw the plane . . . and then he had broken down completely and clung round Ronnie's neck. All persuasions had been useless, they had fallen upon deaf ears; he clung so tightly that he had to be removed by force. It had been a frightful scene.

I was very sorry for Val; I was even more sorry for Ronnie; now that I had time to think about it, I was most sorry of all for myself. What was I going to do with the limp bundle of misery sitting beside me and sobbing uncontrollably? I had tried to comfort him; I had tried to put my arm round him; I had tried to interest him in something else. He lay curled up in the seat and sobbed.

It was late by this time—long past Val's usual bedtime—and I wondered if he would sob himself to sleep. I wondered what the other passengers were thinking. They had seen Val torn from his father's arms and carried into the plane. I had been through a good many miseries and humiliations in my life but this was the worst.

For a long time I sat there, waiting for Val to recover, and at last the sobs grew less. Presently a hoarse voice said, "I suppose I've got to bear it. I mean you couldn't ask the man to go back?"

"I'm afraid I couldn't."

"I've got nobody now," said Val with another sob. "No Mummy and no Daddy."

"You've got Daddy," I told him. "Daddy loves you dearly. He'll come home as soon as ever he can . . . and you've got me. I'll tuck you up in the rug and you'll go off to sleep—"

"No thank you. I'm not a bit sleepy."

"Shall I tell you about Goldilocks and the Three Bears?"

"You can if you like," said Val hopelessly. "I don't think—I'll be awfully—interested—but you can tell me." We had Goldilocks and Red-Riding-Hood and several other nursery classics and although Val showed no signs of going to sleep he allowed me to put my arm round him.

"Shall we have Cinderella now?" I asked in desperation. "If you like," agreed Val.

"Would you rather have Jack the Giant-Killer?"

"I don't mind," he said. "They're nice stories but they aren't true, are they? I like true stories best. Daddy tells me true stories. The one I like best of all is about Jesus cooking the breakfast."

I was so startled that I was dumb.

"Don't you know it, Aunt Jane? They were out all night in the boat, trying to catch some fish, but they didn't catch any at all and they were awfully cold and wet and miserable. Then they saw Jesus on the shore. He had lighted a little fire and was cooking their breakfast."

I recognised it now. It was my favourite story, too, so it was easy to tell it to Val.

"Yes, that's right," he said. "That's just the way Daddy tells it. I'm awfully glad you know it, Aunt Jane." He sighed and added, "I think a breakfast picnic would be lovely. I've never been to a breakfast picnic."

Neither had I; but I promised him one when we got to Timble Cottage—a breakfast picnic on the moor beside a little burn. I would have promised him the moon if it would have done him any good or if it had been within my power to get it for him.

"Tell me the story again," said Val, snuggling closer and putting his head against my shoulder.

I told it again—and yet again. When I had told it four times he was fast asleep so I drew up the rug and tucked it round us both and we were very comfortable together.

Sitting there with Val's warm little body against my side and his silky-soft hair against my cheek I felt happy and peaceful. Before this I had loved Val because he was Ronnie's son, but now I loved him for himself... and I knew there would be no more trouble. He would feel miserable at times, that could not be helped, but he would let me comfort him. And I saw how foolish I had been to fuss and worry about 'the right approach' because of course 'the right approach' to all our fellow creatures is just to love them.

Chapter Twenty-Three

1

"This is a gorgeous place for the picnic," said Val. It was not yet half-past eight but the sun was shining brightly and already there was a pleasant warmth in the air.

The place I had chosen was a little strip of gravel beside a hill-burn which ran down into the Rydd Water. It was sheltered by a high bank and there was a fir-wood close by; one of those straggly woods which had been planted long ago as a wind-break to shelter a little croft. Val and I had left home early and had carried our heavy baskets up the hill, so by this time we were hungry and we wasted no time in setting about our preparations.

My intention had been to make sandwiches and bring a Thermos flask, but when I saw Val's face I knew I had blundered badly and I put them all away. Instead we had brought sausages and thick slices of buttered bread and a small black kettle and tea and milk and sugar and all the other accessories of a 'real proper picnic.' The only concession to modernity was a packet of fire-lighters—for I was not a Girl Guide.

Val took an empty basket and went off to the wood to gather sticks while I set about making a little fireplace. It was not long before we got the fire going and the kettle boiled in due course. In fact everything went according to plan except the cooking of the sausages.

The idea had been to impale the sausages upon sticks and roast them over the hot embers; but this method of cookery, though sound in theory, was found to be unsatisfactory in practice; the sausages were either half raw or charred and in either case unpalatable. Once or twice the flame from a dry piece of drift wood leapt up unexpectedly and burnt the stick and the sausage fell into the fire.

"We should have brought toasting-forks," I said.

Val looked dubious. Obviously he thought toasting-forks were out of place at a 'real proper picnic' but when the last sausage fell into the heart of the flames he changed his mind.

It had been a struggle to get up early but it was worth it, not only because Val was so happy but because it was delightful. The day was new and unspoilt; the sky was blue, the grass was green and a shy little breeze rustled over the moor. Even the burn seemed merrier than usual as it prattled over its bed of pebbles and flung itself into the Rydd Water.

"There's a bird!" exclaimed Val. "What a funny bird! It's got long legs, hasn't it?"

I looked where Val was pointing and saw a heron standing upon a stone at the edge of the burn. I wondered if it could be the same heron that Ronnie and Rosalie had seen . . . but of course it couldn't. It might be the grandson of that famous heron.

There were other birds on the moor and I found that Val was interested to hear about them. He was interested in everything he saw and now that we had got to know each other he was easy to talk to.

When we had finished breakfast Val took off his shoes and socks and splodged about in the burn—as every little boy has loved to do from time immemorial. He saw a tiny brown trout in a peaty pool and tried to catch it in his hand. He spent a long time pursuing the little creature but it eluded him easily. After that we built a dam with stones and turf and watched while the pool filled up with water.

Although Val was quite unlike his father in appearance he had some of Ronnie's mannerisms. He would turn his head quickly and smile . . . and just for a moment Ronnie was there, smiling at me. Sometimes he nodded his head slowly up and down in a thoughtful way . . . and again I saw Ronnie.

Val was so happy playing about in the burn that I was reluctant to drag him home, but by this time he was wet and I was afraid he would get a chill, for he was used to warmer climes than Ryddelton.

"We'll come again, won't we?" said Val as we went down the hill together. "We'll bring twice as many sausages and two toasting-forks and a little net to catch the fish."

2

In a week Val had settled down and become part of the household at Timble Cottage. It was very different from the life in the bungalow at Adruna, but perhaps the fact that it was so utterly different helped him to forget his troubles more quickly. Occasionally he looked wistful and said regretfully, "If only Daddy was here . . ." and sometimes at night he wept a few tears into his pillow before settling down to sleep, but on the whole his contentment was amazing. I was able to write a good account of him to Ronnie.

Fortunately a litter of puppies had arrived quite recently and Val was delighted to help Margaret with them. He was infinitely gentle. He undertook a few small duties in the house and the rest of the time he played in the garden.

Tom Gow had fixed a few planks in the chestnut-tree at the gate and Val spent hours in his 'crows' nest' gazing round the country and pretending to be all sorts of strange and unlikely people. We found an old brass telescope in the antique shop in Ryddelton, and bought it for a few shillings, and Tom Gow put it in order so that it 'really worked'.

Tom Gow could put up a shelf or cure a sick hen or prune a rose-tree . . . but we had never expected him to be able to mend a telescope. When we wanted to pay him for the job he would not take the money.

"Och, it was naethin'," he declared. "I just sorted it for Vull . . . an' I was thinkin' we micht put up a swing in yon aipple tree if you an' Miss Firth ha'e nae objection."

Far from offering any objection Margaret and I were en-chanted with the plan.

All this was very pleasant but I discovered that having Val in the house interfered considerably with my work. I had been in the middle of a new novel when I received Ronnie's letter and had flown out to Adruna; now that I had returned I was anxious to finish the story, but the worry and confusion had broken the sequence and I was completely stuck. Val did not interrupt me when I was shut up in my study—he had been told not to—but I found myself listening for his voice and wondering what he was doing. More often than not I put down my pen and went out to see. More often than not I would find Val in his 'crows' nest' with the telescope, surveying the scene.

"Come up!" he would cry in welcoming tones. "Come up, Aunt Jane. It's frightfully interesting. There are three sheep in Mr. Cow's garden and he's trying to chase them out!"

Or, if it were not sheep in Mr. Gow's garden, it was some-thing else equally enthralling.

Val was never bored. He played by himself for hours . . . and then one day another small boy appeared. He was a grandson of the Gows and they always referred to him as 'Chairley's Chairley'. The Gows had innumerable grandsons and at least three of them were called Chairley—it seemed to be a favourite name in the Gow family. There was Wullie's Chairley (a tall gangling youth who delivered the milk); there was Kate's Chairley, whom we had never seen, and there was Chairley's Chairley whom we knew only too well.

Chairley's Chairley was a fat little boy with red hair and a ruddy complexion. At one time he had haunted the garden whistling untunefully, climbing the trees and searching for birds' nests. He had stolen all our apples (not just a few, which we would not have minded, but the whole crop at one fell swoop) and had sold them to his friends at twopence each.

Margaret and I had a feeling that Chairley's Chairley was on his way to a Big Business Career, but his father had put a stop to that.

"He'll nae dae it agen," said old Tom Gow—and added with relish, "Chairley walloped him proper."

For a time we saw no more of Chairley's Chairley, but now, here he was in the garden playing with Val.

"I don't suppose he'll do Val any harm," said Margaret, peering out of the window.

"He'll do Val all the good in the world," I replied.

3

Mother wrote and said that she and Andrew were looking forward to having Val. He could stay with them and go daily to a very nice little school conveniently near. *"It is much the best plan"* wrote Mother. *"You are not interested in children and you have got your writing so you will not have time to look after Val. I have put down his name for the school and he can start next term."*

Rosalie rang up and said Val must go to Mount Charles. She and Edward would love to have him and of course Mount Charles was an ideal place for a little boy. They had engaged a nursery-governess for Anna—who was now five—and Val could have lessons with her. Rosalie added that I was not very keen on children and of course I had my writing.

Jean said Val was Ronnie's son, so of course Ken wanted to have him. She pointed out that she and Ken were used to children and it would be very lonely for Val at Timble Cottage. I had my writing and Margaret was busy with the dogs.

"It's all true," said Margaret when we had considered these offers. "At least most of it is true."

I knew Margaret was no more anxious than I was to part with Val . . . "He'll have to choose," I said. "Val is a person."

"But how can he know which would be best for him?" asked Margaret with her usual common sense. She added thoughtfully, "I believe Edinburgh would be best—really. It's a very nice little school and it would be good for him to mix with other children, he's too grown-up for his age. It's lovely having him here but he must be educated, Jane."

But Val had been through so many troubles that I thought it was more important for him to settle down quietly and vegetate; more important than schooling.

We were still debating the matter when Val cleared up the problem for himself.

"We'll have to start breakfast earlier next week," said Val, as we sat down to our morning meal. "School begins on Monday and Chairley says we have to be there at half-past eight. Chairley says school is smashing," he added, taking up his spoon and tucking into his porridge and cream.

"School—" I began doubtfully.

"Yes, I can go with Chairley," explained Val. "I'll need to start in the lowest form, but I'll soon work up." Already Val's conversation was slightly tinged with colour borrowed from the conversation of his boon companion.

Margaret and I looked at each other and said nothing but when Val had gone we talked it over—and we sent a long and extremely expensive cable to Ronnie asking what we were to do.

Ronnie's reply was, 'Yes'.

So I went and saw the headmaster and it was settled.

We knew that there would be a storm of protest from the whole family—and there was—but by this time Ronnie's letter had arrived and we stood upon firm ground. Ronnie had written, *"By all means let him go to Ryddelton Academy. If the rough and tumble is too much for him you can take him away, but give it a fair trial. This world is not made for pampered darlings."*

We were both somewhat anxious when we saw him off at the gate, but we need not have worried for Val was a success. Val had lived in Africa; he had seen lions and giraffes and zebras in their native haunts—not just in the Edinburgh Zoo. He had been waited upon, and had flown in an aeroplane—and in spite of all this he did not put on airs (it never occurred to Val that he was better or worse than anybody else). Last but not least he had a staunch and doughty champion in Chairley's Chairley.

During the first week we heard a lot about school, about the lessons and games in the playground, but we heard nothing that gave us cause for anxiety.

On Saturday afternoons the garden was full of small boys rushing about madly all over the flower-beds, climbing the chestnut-tree and uttering strange oaths. We minded nothing except the oaths. They worried us. When Val began to adorn his conversation with them it worried us still more.

"Val, need you say that?" I asked.

"What?" asked Val. "Oh, you mean bloody. But they all say it. They'd think I was a Jaissy if I didn't say it too."

This certainly raised a problem. I thought of Rosalie's face if the word were used in her presence! I thought of Mother's face!

Val was looking at me searchingly. "Perhaps I could say it at school and not at home," he suggested. "It would be awfully difficult to remember, but I could try."

I did not want him to say it at all. "Oh Val! It's such a horrid word! Couldn't you say something in Swahili instead?"

"I might," said Val thoughtfully. Then he giggled and added, "I've just remembered something..."

So Val swore in Swahili and it sounded quite frightful but at least nobody knew what it meant.

Chapter Twenty-Four

1

Now that Val was at school it was reasonable to suppose that I would be able to finish my book but I had got completely bogged and the wheels would not turn.

"Why don't you go and see Miss Smith?" suggested Margaret.

Miss Smith was Mrs. Millard's friend; the woman who 'lived and moved and had her being in the seventeenth century'. I had written to her several times about my books, and she had helped me with historical facts and details about clothes and phraseology, but this time my problem was the plot. Nobody could help me with that. All the same I considered Margaret's suggestion. Perhaps it might help to talk to Miss Smith... and anything was better than sitting at my desk and looking at a blank sheet of paper.

There was nothing to prevent me from leaving home and spending a few days in London. Val was settled in a niche, going to school daily and enjoying the companionship of Chairley; Margaret was here to look after him and to see that all went well.

The first two days of my stay in London were occupied with business matters and shopping; on the third and last day I called on Miss Smith. Her house was situated not far from the Tower. It was a very old house in a street of very old houses. Some of the houses had been modernised, but not Miss Smith's. The front door was of solid oak with iron hinges and an iron knocker.

Miss Smith opened the door herself; she was "a dried up little stick"—as Mrs. Millard had said—but her eyes were bright and her smile was cordial. She was dressed in a dark green smock with a leather belt round her waist; it was a shapeless garment, obviously home-made and certainly not copied from the fine ladies of her favourite period. All the same there was something a little strange about her and almost I expected her to drop a curtsy and say: 'your sarvent, marm' . . . but instead of that she shook hands and invited me to come in, adding that any friend of Augusta Millard's was welcome.

Although we had not met before we had corresponded, so we knew each other and wasted no time in idle talk. I explained my predicament and she replied that she could not help me—fiction was not her line—but she would show me her house and her dolls and would tell me anything I wanted to know.

"All these houses were built in 1668," declared Miss Smith. "Many of them have been modernised but fortunately this one was not much spoilt by alterations and when I bought it, about thirty years ago, I was able to restore it without much difficulty."

It certainly was extremely interesting to me for it was all 'in period' and yet it was a dwelling-place and not a museum. The rooms were small and rather dark, the walls were panelled in dark wood; there were low ceilings and uneven sloping floors. The furniture consisted of oaken chests and cupboards and high-backed chairs. I was particularly interested in the latches on the doors which were made of wood and fastened somewhat clumsily.

"I am afraid I must admit that the latches were made for me by a carpenter," said Miss Smith when she saw me looking at them. "It was impossible to buy latches of the correct pattern . . . and the electric light is an anachronism, but the fact is my eyesight is not good and I found I could not work by candlelight. Another of my concessions to modernity is adequate plumbing. No doubt you are aware that the house should be pervaded by an extremely unpleasant odour."

I glanced at her to see if she were joking but she appeared to be perfectly serious.

She added apologetically, "I have a bathroom with hot and cold water . . . and a gramophone."

It was difficult not to smile. "Seventeenth century music?" I suggested.

"Yes—and not only music. I managed to get some records made by a school of elocution. Perhaps you might like to hear one . . . but first I must show you my dolls."

The dolls were well worth seeing. Miss Smith set them out on the table in a little group; they were about six inches tall and beautifully dressed. There was a lady in travelling costume with a tiny black fur cape and a muff to match; the bodice was tight fitting, the skirt was wide and reached her ankles. Her hat was made of black felt with a wide brim and a scarlet feather. Another little lady was attired for an evening party in a taffeta gown of white and green. The bodice was cut very low and displayed her neck and shoulders and her bare arms. There was a little man in a periwig with a black velvet coat and breeches, black stockings and tiny high-heeled shoes . . . and other little men, more finely attired, in brightly-coloured coats and embroidered waistcoats. All of them wore wigs and broad hats with feathers lying flat along the brims, all of them wore high-heeled shoes with red heels. Some of them had tiny swords.

"I dress them myself," said Miss Smith with pardonable pride. "It is an amusing occupation. The latest addition to my collection is not yet finished." She picked up a little figure in a bright blue coat and breeches and yellow stockings.

"What a long time it must take!" I exclaimed.

She nodded. "The perukes take time and the little shoes—"

"And the swords! How do you make the swords? They aren't much larger than pins!"

"Oh, I get them made by a watchmaker," she replied. "He is interested in my dolls and very neat-fingered. At the moment he is making me a sedan chair. If it is a success—and I have reason to believe it will be—he is going to make a coach."

Somewhat to my surprise I discovered that Miss Smith did not approve of *The Biography of Lady Esmeralda Pie*.

"Augusta's book disappointed me," she declared. "Augusta has an exceedingly good brain but instead of using it to the best advantage she panders to popular taste. Works of history and biography should be approached in a serious manner, not lightly and amusingly."

"They wouldn't sell," I objected.

Miss Smith did not reply. Obviously she thought the remark unworthy of her attention.

"Augusta and I have known each other since we were children," said Miss Smith. "We disagree frequently but in spite of that we continue to be friends."

"She has had a sad life."

"Partly sad and partly gay."

For a few moments there was silence, and then my hostess rose and said she must play one of her records for me.

"Does it take you back to the seventeenth century?" I asked.

"You shall answer that question for yourself, Miss Harcourt," was the reply.

Miss Smith lighted two candles which stood upon the chimney-piece and drew a thick curtain across the window. The record she had chosen was a scene from one of Congreve's plays—an obvious choice—but the phraseology and pronunciation were so strange that at first it was difficult to follow. Then gradually I began to understand; my imagination was gripped. The dimly lit room was filled with voices from the past; I could have sworn I heard the whisper of silken skirts and the chink of swords; I could have sworn I saw people moving in the shadows.

The illusion was so real that it was alarming and to tell the truth I was glad when the scene ended and the needle ran on the waxen disc with the familiar scraping sound.

"Did you go back?" asked Miss Smith as she drew back the curtain and let in the sunshine.

"They came here," I said in a low voice. I saw by her face that it was the right answer.

2

When I returned to the hotel it was nearly five o'clock but I decided not to bother about tea. My head was full of all I had seen and heard, full of ideas for my story, and I wanted to get them on to paper while they were still fresh. I was running up the stairs to find a notebook when the hall-porter called me:

"Miss Harcourt, there's a visitor for you!"

"For me?" I asked in surprise and annoyance.

"He's been waiting more than an hour—in the lounge."

I came down reluctantly. Who could it be? Only Margaret knew I was here.

"It's Dr. Ferguson," said the hall-porter.

"Dr. Ferguson!"

"Yes, miss, that's what he said."

Kenneth! But why had Kenneth followed me to London? Something had happened! Some accident! Val was ill—or Margaret. Kenneth had come to tell me . . .

The hall-porter was looking at me strangely. "He's in the lounge, miss. He seemed very anxious to see you. I said I didn't know when you'd be back but he said he'd wait."

As I pushed open the swing door a tall figure rose from a sofa in the corner of the room and came towards me holding out his hands.

"Ronnie, it's you!" I exclaimed in amazement.

"Didn't the man tell you?"

"He said it was Dr. Ferguson."

"Well, so it is."

"Yes, of course—but I thought it was Kenneth. What on earth are you doing here?"

"Come and sit down and I'll tell you," said Ronnie. "We could have some tea, couldn't we? I've been waiting hours in this dreary hole. Why don't you go to a more comfortable hotel?"

"It's all right," I said. "It's quiet and the people know me. I've been coining here for years."

Ronnie knew that. "Yes, we sat here when I called to see you before we went out to Adruna. A lot of water has flowed under London Bridge since then."

I ordered tea and we sat down on the sofa together. I wanted to know why Ronnie was here, I wanted to hear all his news, but seeing Ronnie unexpectedly had set my heart beating quickly and I was so breathless that it was difficult to speak.

"Miss Firth gave me your address," said Ronnie. "I rang up Timble Cottage this morning. I told her not to tell Val that I was here. It's no good upsetting Val—I'm only here for a few days." He hesitated and then added, "I always seem to be burdening you with my problems, Jane."

"Have you heard from Helen?" I asked him anxiously. She was his principal problem.

"Not a word. I don't know where they are nor what they're doing. I suppose I could find out, but what's the use? I'm just waiting. Sooner or later Helen will write and tell me what she wants."

As usual Helen was to have exactly what she wanted!

"Meantime things have been moving," continued Ronnie more cheerfully. "Orton and I have succeeded in isolating our bug. Of course we can't pack up and leave Adruna until someone else is appointed to take charge of the hospital but we ought to be free in a few months."

"And then?"

"Then Eastringford," said Ronnie smiling. "Yes, really! Orton has been appointed to the bacteriology research laboratories at Eastringford and he's asked for me as his chief assistant."

"Ronnie, how splendid!"

"That's why I came home. They wanted to see me."

"And you've got the post?"

He nodded. "There were half a dozen other fellows after it— some of them much better qualified—but Orton had written and asked for me. It's queer how things happen, isn't it? I never thought I'd get another chance of going to Eastringford."

"You're very pleased?"

"Pleased as Punch," declared Ronnie. "I've always been interested in bacteriological research . . . and the laboratories at

Eastringford are simply wonderful. I could laugh when I think of the way we've been pottering about at Adruna with make-shift equipment." He smiled and added, "Ken will be pleased too. Ken was so angry with me when I gave up the appointment at Eastringford that he would scarcely speak to me. In fact he has never really forgiven me."

"He will, now."

"Yes—and I'm glad. We were such friends, Ken and I."

Ronnie did not stay long but as he was going away he asked me to go out to dinner with him. At first I refused for I had made up my mind that the less I saw of Ronnie the better.

"Do come," said Ronnie. "We'll have dinner at the Savoy. We'll be gay—just for to-night. We'll forget all my problems; we'll pretend they don't exist—just for to-night. It's my birthday."

"Your birthday! Oh Ronnie—"

"So you must come. You will, won't you? Say yes." I said yes.

3

Ronnie and I had arranged to meet at eight o'clock and I was there early, but my host was waiting for me. He was in full rig: white tie, white waistcoat and a white carnation in his buttonhole. He looked absolutely marvellous as he came forward to greet me and I could see that other people thought the same. I was glad I had got a new frock and had put it on for Ronnie's birthday celebration.

"That colour suits you, Jane," said Ronnie. "It's the same colour as the dress you wore at—at—"

"Cherry colour," I told him. "I'm glad you like it. Mother always says it suits me and she's very clever about clothes. As a matter of fact you don't look bad yourself!"

The cloud, which had appeared for a moment, vanished. Ronnie smiled. "Oh well," he said. "If a fellow can't wear a carnation in his buttonhole when he's entertaining a famous author—"

"On his birthday—" I put in.

"On his birthday," agreed Ronnie.

We went in to dinner laughing.

We had a table in the corner farthest from the band and we sat and watched the other people—neither of us wanted to dance. We talked about ourselves and the things that interested us; we talked about Val; we talked about my books. I discovered that Ronnie had read all my books and enjoyed them.

"They're an entertainment," he declared. "You say they're 'just stories'—well, of course they are! I like stories. Everybody likes stories."

"Not everybody."

"Everybody with any sense. The story-teller has always been a valuable member of society. Even in prehistoric times when men hunted wild beasts and lived in caves they sat round the camp-fire at night and listened to stories. Your profession is one of the oldest in the world and one of the most useful."

"Away!" I cried, laughing.

"It is, really. And we need stories more than ever now. We need stories to entertain us, to help us to forget our troubles, to fill our lives with colour." He paused and then added, "The period you've chosen is very colourful."

"Would you like to have lived then, Ronnie?"

"It must have been fun. Awful fun to wear all those queer clothes and swagger about with a sword."

"Not so much fun if you got ill."

"Oh, you hadn't a hope if the doctor got you into his clutches. If you were wounded and lost a lot of blood the doctor bled you; if your lungs went wrong he shut the window and pulled the curtains and kept out the fresh air . . ." For a moment Ronnie looked quite upset at the stupidity of his predecessors.

"Talking of curtains," I said. "You will be interested to hear about a most astonishing experience I had this afternoon. I went to see a woman who lives in a queer old house near the Tower and summons up ghosts from the past—"

"Not really!"

"She did—for me. I'm not sure she isn't a witch . . ."

Ronnie listened to my story and asked several questions. He said, "The play was spoken by actors; but how do they know the way people spoke in those days."

"From old diaries and letters—people spelt words as they were pronounced—and from verses. For instance:

> 'Love's but a frailty of the mind
> When 'tis not with ambition join'd.'"

I added, "Obviously Congreve pronounced the words as if they rhymed."

"You know a lot about it," said Ronnie in surprise.

"Oh well, my books are 'just for fun', but I like to have the background right."

"Where do you get your characters, Jane? They're awfully real. I liked that fellow, Ralph, in *The Mulberry Coach*."

"Did you?"

"He was my sort of chap," declared Ronnie. "If I had met him in real life I would have liked him—if you know what I mean."

I nodded. I knew what he meant.

"Where did you get him?" repeated Ronnie. "Is he a real live person?"

It was difficult to answer. "He was a dream," I said vaguely.

"You mean you dreamt about him?"

"I dreamt about him for months, sleeping and waking."

Ronnie gazed at me for a moment without speaking. I thought he was going to ask more about Ralph but fortunately the subject was changed by the arrival of a large party at the next table. They wanted two tables put together and the seats changed round and there was a lot of talk and confusion.

"My goodness!" exclaimed Ronnie. "Look at that woman with blue hair! Does she think it's pretty?"

"She thinks it's arresting—and how right she is!"

"What do you mean?"

I laughed and said, "Well, you stared at her didn't you? You're talking about her. If she hadn't got blue hair you wouldn't have looked at her twice."

"That's true," he agreed. "Take away the blue hair and there's nothing much left. You're rather a devil, Jane."

"You didn't know I was a devil, did you?"

"I didn't know much about you—until to-night," said Ronnie seriously.

Presently Ronnie leant forward and said, "You're enjoying yourself, aren't you? You're glad you came?"

I was glad I had come. Later I should be miserable, but I put it out of my mind. We were gay—just for to-night—because it was Ronnie's birthday.

Chapter Twenty-Five

1

The next day I went home to Ryddelton. Ronnie came to Euston to see me off; he had tried to persuade me to stay in London for the week-end and go out with him again, but I refused firmly. We had had our gay evening together and it had been perfect—that was enough.

At the very last moment, when the train was about to start, Ronnie repeated his plaint.

"I can't think why you won't stay," he declared. "There's nothing to prevent you. Even now it isn't too late. Stay till Monday. We could have another binge—"

"The traveller cannot bathe twice in the same stream," I told him.

"That sounds like a proverb."

The train had started to move.

I put my head out of the window and said, "Chinese philosophy, Ronnie."

Ronnie took his hat off and waved. I watched him standing there and waving until I could see him no longer. I wondered when I should see him again.

There was a warm welcome waiting for me at Timble Cottage. Margaret and Val had got on very well but all the same they were very pleased to see me. Val's hug nearly strangled me.

"How's Chairley?" I asked when I could speak.

"He's fine," said Val. "He has got a new baby at his house. I think it would be rather nice to have a baby, but Chairley says they're no use at all. They can't do anything except lie and stare. Chairley says he'd much rather have a bike. Did you remember my bike, Aunt Jane?"

"It's coming," I said. "It's a red one—with a bell."

"Oh joy!" cried Val and he hugged me again.

"You didn't forget the electric cooker, I hope," asked Margaret anxiously.

"It's coming," I said. "It's a white one with a glass door."

"Oh joy!" exclaimed Margaret, laughing.

"No hug?" I asked . . . so Margaret hugged me, too.

It was all very pleasant. I knew I was lucky to have Margaret and Val (some people seemed to think ours was a strange household, consisting as it did of three generations, but no household could have been more harmonious); I knew I was lucky to have my work. The new story which had stuck so badly began to move and I settled down to a daily routine. Writing in the morning, walking the dogs in the afternoon, playing with Val after tea.

There were interruptions of course, social occasions such as tea at Mount Charles and an occasional visit to Edinburgh. In August there was the Tennis Tournament and the Flower Show and a dance at Tocher House.

So the summer passed and the heather bloomed purple on the hills and it was September.

2

One morning when I was hard at work a car drove up to the door. I was alone in the house, for Val was at school and Margaret was shopping in Ryddelton, so I had to put down my pen and answer the bell myself. My visitor was Andrew.

"Hallo!" I exclaimed. "What good wind has blown you to Ryddelton? Where's Mother?"

"I didn't bring your Mother—she doesn't know I've come. I wanted to talk to you, Jane. Are you alone?"

This sounded mysterious, to say the least of it, and I wondered what had happened.

"I can't stay long," said Andrew as he followed me into the sitting-room. "No, I can't stay to lunch. I just wanted to see you and have a chat. I suppose Ronnie is still in Kenya?"

"Yes," I said. "They haven't found anyone to take charge of the hospital yet."

"Have you had a letter from him lately?"

"Last week," I replied. Ronnie and I corresponded regularly for he liked to hear about Val's doings.

"And you saw him in London, didn't you?"

"Yes."

"Jane, what is he going to do about Helen?"

"Nothing," I said. "Nothing until he hears from her. He hasn't heard a word from Helen since she left him."

"It's most unsatisfactory," declared Andrew. "If he intends to divorce Helen he should start proceedings and not leave it too long."

I explained that Ronnie did not intend to start proceedings until he knew quite definitely what Helen wanted.

"What Helen wants is neither here nor there," said Andrew.

"He thinks it matters a lot."

"Well, he ought to find out. He ought to get moving. The best way would be to send her a lawyer's letter."

"How can he when he doesn't know where she is?" Andrew hesitated for a moment and then he said, "I know where she is. As a matter of fact I've been keeping track of them. Perhaps you think it was none of my business; but Anna is very much my business, and Helen is Anna's daughter, so I thought it essential to know what was happening. They were in London for a time, going the pace and spending money like water, then they went to Paris and Rome—"

"Do you mean you engaged a detective?"

Andrew laughed, not very merrily. "It wasn't necessary," he said. "They haven't been in hiding—far from it. They've been throwing their weight about; they've been seen everywhere. I made a few inquiries from time to time, that was all."

"Where are they now?" I asked.

"Lancaster is in London on business. He's well known in the financial world. Helen is staying at a clinic in Switzerland."

"Is she ill?" I exclaimed.

"She may be ill or she may have gone there for a rest. I can't tell you. Anyway that's where she is."

"Have you got her address?"

"Oh yes, it's that clinic where she went when she was a child." Andrew hesitated and then added, "I haven't said a word about it to your Mother—and you're not to tell her, Jane. I won't have her worried. She has worried quite enough about Helen. You can tell Ronnie if you like, but he had better be careful what he does. If he writes to Helen or goes and sees her it will complicate matters considerably."

"Perhaps I should go and see her."

"You had better keep clear of the whole affair," said Andrew.

I was silent for a few moments and then I said, "Honestly, I think I should go and see her."

At first Andrew said no, but after some argument he agreed reluctantly that it could do no harm for me to go and see Helen—if I were careful. I was not to say I was an emissary from Ronnie nor to commit him to any course of action; I was on no account to tell her that I had stayed unchaperoned in Ronnie's bungalow. In fact I received so many instructions about what I was not to say to Helen that it seemed as if there was little left to say.

That night I talked it over with Margaret, for I had come to depend upon her solid common sense.

"Yes, I see," said Margaret thoughtfully. "Of course Andrew is usually right, but he's looking at the matter from a legal point of view and to my mind it's a human problem. She's your sister so it's only natural for you to go and see her when she's ill."

"I feel I ought to."

"I think you ought to," agreed Margaret. "You don't need to mix yourself up in her affairs. It will just be a sisterly visit . . . and when you've seen her you'll be able to write and tell Ronnie all about her. Then he can do what he thinks best. That would clear up the whole situation, wouldn't it?"

"Yes, it would," I said.

"So your book gets shelved again," said Margaret with a rueful smile. "Your family is a great nuisance to you, Jane."

Chapter Twenty-Six

1

The clinic where Helen was staying was situated on a hill above the town. It was not a very large building. Round it, but not very near, there were pinewoods and beyond the pinewoods were snow-capped mountains glistening in the sunshine. Quite a number of patients were walking about in the beautifully laid-out gardens, others were lying on balconies, wrapped in rugs. There was an atmosphere of peacefulness and cheerfulness about it, so that it did not seem like an ordinary hospital at all. I gave my name to the girl at the desk and after a few minutes delay she said that Madame Ferguson would be happy to see me.

"Madame is not really allowed to have visitors but a sister is different," she explained.

Helen was lying propped up with pillows and enveloped in a white fleecy shawl. She was as lovely as ever—indeed she was lovelier for her expression was softer.

The nurse put a chair for me and went away.

"It was good of you to come," said Helen with a welcoming smile. "When they told me you were here I was surprised. I thought you would be angry with me." Her voice was very soft and husky and her face was thinner, but she did not look really ill.

"I came at once," I told her. "I only heard a few days ago that you were here."

"How did you hear?"

"Andrew told me."

"Andrew!" she exclaimed. "I used to like Andrew at one time but he's far too nosy. He interferes in things that don't concern him. He thinks because he married Mother it gives him the right to interfere with me." She smiled and added, "But I'm glad you came."

"I was so sorry to hear you were ill."

"Yes, it's a nuisance. Some days I feel ghastly, but I'm much better really. Of course Madame Monet is rather a fuss-pot and so are the nurses, but I want to get well quickly so I do what they say." She paused for a few moments and then added, "When I'm better I want to go back to Ronnie."

I was silent.

"Jane, I want to see Ronnie. I want to say I'm sorry. It was all a mistake. It was because I was lonely and Dick was kind and amusing. That was how it happened."

"You mean you've left Mr. Lancaster?"

She nodded. "Yes, but we're still friends. He's very fond of me and we had a good time together until I began to get ill. Then I realised that Dick wasn't all I thought." She moved uneasily and added, "I don't mean he wasn't kind, but he just—wasn't—Ronnie."

For a moment I was too angry to speak; all sorts of horrible feelings boiled up inside me but I managed to swallow them down.

"I see you're annoyed," said Helen with a little sigh. "You don't understand, that's all. I think Ronnie will understand if I tell him about it. That's why I want to see him."

"Yes, I expect Ronnie will understand."

"You mean it will be all right?" Her eyes were looking at me anxiously and I realised that for once in her life Helen was not sure she was going to get exactly what she wanted—but of course she would. If she wanted to go back to Ronnie he would take her. He had said so.

"Why don't you write to him?" I asked. "You could explain—"

"They won't let me write letters . . . and it isn't the sort of letter I could dictate. But you could write to him, couldn't you?"

"Yes, I'll write."

"Write to-night, Jane. Tell him I want to see him. Tell him I'll be better soon. Nobody could help getting better quickly in this lovely place."

I had felt the same. It was a lovely place and Helen's room was extremely pleasant; large and airy. It was bare except for necessities but that was as it should be. The windows were wide open and the view was incredibly beautiful. The sun was shining and the air was clear as crystal.

"You're quite comfortable—I mean you've got all you want?" I asked.

"Oh yes, and everyone is very kind. I was here before—when I was a child—and I got well very quickly. You remember?"

"Yes, I remember."

"That's why I wanted to come back."

I thought she was getting tired so I rose and said I must go.

Helen gave a little sigh. "I suppose Ronnie is still at that ghastly Adruna, but he'll be coming home soon, won't he?"

"Yes, he's going to Eastringford," I told her. "It's good, isn't it? He's very pleased about it. Dr. Orton has been appointed to the bacteriological laboratories and Ronnie is going as his chief assistant."

"That wouldn't do," said Helen. She said it quietly and calmly.

"Wouldn't do!"

"No, it wouldn't do at all. For one thing I don't like the Ortons and for another they don't like me. Ronnie will have to find a practice somewhere in England where nobody knows anything about us. Then we can start afresh."

She spoke with confidence, as if it were all settled.

"Oh Helen!" I exclaimed. "Surely you wouldn't—"

"Wouldn't what?"

I had been going to say, 'Surely you wouldn't make him give it up again' but I remembered Andrew's warning. Andrew had said I was not to talk about Ronnie's future plans.

"What is it, Jane?" asked Helen a trifle anxiously.

"I can't promise anything—for Ronnie," I told her.

"Oh, is that all?" said Helen. "There's no need to worry about that. Ronnie knows I don't like the Ortons." She added, "You'll come again to-morrow, won't you? Oh, and don't forget to write to Ronnie and tell him what I said."

2

The letter was not difficult to write. I told Ronnie that I had been to see Helen and that she seemed quite cheerful and comfortable and hoped to be better soon. I told him what she had said and added that Andrew had warned me not to make any promises, so I had been careful not to do so . . . and I passed on Andrew's advice about a lawyer's letter. It was no use saying more. I knew Ronnie would write to Helen himself. He would do exactly as Helen wanted. He would do it, not because he loved her (she had killed his love long ago) but because of the promises he had made at his marriage.

I wrote quite cheerfully but I did not feel cheerful. Helen had said they could start afresh in a new place . . . but was it possible to put aside all that had happened? Was it possible for them to settle down together and be happy? I thought of Val. It was remarkable that Helen had never mentioned Val; she had never even asked how he was! I wondered if she would allow Val to stay with me at Timble Cottage. Certainly this plan would be very much better for Val, for even if Helen and Ronnie were able to settle down together there was bound to be stress and strain. It could not be the right sort of home for a sensitive child.

The future was dark and full of difficulties—or so it seemed to me.

That night I lay for hours thinking about Ronnie and Helen and Val and wondering what I could do . . . but gradually my ideas grew clearer and I realised I could do nothing for I had no right to interfere; they must work out the problem themselves. Ronnie had forgiven Helen before, he would forgive her again—and again if necessary—but perhaps she had learnt her lesson. Perhaps after this she would appreciate Ronnie and make him happy.

It was in this more hopeful mood that I went to see Helen again.

My visit was much the same as yesterday except that I did most of the talking. I told her I had written to Ronnie and posted the letter by air mail.

"That's good," she said.

Then I told her I had flown out to Adruna and brought Val home.

"Do you mean Val is at Timble Cottage?" said Helen in surprise. "How very strange! I thought the Ortons would look after him."

"How could they?"

"Oh well, Mrs. Orton was always going on about Val—saying I didn't look after him properly and all that—but of course it was absolute nonsense. Val was quite happy with the servants. Did you stay in the bungalow, Jane?"

I had expected this question and had my answer ready. "Yes, and I thought it was a delightful bungalow. Mrs. Orton was there when I arrived."

"She's ghastly, isn't she? I simply couldn't stand the woman; she got on my nerves and made me want to scream."

"She means well," I said . . . but as a matter of fact I sympathised with Helen over this. If I had seen too much of Mrs. Orton I should have wanted to scream.

"She's so marvellous in her own estimation!"

I could not help smiling,

"You can smile," said Helen. "I don't suppose you were there very long. If you had lived next door to her for years you wouldn't have felt like smiling. She was always popping in at unexpected moments and finding fault with everything; asking why I did this and didn't do that. She used to tell me that whatever time of night Dr. Orton came home from the hospital she was waiting for him with a hot meal."

"It was true—" I began.

"Oh yes, it was true. She was so worthy, and of course I was unworthy of Ronnie. They both thought that." Helen sighed and added, "I suppose they were right . . . but I really am going to be quite different in future. I'm going to settle down and be a model wife."

"And a model mother?"

"Oh yes, of course," said Helen.

We were silent for a few minutes after that, but it was a companionable silence. Obviously Helen meant to turn over a new leaf. I felt more in sympathy with her than I had ever felt before, and I think she had the same feeling about me.

"You needn't rush home, need you?" said Helen when I rose to go.

I hesitated. The fact was I had not intended to stay in Switzerland more than a few days. I wanted to get home. I wanted to finish my book which had been hanging fire for so long.

"You haven't anything important to do at home, have you?" said Helen.

"N-no," I said doubtfully. Helen would not think my book was important.

"Please, Jane," said Helen. "It's so dull lying here all day with nothing to do. I like seeing you."

"Yes," I said. "Yes, of course I'll stay—if you want me."

"Come to-morrow."

"Yes," I said.

Chapter Twenty-Seven

1

When I was coming away the nurse ran after me and said that the matron would like to see me for a few minutes. She added, "Madame Monet speaks no English but perhaps Mademoiselle Harcourt speaks French?"

"Yes, a little," I replied cautiously. It was always risky to say that one 'spoke French'—or so I had found.

As a matter of fact I was glad to have the opportunity of seeing Madame Monet, and asking her about Helen, and the clinic was so well run that I thought she would be worth seeing on her own account. She must be a wonderful woman to take on a job like this and do it so efficiently.

When Madame rose to greet me I was not disappointed; she looked like a woman with a vocation. In a way she looked like a nun, with her clear pallor and fine features and her sweet expression. Her dark hair was smooth and parted in the middle of her forehead. Her eyes were soft and kind.

She motioned me to a comfortable chair and we both sat down.

"Parlez vous français, Mademoiselle Harcourt?" she asked.

I replied that I spoke French a little and went on to say that I had seen my sister and found her very comfortable and cheerful.

"Elle est très malade, votre soeur," said Madame Monet sadly.

It was not so much the words as the tone in which they were spoken that brought a chill to my heart. I was so shocked that I was dumb. I could only sit there staring at her.

"You are surprised," she said gently. "Yes, I can see that. I am so very sorry to give you this bad news but it is necessary you should know."

"You mean—seriously ill?"

She nodded.

"But—but I can't believe it! She was talking to me—"

"It is true, Mademoiselle Harcourt. Do you think I would alarm you like this if it were not true?"

"No, of course not . . . but surely she could have treatment! There are all sorts of treatments—modern methods of treatment—"

"If it is taken in time, yes, but in her case it was too late. Modern science can accomplish marvels but not miracles. Your sister was so very ill when she came to us that it was impossible to do anything. It was madness to leave it so long. There was no hope of healing."

"No hope!"

Madame Monet began to explain; I heard her voice through a haze. I was too dazed to listen properly. Only a phrase here and there was comprehensible . . . but although I could not understand the detailed explanation there was no doubt about the meaning of it all.

"It is incredible!" I cried. "She doesn't look very ill—"

"At times she looks very ill. This is one of her good days." Madame Monet hesitated and then added, "I think you do not understand all I say. It is difficult in a foreign language."

I tried to explain that it was difficult, not so much because I had failed to understand all she told me, but because Helen had seemed so hopeful. "She was talking so cheerfully of all she will do when she is better," I said desperately.

"Yes, it is very sad. She has talked to me like that also."

Madame Monet rose as she spoke and took a tray from a side table. "You will have some coffee, it will do you good," she added.

The coffee was hot and strong and I was very thankful for it—but there was something I had to say.

"Madame, is it right—" I began, searching for words.

"Yes, it is right," said Madame Monet nodding. 'In this case it is much better that she should talk hopefully of all she intends to do."

"In this case?"

"Yes. In some cases it is right that the patient should know the truth, but your sister would be frightened and unhappy. She has her treasure in this world."

"She has her treasure in this world!"

"It is true, isn't it?"

"Yes," I said doubtfully. "Yes, but still—"

"Believe me, it is much better that she should not know."

"It seems terrible!"

"It is terrible," said Madame Monet gently. "But the Good God is merciful. Do you think the Good God is less merciful than you?"

"I don't understand."

"I mean you are merciful. You understand that it is her nature to have her treasure in this world. That is so, isn't it? She has not been good. Oh yes, she has told me about it—but still you love her in your heart and are sorry. Do you think the Good God is less loving and sorry than you?"

"Thank you," I said humbly.

"You will not be too unhappy? You will remember?"

"Yes, I will remember."

I thanked her again and said good-bye but she came out to the door with me to see me off.

"Where is her husband?" asked Madame Monet. "Do you think he will come?"

"He is in Africa, but he will come as soon as he can."

"It must be soon."

"He will fly," I said.

Madame Monet offered to send for a *fiacre* to take me to the hotel but I told her I would rather walk. When I got to the gate I looked back and saw her standing on the steps watching me.

I still could not believe it. I still felt dazed and incredulous, as if it were all a terrible dream. Even when I had found the post office and stood at the desk trying to write the cable I could not believe it was true.

I wrote, *Helen is dying. She wants to see you. They say you must fly.*

It was horribly bare and bald, but I could think of no other words in which to break the news. I added my name and the address of the hotel where I was staying and let it go.

Ronnie came at once by the first plane he could get but he arrived too late.

2

I was having tea in the hotel lounge when Ronnie came in. It had been impossible to meet him at the station for I did not know what train he would be able to get. I had wondered how to tell him, but there was no need to tell him anything.

"Too late?" he said as he took my hand.

"Yes."

"I thought it would be. Everything has been too late."

He sat down beside me and I told him all about it. We were in a corner of the lounge and it was not crowded, so we could talk privately—nobody bothered about us. I told him that Madame Monet had explained the whole course of Helen's illness but I had not understood the details—just that it was too late.

"Everything has been too late," repeated Ronnie. "I was too late in getting to Nairobi. If I had managed to get there earlier I could have stopped them before they flew to Rome. It's all my fault."

"Your fault? Oh no!"

"I failed Helen. If I could have stopped them—"

"It goes back much further," I told him. "All that happened to Helen had roots in the past—long before you ever saw her. It all happened because she was the sort of person she was."

"'All in our stars'?" asked Ronnie. "Is that what you mean?"

"Oh no, not that! All in our natures; all in the way we think and live our lives!"

"If I could believe that . . ." said Ronnie in doubtful tones.

"It's true!" I said desperately, for indeed I knew it to be true, and it seemed dreadful that Ronnie should feel it was 'all his fault' and allow the shadow of it to darken his life.

"All in our natures?" said Ronnie thoughtfully.

"Yes, and it was especially true of Helen. Even when she was a child she thought it was her right to enjoy herself and have a good time. She thought that was the only thing that mattered. I remember Mother saying, 'Helen can never be happy unless she's enjoying herself'. It sounds a silly thing to say but there was a lot of truth in it."

"Your mother never says silly things."

"Not often," I agreed. "And of course Helen was so pretty that it all came easily."

"It all came too easily. Everybody loved her. There was a sort of magic in Helen that nobody could resist."

"An enchantment."

"Yes, an enchantment. I was enchanted the first time I saw her. I shall never forget the picture she made when she came into the room. She looked like an angel straight from Heaven. Even when I found she wasn't—an angel—I went on loving her for a long time. I went on loving her long after she stopped loving me. It's a miserable business loving someone who doesn't care twopence about you, Jane."

"Yes, I know," I said.

We did not talk much more. Ronnie sat staring into vacancy with the bewildered air of a child that has been punished unjustly—his pipe, unlit, was clenched between his teeth.

Presently he rose and said he would go up to the clinic, and I did not offer to go with him as I thought he would rather go alone.

There were various arrangements to be made, as there always are on these sad occasions. I had made some arrangements already and had chosen a quiet corner in the little cemetery near the English Church for Helen's grave. I had spoken to Andrew on the telephone (I thought some of the family might want to come to the funeral). They decided not to come, but they told me to order flowers.

It was very wet that day, the rain came down in a steady drizzle and the hills were veiled in mist. The English chaplain—a young delicate-looking creature—read the service. Ronnie had borrowed an umbrella and we stood there together beneath its shelter listening to the solemn words. I noticed that there was another wreath, besides those I had ordered for the family. It was a large beautiful wreath of red roses, and I wondered who had sent it, for there was no card.

The service did not take long and we were just turning away when Ronnie pressed my arm and said, "Wait a moment, Jane."

He left me with the umbrella and went and spoke to a man in a burberry coat who had been standing in the background.

When he came back he said, "That was Lancaster. I felt I ought to speak to him. That wreath is from him. I just thanked him for it. I didn't know what else to say. He didn't say anything. He was too upset—he was terribly upset. Perhaps it was foolish of me to speak to him, but I didn't want there to be any—any rancour. It's all over now."

It was all over. There was nothing else to do. I think those few words in the cemetery to the man who had wronged him helped Ronnie to turn the page and put the past behind him, for the shadow on his brow had lifted and when we got back to the hotel he began to talk quite cheerfully about his plans.

I asked if he were coming back to Ryddelton with me.

"Not now, I'm afraid," said Ronnie. "I must fly back to Adruna to-morrow—but I shall be free quite soon. I've been making inquiries about Eastringford and I find I can get comfortable lodgings in the town. Fortunately there's a very good school. Val can go there daily. Orton knows the headmaster so it's all laid on."

"That sounds splendid," I said. I tried to speak as if I were pleased about it; but it was difficult, for I had been hoping that Ronnie would let me keep Val—at least for a time. I had told myself that Ronnie would be far too busy to want Val, but I might have known better.

"I shall come home by sea," continued Ronnie. "Flying is too expensive except in an emergency. I shall sell most of the furniture but there's a lot of luggage and stuff that I must bring. I ought to be home before Christmas."

"Val will be pleased," I said.

3

Ronnie and I had dined together and were leaning on the balcony of the hotel watching the moon rising from behind the mountains. It was so beautiful that it seemed unreal—and all the more unreal because there was a dance in the hotel that evening. We could hear the talk and laughter and the music from the band playing the latest samba.

Presently Ronnie said, "The traveller cannot bathe twice in the same stream. Do you remember saying that, Jane?"

"At Euston."

"Yes, in all the noise and fuss and bustle. At first I thought it superficial, but it came back to me again and again, and every time I saw more in it."

"We're all travellers, aren't we?"

"Yes, and there are hundreds of streams, some pleasant and others not. The traveller toils along the dusty road and then, far off, he sees a stream. He's hot and thirsty so he looks forward to his bathe, but when he gets there the stream is muddy and weedy so he doesn't enjoy his bathe as much as he expected . . . but sometimes he comes to a stream quite suddenly, a different sort of stream; he sees a pool of crystal clear water—"

"The sun is shining on the ripples and there are primroses growing on the bank."

"Yes, sunshine and primroses," agreed Ronnie. "It's a perfect place for a bathe. The traveller would like to linger here, of course, but he has to press on . . . so on he goes. He looks back over his shoulder and wishes he could bathe twice in the sunlit pool."

"There's another kind of stream—" I began.

"Yes, I know," agreed Ronnie. "It runs in a deep gully amongst jagged rocks—the water is icy cold and the current nearly sweeps him off his feet—but somehow or other the traveller struggles through and crawls out on the other side."

"But he doesn't have to bathe in it again."

Ronnie sighed and said, "No, never again. It's behind him."

Chapter Twenty-Eight

1

"Aunt Jane," said Val. "Do you think there will be snow for Christmas?"

Val had asked the same question a dozen times at least. He had never seen snow; he was yearning to see it; he was especially anxious that the ground should be white with snow at Christmas.

"Daddy would like it," explained Val. "Daddy hasn't seen snow for years and years. If there was snow we could go tobogganing. Mr. Gow says he can easily make me a toboggan. Oh dear, I wish the snow would come!"

I was not yearning for snow (it is cold and uncomfortable and messy when you have to go out in it and dig a path to the gate and carry in wood for the fire) and I was not at all sure that Ronnie would appreciate it either. At any rate I could do nothing about it. I could buy a turkey; I could help to make plum-puddings and to decorate the house but I could not order snow.

The preparations for Ronnie's arrival at Timble Cottage were on an elaborate scale. Val staggered in with loads of holly and Tom Gow found a 'Christmas Tree' in the woods and planted it in a pot. We decorated it with tinsel and coloured balls and candles. Margaret had a little model of Father Christmas in his sleigh, drawn by reindeer, so we wired it carefully on to the top branch.

"But he's not real," said Val regretfully. "I mean Chairley says he's just a fairy tale—for kids. I suppose Chairley's right, Aunt Jane?"

"Yes, I'm afraid so, Val."

"Och well, I don't care," declared Val. "I'll have my own Daddy and he's better than a hundred million silly old Father Christmases."

It seemed a pity that the lovely old legend of Santa Claus should be exposed as a myth to a seven-year-old child (I remembered what fun it had been unpacking my Christmas stocking) and I was all the more disappointed because I had laid in a store of fascinating gew-gaws to fill a stocking for Val; but I had promised Val, cross my heart, that I would never lie to him.

"He can still have his stocking," said Margaret consolingly. "Even if he knows we've filled it for him it will be fun."

Ronnie was coming to Timble Cottage on Christmas Eve. He was coming for a few days only, to spend Christmas with us and to fetch Val. His plans had all gone smoothly; he had found rooms in Eastringford and had arranged with the landlady to cook and cater and to keep an eye on Val when he was out. He had been to see the headmaster of the school and had liked him immensely so he had arranged for Val to start there next term. It was all fixed without the slightest difficulty; it sounded ideal.

Val was so excited that he could talk of nothing else.

"Fancy seeing Daddy!" Val would exclaim. "I haven't seen Daddy for ages and ages. I've grown, haven't I? Won't Daddy be surprised when he sees how big I am? Oh dear, I hope the train won't be late. The train won't be late, will it, Aunt Jane?"

"It might be late."

"But I don't need to go to bed until Daddy comes, do I? I couldn't go to bed till I've seen Daddy. I want to meet him at the gate, you see."

In the morning, when Val came down to breakfast, he would cry, "Only two more days till Daddy comes! I wish I could push on the time. I wish to-day was the day after to-morrow. I don't know how I'm going to bear waiting two more days . . ."

Margaret and I suffered in patience, but Chairley did not.

"Other folks have Dads besides you," grumbled Chairley. "What's all the fuss?"

"There's nobody like my Daddy. He's smashing," declared Val earnestly. "Wait till you see him!"

"I'm not wanting tae see him."

"But Chairley, I've told you—he's smashing! Oh joy!" cried Val, hopping about in excitement. "Oh joy, Daddy's coming! He's coming to fetch me—"

"I ken that fine. You've telt me a dizzen times. I'm sick of hearing aboot it—and that's the truth."

"But Chairley—"

"You're going tae live in England," said Chairley scornfully. "You're going tae an English school. You'll be a toff."

"Oh, no, Chairley!"

"Aye, ye will so. You'll forget all aboot me."

"No, honestly. Listen, Chairley, I'll come back often—for the holidays—Aunt Jane says I can."

"You'll not be wanting tae play with me."

"I will! I will so! I'll never forget you. We'll play together in the holidays—when I come—"

"What's holidays?" said Chairley miserably. "What'll I dae all the rest of the time when you're not here?"

Chairley was not the only person who was wondering what he would do when Val was not here.

"It will be frightful," declared Margaret. "But of course we mustn't show him that we mind. I shall have to find a mate for Bess; there's nothing so comforting as a litter of spaniel puppies. You've got your work to keep you happy."

"I've finished my book," I reminded her.

"Oh I know, but you can start a new one."

"It will be a dashed dull book," I said, trying hard to smile.

2

There was no snow for Christmas but everything else was ready for Ronnie's arrival. The bed was aired, the turkey was waiting in the larder and there were masses of holly all over the house. We had placed the tree in the window of the sitting-room and drawn back the curtains so that it could be seen from the gate. All that remained to be done was to light the candles when our visitor arrived.

Ronnie was due at five o'clock but the train was delayed and it was nearly seven when the taxi was heard in the distance, grinding up the hill.

"That's him!" shrieked Val. "That's Daddy at last! Quick, quick, light the candles! Light the candles for Daddy! Isn't it a good thing that the taxi makes such a row!"

Margaret and I hastened to light the candles while Val rushed out to the gate . . . we heard the ecstatic greetings—Ronnie's deep voice and Val's shrill treble—and a few moments later Ronnie came up the path with Val hanging round his neck. Ronnie was laughing; he seemed almost as excited as the child.

"Val, you're strangling me!" he exclaimed. "Val, you weigh a ton—what has Aunt Jane been feeding you on? Val, get down and let me speak to Aunt Jane!"

But Val was too excited to listen.

"Daddy, you like the tree! Weren't you surprised when you saw it? Didn't it look lovely when you drove up to the gate? Look at the holly, Daddy! I climbed up the ladder myself and fixed it with a nail—and Chairley helped me. You haven't seen Chairley, have you? Chairley's my very best friend—you'll see him to-morrow! And wait till you see the plum-pudding! Daddy, I helped to stir it—and I helped Aunt Margaret to stuff the turkey—"

By this time he had released his stranglehold and was capering about in the hall. "Hurrah, hurrah!" he shouted. "Daddy's come! Hurrah, hurrah!"

Val was shouting, we were all laughing and the taxi-driver was waiting for his fare. The noise and confusion created by one small crazy boy was quite incredible.

Gradually the excitement abated and we were able to make ourselves heard; to speak in a rational manner and to show Ronnie his room. Ronnie was delighted with everything and especially delighted with his son.

"He's simply splendid," declared Ronnie.

"He's put on weight," said Margaret proudly; she was the cook!

"Yes, but it isn't only that."

"You mean he's noisier?" I suggested.

"Definitely noisier," chuckled Ronnie. "It's a good sign for a little boy to be noisy. He was far too quiet before."

Yes, he had been far too quiet. When I looked back and remembered the pale little ghost in the bungalow at Adruna I realised the difference in Val. He looked a different child. "I'm glad you're pleased," I said.

"Pleased!" echoed Ronnie. "I simply can't thank you enough. He's better in every way."

I was glad to see that Ronnie himself looked a great deal better. His eyes had lost the bewildered expression which had worried me so much. Obviously he had put the past behind him and was looking forward to the future. A future full of useful work; the kind of work in which he was interested; the kind of work he could do well.

We had promised Val that he should stay up late that night, but he was so tired with all the excitement that soon after supper his head began to nod and his eyes would not stay open.

"Maybe I'd better—go to bed," said Val sleepily. "You'll come up—won't you, Daddy—and tell me—a story."

But Val was asleep almost before his head touched the pillow and the story remained untold.

Margaret, also, went off to bed early and after that Ronnie and I were alone, sitting by the fire and talking. There was nothing particularly interesting about our conversation (it was mostly about Val's clothes for his new school and the arrangements Ronnie had made at Eastringford) but somehow it did not seem to matter what we talked about. It was enough to see Ronnie sitting by the fire smoking his pipe, and to listen to his voice.

"About Val's shoes," I said. "When you buy Val a new pair of shoes you must tell them to put a little piece of leather to support the arch of his left foot. Don't forget, will you? It's important."

"I won't forget," said Ronnie. He smiled and added "Shoes or ships or sealing-wax. Do you remember, Jane? The first time I saw you I suggested these curious objects as a subject for conversation."

"But we talked about brass knobs and buttons instead—and all the time I was longing to ask your name."

"If only I had known . . ." said Ronnie with a rueful smile.

It was the custom in Ryddelton for the choir of the church to go round the town on Christmas Eve and to sing carols, so I was not surprised when we heard the sound of footsteps on the gravel path.

"What's that?" asked Ronnie. "There's somebody in the garden!"

"Listen, Ronnie," I said.

For a few moments there was silence and then the silence was broken by voices raised in harmony. The choir had begun with the age-old favourite, "While Shepherds Watched their Flocks by Night."

"That's lovely!" said Ronnie softly. "It only wanted that . . ." He rose as he spoke and drawing aside the curtain, opened the window.

It was a quiet night, very mild and cloudy, but we could see the shadowy forms of the singers standing in a semi-circle on the lawn.

When the hymn ended I signed to Ronnie to speak to the singers—usually I thanked them myself, but to-night I felt so moved that I could not trust my voice—so Ronnie thanked them, and told them that he had just returned from Africa and it was a great pleasure to hear Scottish voices singing his favourite hymn.

"Maybe you'd like another?" suggested one of the men. "If you'd care for it we could sing, 'O, Little Star of Bethlehem.'"

"Please do," said Ronnie.

They sang it for him and it seemed so beautiful that it was almost more than I could bear; the quiet peaceful night, and the voices singing in the darkness, and Ronnie standing at the open window.

They went away after that, for it was getting late and they had a long road home. They called out, "Good night—and a happy Christmas!" We heard their footsteps on the gravel and the click of the gate and the sound of their conversation getting fainter and fainter and dying away in the distance.

For a time neither of us moved nor spoke and then Ronnie said, "It's Christmas Day, Jane. A happy Christmas, my dear."

3

Ronnie and I shut up the house, bolting the front door and snibbing the windows, and then we went upstairs.

"Jane!" exclaimed Ronnie, halting on the landing. "That's Val! He's awake—he's crying!"

It was true; I could hear Val sobbing as if his heart would break.

I opened the door and we went in and turned on the light.

"Val, what's the matter?" asked Ronnie. "Did the singing waken you? What's the matter, old chap?"

"Aunt Jane!" sobbed Val. "Aunt Jane—"

I sat down on the edge of the bed. "What's the matter, darling?" I asked. "You were so happy when you went to bed. Did you have a bad dream? Tell me about it, Val."

He knelt and hugged me. His arms were round my neck and his face, pressed to mine, was wet with tears.

"Tell me about it," I repeated. "Tell me what's the matter."

"It's you!" he cried incoherently. "It's you, Aunt Jane! I didn't think before—but now I've thought! I can't bear it—I can't bear it! I want—I want—"

"Darling, what do you want?"

"I don't know what I want! I want to go with Daddy—and I want to stay with you. Oh dear!" sobbed Val. "Oh dear, it's awful to love two people!"

"You'll have Daddy—" I began, but I could not go on.

My face was wet and I was not sure whether they were Val's tears or mine.

"But I won't have you! I want you—and Daddy. I want both of you—at once. Oh, why can't we all be together!"

"I've been wondering the same thing," said Ronnie in a low voice. "I've been wondering if—if we could all be—together."

I could not speak. I could not have spoken to save my life.

"Jane," said Ronnie. "Jane, you see how it is. Here are two people who want you. Here are two people who love you so much that they can't be happy without you."

"Too soon," I whispered. "It's too soon—for that."

"I know," he said. "I know it's too soon, but we can wait. We can wait as long as you like. If Val and I know you're coming—some day—we don't mind waiting."

"Will you?" asked Val, squeezing me tightly. "Oh, please say yes. Will you come some day—cross your heart?"

"Yes—some day—cross my heart," I whispered.

THE END

AN AUTOBIOGRAPHICAL SKETCH
by D.E. Stevenson

EDINBURGH was my birthplace and I lived there until I was married in 1916. My father was the grandson of Robert Stevenson who designed the Bell Rock Lighthouse and also a great many other lighthouses and harbours and other notable engineering works. My father was a first cousin of Robert Louis Stevenson and they often played together when they were boys.

So it was that from my earliest days I heard a good deal about "Louis", and, like Oliver Twist, I was always asking for more, teasing my father and my aunts for stories about him. He must have been a strange child, a dreamy unpredictable creature with a curious fascination about him which his cousins felt but did not understand. How could ordinary healthy, noisy children understand that solitary, sensitive soul! And as they grew up they understood him even less for Louis was not of their world. He was born too late or too early. The narrow conventional ideas of mid-Victorian Edinburgh were anathema to him. Louis would have been happy in a romantic age, striding the world in cloak and doublet with a sword at his side, he would have sold his life dearly for a Lost Cause—he was ever on the side of the underdog. He might have been happy in the world of today when every man is entitled to his own opinions and the Four Freedoms is the goal of Democracy.

My father was old-fashioned in his ideas so my sister and I were not sent to school but were brought up at home and educated by a governess. I was always very fond of reading and read everything I could get hold of including Scott, Dickens, Jane Austen and all sorts of boys' books by Jules Verne and Ballantyne and Henty.

When I was eight years old I began to write stories and poems myself. It was most exciting to discover that I could. At first my family was amused and interested in my efforts but very soon they became bored beyond measure and told me it must stop. They said it was ruining my handwriting and wasting my time. I argued with them. What was handwriting for, if not to write?

"For writing letters when you're older," they said. But I could not stop. My head was full of stories and they got lost if I did not write them down, so I found a place in the box-room between two large black trunks with a skylight overhead and I made a little nest where I would not be disturbed. There I sat for hours—and wrote and wrote.

Our house was in a broad street in Edinburgh—45 Melville Street—and at the top of the street was St. Mary's Cathedral. The bells used to echo and re-echo down the man-made canyon. My sister and I used to sit on the window-seat in the nursery (which was at the top of the house) and look down at the people passing by. I told her stories about them. Some of the memories of my childhood can be found in my novel, *Listening Valley*, in which Louise and Antonia had much the same lonely childhood.

Every summer we went to North Berwick for several months and here we were more free to do as we wanted, to go out by ourselves and play on the shore and meet other children. When we were at North Berwick we sometimes drove over to a big farm, close to the sea. We enjoyed these visits tremendously for there were so many things to do and see. We rode the pony and saw the farmyard animals and walked along the lovely sands. There were rocks there too, and many ships were wrecked upon the jagged reefs until a lighthouse was erected upon the Bass Rock—designed by my father. Years afterwards I wrote a novel about this farm, about the fine old house and the beautiful garden, and I called it *The Story of Rosabelle Shaw*.

As we grew older we made more friends. We had bathing picnics and tennis parties and fancy dress dances, and of course we played golf. I was in the team of the North Berwick Ladies' Golf Club and I played in the Scottish Ladies' Championship at Muirfield and survived until the semi-finals. I was asked to play in the Scottish Team but by that time I was married and expecting my first baby so I was obliged to refuse the honour.

Every Spring my father and mother took us abroad, to France or Switzerland or Italy. We had a French maid so we spoke French easily and fluently—if not very correctly—and it was very pleasant to be able to converse with the people we met. I liked Italy best, and especially Lake Como which seemed to me so beautiful as to be almost unreal. Paris came second in my affections. There was such a gay feeling in Paris; I see it always in sunshine with the white buildings and broad streets and the crowds of brightly clad people strolling in the Boulevards or sitting in the cafés eating and drinking and chattering cheerfully. Quite often we hired a carriage and drove through the Bois de Boulogne. My sister and I were never allowed to go out alone, of course, nor would our parents take us to a play—as I have said before they were old-fashioned and strict in their ideas and considered a "French Play" an unsuitable form of entertainment for their daughters—but in spite of these annoying prejudices we managed to have quite an amusing time and we always enjoyed our visits to foreign countries.

In 1913 I "came out" and had a gay winter in Edinburgh. There were brilliant "Balls" in those far off days, the old Assembly Rooms glittered with lights and the long gilt mirrors reflected girls in beautiful frocks and men in uniform or kilts. The older women sat round the ballroom attired in velvet or satin and diamonds watching the dancers—and especially watching their own offspring—with eyes like hawks, and talking scandal to one another. We danced waltzes and Scottish country dances and Reels—the Reels were usually made up beforehand by the Scottish Regiment which was quartered at Edinburgh Castle. It was a coveted honour to be asked to dance in these Reels and one had to be on one's toes all the time. Woe betide the unfortunate girl who put a foot wrong or failed to set to her partner at exactly the right moment!

The First Great War put an end to all these gaieties—certainly nobody felt inclined to dance when every day the long lists of casualties were published and the gay young men who had been one's partners were reported dead or missing or returned wounded from the ghastly battlefields.

In 1916 I married Major James Reid Peploe. His family was an Edinburgh family, as mine was. Curiously enough I knew his mother and father and his brothers but had never met him until he returned to Edinburgh from the war, wounded in the head. When he recovered we were married and then began the busiest time of my life. We moved about from place to place (as soldiers and their wives and families must do) and, what with the struggle to get houses and the arrival—at reasonable intervals—of two sons and a daughter I had very little time for writing. I managed to write some short stories and some children's poems but it was not until we were settled for some years in Glasgow that I began my literary career in earnest.

Mrs. Tim was my first successful novel. In it I wrote an account of the life of an Officer's wife and many of the incidents in the story are true—or only very slightly touched up. Unfortunately people in Glasgow were not very pleased with their portraits and became somewhat chilly in consequence. After that I wrote *Miss Buncle's Book* which has been one of my most popular books. It sold in thousands and is still selling. It is about a woman who wrote a book about the small town in which she lived and about the reactions of the community.

All the time my children were growing up I continued to write: *Miss Buncle Married, Miss Dean's Dilemma, Smouldering Fire, The Story of Rosabelle Shaw, The Baker's Daughter, Green Money, Rochester's Wife, A World in Spell* followed in due succession—and then came the Second Great War.

Hitherto I had written to please myself, to amuse myself and others, but now I realised that I could do good work. *The English Air* was my first novel to be written with a purpose. In this novel I tried to give an artistically true picture of how English people thought and felt about the war so that other countries might understand us better, and, judging by the hundreds of letters I received from people all over the world, I succeeded in my object—succeeded beyond my wildest hopes. My wartime books are *Mrs. Tim Carries On, Spring Magic, Celia's House, Listening Valley, The Two Mrs. Abbotts, Crooked Adam* and *The Four Graces*. In these books I have pictured every-day life in Britain during the war and have tried to show how ordinary people stood up to the frightfulness and what they thought and did during those awful years of anxiety. One of my American readers wrote to me and said, "You make us understand what it must be like to have a tiger in the backyard." I appreciated that letter.

Wartime brought terrible anxieties to me, for my elder son was in Malta during the worst of the Siege of that island and then came home and landed in France on D-Day and went through the whole campaign with the Guards Armoured Division. He was wounded in ten places and was decorated with the Military Cross for outstanding bravery. My daughter was an officer in the Women's Royal Naval Service and was commended for her valuable work.

In addition to my writing I organised the collection of Sphagnum Moss for the Red Cross and together with others went out on the moors in all weathers, wading deep in bog, to collect the moss for surgical dressings. This particular form of war-work is described in detail in *Listening Valley*.

After the long weary years of war came victory for the Allies, but my job of writing stories went on. I wrote *Mrs. Tim Gets a Job, Kate Hardy, Young Mrs. Savage* and *Vittoria Cottage*. All these books were quite as successful as their predecessors and *Young Mrs. Savage* was chosen by the American Family Reading Club as their Book of the Month. My new novel *Music in the Hills* is in the same genre and all those who have read it think it is one of my best. A businessman, who lives in London, wrote to me saying '*Music in the Hills* is as good as a holiday and, although I have read several other books since reading it, the peaceful atmosphere lingers in my mind. I hope your next book will tell us more about James and Rhoda and the other characters for they are so real to me and have become my friends." The scene of this book is laid in the hills and valleys of the Scottish Borders and the people are the rugged individualistic race who inhabit this beautiful country. For a long time it has been in my mind to write a story with this setting and to try to describe the atmosphere, to paint an artistically true picture of life in this district. Now it is finished and I hope my large and faithful public will enjoy reading it as much as I have enjoyed writing it.

Sometimes I have been accused of making my characters "too nice". I have been told that my stories are "too pleasant", but the fact is I write of people as I find them and am fond of my fellow human beings. Perhaps I have been fortunate but in all my wanderings I have met very few thoroughly unpleasant people, so I find it difficult to write about them.

We live in Moffat now. Moffat is a small but very interesting old town which lies in a valley between round rolling hills. Some of the buildings are very old indeed but outside the town there are pleasant residential houses with gardens and fine trees of oak and beech and elm. From my window as I write I can see the lovely sweep of moorland where the small, lively, black-faced sheep live and move and have their being. Every day the hills look different: sometimes grey and cold, sometimes green and smiling; in winter they are often white with snow or hidden in soft grey mist, in September they are purple with heather, like a royal robe. Although Moffat is isolated there is plenty of society and many interesting people to talk to and entertain and it is only fifty miles from Edinburgh so, if I feel dull, I can go and stay there at my comfortable club and see a good play or a film and do some shopping.

There are several questions which recur again and again in letters from friends and acquaintances. Perhaps I should try to answer them. The first is, why do you write? I write because I enjoy writing more than anything. It is fascinating to think out a story and to feel it taking shape in my mind. Of course I like making money by my books—who would not?—but the money is a secondary consideration, a by-product as it were. The story is the thing. Writing a book is the most exciting adventure under the sun.

The second question is, how do you write? I write all my books in longhand, lying on a sofa near the window in my drawing room. I begin by thinking it all out and then I take a pencil and jot it all down in a notebook. When that stage is over I begin at the beginning and go on like mad until I get to the end. After that I have a little rest and then polish it up and rewrite bits of it. When I can do no more to it I pack it up, smother the parcel with sealing wax, and despatch it to be typed. I am now free as air and somewhat dazed, so I ring up all my friends (who have been neglected for months) and say, "Come and have a party."

Another question is, do you draw your characters from real life? The answer is definitely NO. The characters in a novel are the most interesting part of it and the most mysterious. They must come from Somewhere, I suppose, but they certainly do not come from "real life". They begin by taking shape in a nebulous form and then, as I think about them and live with them, they become more solid and individualistic with definite ideas of their own. Sometimes I get rather annoyed with them; they are so unmanageable, they flatly refuse to do as I want and take their own way in an arbitrary fashion.

All the people in my books are real to me. They are more real than the people I meet every day for I know them better and understand them more deeply. It is difficult to say which is my favourite character, for I am fond of them all, but the most extraordinary character I ever had to deal with was Sophonisba Marks (in my novel *The Two Mrs. Abbotts*.) I intended her to be a subsidiary character, an unimportant person in the story, but Miss Marks had other ideas. In spite of the fact that she was plain and elderly and somewhat deaf and suffered severely from rheumatism, Miss Marks walked straight into the middle of the stage and stayed there. She just wouldn't take a back seat. She is so real to me that I simply cannot believe she does not exist. Somewhere or other she must exist—perhaps I shall meet her one day! Perhaps I shall see her in the street, coming towards me clad in her black cloth coat and the round toque with the white flowers in it and carrying her umbrella in her hand. I shall stop her and say loudly (because of course she is deaf) "Miss Marks, I presume!"

It will be seen from the foregoing sketch that my life has not been a very eventful one. I have had no hair-raising adventures nor travelled in little-known parts of the world, but wherever I have been I have made interesting friends and I still retain them. Friends are like windows in a house, and what a terribly dull house it would be that had no windows! They open vistas, they show one new and lovely views of the countryside. Friends give one new ideas, new values, new interests.

Thank God for friends!

Someday I mean to write a book of reminiscences; to delve into the cupboard of memory and sort out all the junk. There is so much to write about, so many little pictures grave and gay, so many ideas to think about and disentangle and arrange. Looking back is a fascinating pastime; looking back and wondering what one's life would have been if one had done this instead of that, if one had turned to the left at the crossroads instead of to the right, if one had stayed at home instead of going out or had gone out five minutes later. Jane Welsh Carlyle says in one of her letters, "One can never be too much alive to the consideration that one's every slightest action does not end when it has acted itself but propagates itself on and on, in one shape or another, through all time and away into eternity."

FICTION BY D.E. STEVENSON

Published by Dean Street Press

Mrs. Tim Carries On (1941)
Mrs. Tim Gets a Job (1947)
Mrs. Tim Flies Home (1952)

Smouldering Fire (1935)*
Spring Magic (1942)

Vittoria Cottage (1949)
Music in the Hills (1950)
Winter and Rough Weather (1951, aka *Shoulder the Sky*)

The Fair Miss Fortune (written c. 1938, first published 2011)
Green Money (1939, aka *The Green Money*)
The English Air (1940)
Kate Hardy (1947)
Young Mrs. Savage (1948)
Five Windows (1953)
Charlotte Fairlie (1954, aka *The Enchanted Isle*, aka *Blow the Wind Southerly*)
The Tall Stranger (1957)
Anna and Her Daughters (1958)
The Musgraves (1960)
The Blue Sapphire (1963)

Other Titles

Jean Erskine's Secret (written c. 1917, first published 2013)
Peter West (1923)
Emily Dennistoun (written c. 1920s, first published 2011)
Mrs. Tim of the Regiment (1932)*
Golden Days (1934)*
Miss Buncle's Book (1934)
Divorced from Reality (1935, aka *Miss Dean's Dilemma*, aka *The Young Clementina*)

Miss Buncle Married (1936)
The Empty World (1936, aka *A World in Spell*)
The Story of Rosabelle Shaw (1937)
The Baker's Daughter (1938, aka *Miss Bun the Baker's Daughter*)
Rochester's Wife (1940)
Crooked Adam (1942)
Celia's House (1943)
The Two Mrs Abbotts (1943)
Listening Valley (1944)
The Four Graces (1946)
Amberwell (1955)
Summerhills (1956)
Still Glides the Stream (1959)
The Musgraves (1960)
Bel Lamington (1961)
Fletcher's End (1962)
Katherine Wentworth (1964)
Katherine's Marriage (1965, aka *The Marriage of Katherine*)
The House on the Cliff (1966)
Sarah Morris Remembers (1967)
Sarah's Cottage (1968)
Gerald and Elizabeth (1969)
House of the Deer (1970)
Portrait of Saskia (collection of early writings, published 2011)
Found in the Attic (collection of early writings, published 2013)

* see Explanatory Notes

EXPLANATORY NOTES

MRS. TIM

Mrs. Tim of the Regiment, the first appearance of Mrs. Tim in the literary world, was published by Jonathan Cape in 1932. That edition, however, contained only the first half of the book currently available from Bloomsbury under the same title. The second half was originally published, as *Golden Days*, by Herbert Jenkins in 1934. Together, those two books contain Mrs. Tim's diaries for the first six months of the same year.

Subsequently, D.E. Stevenson regained the rights to the two books, and her new publisher, Collins, reissued them in the U.K. as a single volume under the title *Mrs. Tim* (1941), reprinted several times as late as 1992. In the U.S., however, the combined book appeared as *Mrs. Tim of the Regiment*, and has generally retained that title, though a 1973 reprint used the title *Mrs. Tim Christie*. Adding to the confusion, large print and audiobook editions of *Golden Days* have also appeared in recent years.

Fortunately no such title confusions exist with the subsequent Mrs. Tim titles—*Mrs. Tim Carries On* (1941), *Mrs. Tim Gets a Job* (1947), and *Mrs. Tim Flies Home* (1952)—and Dean Street Press is delighted to make these long-out-of-print volumes of the series available again, along with two more of Stevenson's most loved novels, *Smouldering Fire* (1935) and *Spring Magic* (1942).

SMOULDERING FIRE

Smouldering Fire was first published in the U.K. in 1935 and in the U.S. in 1938. Until now, those were the only complete editions of the book. All later reprints, both hardcover and paperback, have been heavily abridged, with entire chapters as well as occasional passages throughout the novel cut from the text. For our new edition, Dean Street Press has followed the text of the first U.K. edition, and we are proud to be producing the first complete, unabridged edition of *Smouldering Fire* in eighty years.

FURROWED MIDDLEBROW

FM1. *A Footman for the Peacock* (1940) . . . . RACHEL FERGUSON
FM2. *Evenfield* (1942) . . . . RACHEL FERGUSON
FM3. *A Harp in Lowndes Square* (1936) . . . . RACHEL FERGUSON
FM4. *A Chelsea Concerto* (1959) . . . . FRANCES FAVIELL
FM5. *The Dancing Bear* (1954) . . . . FRANCES FAVIELL
FM6. *A House on the Rhine* (1955) . . . . FRANCES FAVIELL
FM7. *Thalia* (1957) . . . . FRANCES FAVIELL
FM8. *The Fledgeling* (1958) . . . . FRANCES FAVIELL
FM9. *Bewildering Cares* (1940) . . . . WINIFRED PECK
FM10. *Tom Tiddler's Ground* (1941) . . . . URSULA ORANGE
FM11. *Begin Again* (1936) . . . . URSULA ORANGE
FM12. *Company in the Evening* (1944) . . . . URSULA ORANGE
FM13. *The Late Mrs. Prioleau* (1946) . . . . MONICA TINDALL
FM14. *Bramton Wick* (1952) . . . . ELIZABETH FAIR
FM15. *Landscape in Sunlight* (1953) . . . . ELIZABETH FAIR
FM16. *The Native Heath* (1954) . . . . ELIZABETH FAIR
FM17. *Seaview House* (1955) . . . . ELIZABETH FAIR
FM18. *A Winter Away* (1957) . . . . ELIZABETH FAIR
FM19. *The Mingham Air* (1960) . . . . ELIZABETH FAIR
FM20. *The Lark* (1922) . . . . E. NESBIT
FM21. *Smouldering Fire* (1935) . . . . D.E. STEVENSON
FM22. *Spring Magic* (1942) . . . . D.E. STEVENSON
FM23. *Mrs. Tim Carries On* (1941) . . . . D.E. STEVENSON
FM24. *Mrs. Tim Gets a Job* (1947) . . . . D.E. STEVENSON
FM25. *Mrs. Tim Flies Home* (1952) . . . . D.E. STEVENSON
FM26. *Alice* (1949) . . . . ELIZABETH ELIOT
FM27. *Henry* (1950) . . . . ELIZABETH ELIOT
FM28. *Mrs. Martell* (1953) . . . . ELIZABETH ELIOT
FM29. *Cecil* (1962) . . . . ELIZABETH ELIOT
FM30. *Nothing to Report* (1940) . . . . CAROLA OMAN
FM31. *Somewhere in England* (1943) . . . . CAROLA OMAN

FM32. *Spam Tomorrow* (1956) . . . . VERILY ANDERSON
FM33. *Peace, Perfect Peace* (1947) . . . . JOSEPHINE KAMM
FM34. *Beneath the Visiting Moon* (1940) . . . . ROMILLY CAVAN
FM35. *Table Two* (1942) . . . . MARJORIE WILENSKI
FM36. *The House Opposite* (1943) . . . . BARBARA NOBLE
FM37. *Miss Carter and the Ifrit* (1945) . . . . SUSAN ALICE KERBY
FM38. *Wine of Honour* (1945) . . . . BARBARA BEAUCHAMP
FM39. *A Game of Snakes and Ladders* (1938, 1955) . . . .
. . . . DORIS LANGLEY MOORE
FM40. *Not at Home* (1948) . . . . DORIS LANGLEY MOORE
FM41. *All Done by Kindness* (1951) . . . . DORIS LANGLEY MOORE
FM42. *My Caravaggio Style* (1959) . . . . DORIS LANGLEY MOORE
FM43. *Vittoria Cottage* (1949) . . . . D.E. STEVENSON
FM44. *Music in the Hills* (1950) . . . . D.E. STEVENSON
FM45. *Winter and Rough Weather* (1951) . . . . . . D.E. STEVENSON
FM46. *Fresh from the Country* (1960) . . . . MISS READ
FM47. *Miss Mole* (1930) . . . . E.H. YOUNG
FM48. *A House in the Country* (1957) . . . . RUTH ADAM
FM49. *Much Dithering* (1937) . . . . DOROTHY LAMBERT
FM50. *Miss Plum and Miss Penny* (1959) . DOROTHY EVELYN SMITH
FM51. *Village Story* (1951) . . . . CELIA BUCKMASTER
FM52. *Family Ties* (1952) . . . . CELIA BUCKMASTER
FM53. *Rhododendron Pie* (1930) . . . . MARGERY SHARP
FM54. *Fanfare for Tin Trumpets* (1932) . . . . MARGERY SHARP
FM55. *Four Gardens* (1935) . . . . MARGERY SHARP
FM56. *Harlequin House* (1939) . . . . MARGERY SHARP
FM57. *The Stone of Chastity* (1940) . . . . MARGERY SHARP
FM58. *The Foolish Gentlewoman* (1948) . . . . MARGERY SHARP
FM59. *The Swiss Summer* (1951) . . . . STELLA GIBBONS
FM60. *A Pink Front Door* (1959) . . . . STELLA GIBBONS
FM61. *The Weather at Tregulla* (1962) . . . . STELLA GIBBONS
FM62. *The Snow-Woman* (1969) . . . . STELLA GIBBONS
FM63. *The Woods in Winter* (1970) . . . . STELLA GIBBONS
FM64. *Apricot Sky* (1952) . . . . RUBY FERGUSON
FM65. *Susan Settles Down* (1936) . . . . MOLLY CLAVERING
FM66. *Yoked with a Lamb* (1938) . . . . MOLLY CLAVERING
FM67. *Loves Comes Home* (1938) . . . . MOLLY CLAVERING

FM68. *Touch not the Nettle* (1939) .... MOLLY CLAVERING
FM69. *Mrs. Lorimer's Quiet Summer* (1953) ... MOLLY CLAVERING
FM70. *Because of Sam* (1953) .... MOLLY CLAVERING
FM71. *Dear Hugo* (1955) .... MOLLY CLAVERING
FM72. *Near Neighbours* (1956) .... MOLLY CLAVERING
FM73. *The Fair Miss Fortune* (1938) .... D.E. STEVENSON
FM74. *Green Money* (1939) .... D.E. STEVENSON
FM75. *The English Air* (1940)* .... D.E. STEVENSON
FM76. *Kate Hardy* (1947) .... D.E. STEVENSON
FM77. *Young Mrs. Savage* (1948) .... D.E. STEVENSON
FM78. *Five Windows* (1953)* .... D.E. STEVENSON
FM79. *Charlotte Fairlie* (1954) .... D.E. STEVENSON
FM80. *The Tall Stranger* (1957)* .... D.E. STEVENSON
FM81. *Anna and Her Daughters* (1958)* .... D.E. STEVENSON
FM82. *The Musgraves* (1960) .... D.E. STEVENSON
FM83. *The Blue Sapphire* (1963)* .... D.E. STEVENSON

*titles available in paperback only

www.ingramcontent.com/pod-product-compliance
Ingram Content Group UK Ltd.
Pitfield, Milton Keynes, MK11 3LW, UK
UKHW041943230426
12048UKWH00008B/99